THE GOLD FEATHER

BOOK ONE IN SERIES

DANI PASQUINI

This book is dedicated to my PB&J team. I could not have done this without your love, understanding and support. I love you all ferociously.

You have to die a few times before you can really live.

— CHARLES BUKOWSKI

THE REMAINING DREAMS

1

When I was a child, I would have nightly dreams of flying. My body would lift effortlessly out of bed to then float through the kitchen and the other small rooms in our home until I flew straight out the back door. The ability to remain in the air felt innate. As if it were a perfectly natural thing to do. Something I had been born to do.

These dreams were vivid in my mind. The feel of the wind on my bare legs as my nightgown flipped and flitted around my body as the cold winter air licked my body. I would will myself to keep moving higher and higher in the star filled sky until not a sound could be heard except for my beating heart and the soft lulling whisper of the wind as it embraced me like an old friend. I felt joyous as the constraints of gravity set me free.

As vivid as these dreams had been and despite the freedom and joy I experienced each night, it was the last of these experiences that held the most weight in my mind. It began like any other night, I pushed my body to soar higher and higher into the bright moonlit sky, embracing the euphoria that consume my senses until quite suddenly the feeling of terror ran through my veins, paralyzing me with fear. My body began to jerk as an invisible string that felt as if it were tethered inside of my chest began to pull me back to Earth with ferocious speed. With a grunt, I plummeted down in a blur until finally it all turned to black just as my body forcefully landed on my mattress. With a painful jolt, I opened my eyes as I sat on the bed clutching my chest while panting painfully for breath.

BROOKLYN, NY

2

Looking back, I lived my life like a majority of people do in developed parts of the world do. Like many, my life was bookmarked by a series of tragedies, adventures, loves and losses. I had always been seeking that elusive dream of what life, as described by society, was supposed to look like for normal people. I had the successful job, the spouse, the children, and the beautiful home with a dog, friends and even the occasional weekend getaway.

The motions of my life had all been premeditated and contrived by others ideals of what the life of a responsible adult should be. I always felt as if I were trying to survive the mundaneness by doing as I was told while also mimicking what I saw. I behaved as others did in relationships. I cared for my husband and adored my children as others did. It was with great conscious effort that I tried to be a good mother and an acceptable partner. Admittedly, I had moments where I felt happiness. The children were often the source of these experiences. These fleeting moments where I felt joy were the moments that kept me moving forward in the hopes that I would be able to stumble into those feelings again.

But despite all of my efforts, I couldn't help but feel as if I were living someone else's life and that the person I had become was only a hardened external shell going through the motions of life while the real me lay dormant in a cold and dark corner of my brain. More often then I care to admit, I would find myself pulled into such a deep depression that it felt as if I were having an affair with the dark parts that resided within me.

My husband Philip would become incensed whenever I would try to talk to him about how I felt. These conversations would always end with him yelling, filled with rage while telling me that deep down I didn't think he was good enough for me and that I hated the life we had created together. The guilt I felt would consume me as I listened to his words, trying desperately to disagree with what he was saying while deep down, shamefully knowing that he was right. These sessions would last until I apologized and pretended that we hadn't argued while the blanket of melancholy that continued to threaten to cover me, temporarily concealed these thoughts and feelings I had so desperately been trying to find resolution to.

I desperately tried to force myself into believing that I had achieved everything that I had set out to. I had arrived, the journey was complete. I had found the love I had sought in a husband and the children I had yearned for after so many years of trying. But despite it all, none of it seemed to matter. There seemed to be nothing that the self-help books, therapy sessions and pharmaceuticals could do. The feeling of loss and emptiness always remained within me, lulling me into the darkest parts of my being.

Now, several years after the accident and several suicide attempts later, I found myself walking in the pouring winter rain without a coat, purposefully not using the umbrella I carried in my purse, begging the cold winter air to penetrate through my thin wet scrubs and to drench my skin in the hopes that I could feel the ice rip through my external barriers only to then tear through muscle and tendons all the way to my bones so that I could feel the pain I so desperately sought. As I walked, I prayed that hypothermia would consume my body and that it would kill me because I was a piece of shit and I didn't deserve to live.

Pain was my punishment for not realizing how lucky I had been for having had found joy and love all of those years ago. Desperately, I wished that I had been present emotionally more often back then and that I had kept my head out of the sky so that I could have actually enjoyed it all while I had the chance. To love my time with them as much as they had loved me.

I had become completely lost. My heart had turned into an empty shell and my lackluster brown eyes had become incapable of seeing anything but pain. I arrived in my apartment in the city completely drenched, dripping rainwater as I made my way up the four flights of stairs all while remembering our warm country home. That home had always been filled with the laughter of children running in the yard, birds chirping and the smell of freshly cut grass on bright spring mornings. Seeking refuge from the quiet and the memories that the walls contained, I sold the house not long after the accident. Wanting nothing around me that would remind me of the time I had spent there with them, when I was loved and warm but too blind to see it then. I had been so stupid and ungrateful. Such a cliché. Such disgrace that I did not realize what I had until it was all gone. I was so ashamed of who I was then and detested myself now more than ever before.

All that awaited me now in my walk-up studio apartment was a bed, a TV and a kitchen table. Walking passed the mirror in the entry hall, I caught site of my dripping long brown hair as it clung to my pale face. I gazed at my sunken brown eyes as they reflected back at me containing no glimmer of life. Turning away from the emaciated horror I had become, I walked into my dark depressing apartment filled with cold emptiness wanting nothing of comfort around me as I embraced my solitude and despair.

The daily phone call from the three friends I had left reminded me of their fear and concern. My last suicide attempt had really hit them hard and I knew that they were filled with angst as the phone rang during their daily check-ins as the phone rang, fearing I wouldn't answer. They were always offering to meet me for coffee or dinner, anything to have me not sit alone in my depression filled apartment. But I would only feel slightly guilty for always finding an excuse to not take them up on their offers. I dreaded the sight of their shocked eyes looking at me full of pity and sadness at what I had become. As more time passed, it had become more difficult to reassure them that everything was in fact all right. That all I needed was some more time to recover.

They felt somewhat reassured that I was on my way back to my old self when I told one of them that I had started to run again. But in all honesty, I would run for miles, hard and fast to the point where I would experience intense body pain. Little did they know that the last thing I wanted to do was get better. My punishments and exertions had made my body rail thin, where once upon a time my body had been full of curves and I would have even considered myself beautiful once. But there was nothing left of my old self now. My tall stature and pale skin made me look sickly with my sallow eyes and thinning long brown hair. I would rarely eat, sustaining myself on coffee and the occasional apple. Hoping and praying that my body would just give out on its own.

Through my desperate attempts at self-destruction, I continued to work as a nurse in a busy inner city emergency room. The fast pace and intensity left little time to form connections with patients and colleagues. It had been exactly what I needed and it offered lots of overtime opportunities, which I welcomed. Anything to not go home and sit in my dreary apartment waiting for the phone to ring or the incessant pinging from text messages from my well-intentioned friends.

The noise, dirt and chaos that I found in the city streets would consume me, filling me with its pollution of negativity as I sat on the park bench during my breaks from work listening to the sirens, car horns, drunks yelling at each other as the subway rumbled beneath my feet and the cold wind blew on my face until my skin felt numb. It all helped my dig deeper and deeper into my pit of blackness in an ignorant attempt to shelter myself from the realities of my life.

The hours and days had become predictable and monotonous. I would leave for work early in the morning, walk the several blocks to the subway station, work my twelve to fourteen hour shifts and then head back to my apartment as late as possible at night where I would just sit and stare at the black TV screen. My nightly bathing had also become routine as I would sit on the shower floor with the scalding hot water running over my reddened skin while contemplating if I should let the scalpel that I held over my wrist penetrate my skin. I had become intensely self-deprecating of my passed suicide failures. I couldn't even get that shit right, I would say to myself while pondering if on a subconscious level fear had held me back all of those other times from succeeding.

The antidepressants that the psychiatrists had started me on made me feel as if I were sleepwalking through a thick numbing fog. Without disclosing to anyone, I quickly weaned myself off of those medications so that I could plan my next attempt with the hope and determination that this next attempt would be my absolute last. I had to be present within my body and mentally focused so that I could get it right and be successful. Once the plans had been made, the next step would be to decide when.

3

One nondescript night, as I walked home from the subway after a long shift at work, I stepped over a homeless man who was obviously very intoxicated. His stench assaulted my senses as I stepped over his outstretched legs with its filthy pants and bare feet. "You are an ugly bitch that just needs to die," he slurred drunkenly.

Silently agreeing with his assessment, I nodded and thanked him as I took his outburst as my sign that the time had come for me to pull the trigger one last time. With a sense of relief and purpose, I continued on my path to the apartment having made peace of my decision knowing that I had truly tried to make my life meaningful again, but had intensely and repeatedly failed. There was nothing keeping me here anymore. I had kept myself alive because of a promise I had made to my girlfriends a they wept at my hospital bed after my last attempt. A simple drug overdose had been my last plan, with old pills I had found in the house. A combination of narcotics that we had stowed away over the years from random injuries and oral procedures. If my friends had truly understood why I had done it, they would have forgiven me and let me go. I told myself that deep down they already knew that one day I would be successful and that they had already forgiven me.

My preparations were all very unceremonious. I walked around the apartment and made sure that everything was clean, my bed made and that my clothes were put away neatly. After slowly undressing in front of the full length mirror in the bathroom, I noticed the gold feather necklace my mother had given me faintly glittering in my frail chest. I held onto it tightly deciding that I couldn't bear to take it off, desperately wishing that she were still around for me.

As I slid my delicate body into the scalding hot tub, I tightly clutched the bottle of narcotics that I had secretly been hoarding, along with a bottle of wine to wash it all down and a scalpel for good measure. What I was about to do felt final and most importantly it felt right. After taking a big delicious gulp of my wine, I plunged into the water, fully submerging my body so that my lusterless brown hair floated around me and my skin became soft from the heat.

I gulped down the 30 or so pills as I finished the bottle of wine. Just as the pills began to take effect and my muscles began to soften, I unplugged the drain until it emptied about half way before rein-serting the plug and turning the scalding hot water on again until sweat ran down my scalp and my body filled with heat as my skin reddened, softened and wrinkled from the swelter. Before my mind faded into a drugged and drunken euphoric state, I reached for the scalpel and without hesitation plunged the knife deeply into my wrists cutting easily as I pulled it through my skin and into the both arteries on each of my wrists following their path up my arms. Once the cuts had been made, I dropped the scalpel into the tub and sat back as I watched the water turn to blood.

With a sluggish mind, weakening limbs and shallow breathing, my peripheral vision began to darken and fade as it closed in around me. Despite the heat of the water, my body began to shiver slightly with the little life it still contained as I slowly began to slide beneath the bloody water.

Just as I was about to fully submerge, I experienced a hallucination of a beautiful tall man who came rushing into my bathroom, loudly slamming the door open and saying with a gasp, "No!"

THE BIRCHES

4

I woke up in a stark white room with white subway tiles lining the walls and white linoleum covering the floor. Everything was white and sterile, making me feel as if I were drowning in a bright snowstorm. Through squinting eyes, I could see that I was lying on a white metal bed situated in the middle of the bright room. The blankets and sheets that covered my body were white. The window to my right beamed in bright sunlight through sheer white curtains.

As my mind began to regain lucency, I searched around the room for anything familiar as panic began to build making my body shake softly. As the strangeness of the room began to take shape in my mind, I was startled to discover someone breathing next to me on my left side. There was a man snoring slightly as he slept, slouched over in an armchair beside me. Alarmed, I quickly tried to push myself up to sitting only to be painfully reminded of what I had yet again failed to do as I stared at my bandaged arms. My level of panic level soared as I realized where my likely present location was... I was in hospital psych ward, I screamed in my mind.

The feeling of failure filled me with dread as I recalled what I had done. Remembering the scalpel as it cut through my skin like butter and the thick hot blood enveloped my body before it all faded to black. As my breathing quickened, I tried to make sense of how this could have happened. That was when I remembered seeing someone in my bathroom. Had I been hallucinating? Or was this man the same figure I saw storming into my very private and hopeful final attempt to die? Had he doomed me to fail again? Did he bring me here? Am I in a psychiatric hospital again? My heart rate quickened and my breathing became labored as I silently kept asking myself, how could I have failed yet again after all of the planning and preparation? How could this be happening again? I could not bear the thought of having to face my friends in this situation again.

The tears began to unnoticeably and silently run down my cheeks as my breathing turned to pants and my ribs seemed to tighten around my lungs. The overwhelming feeling of sadness as my failure became evident overtook me, making my vision blur as I unintentionally began to make a horrific sound of anguish and pain.

I felt myself begin to spiral down the black abyss I contained within my mind while sliding on a river of despair, until the oddest thing began to happen. It felt as though the blackness within my body and mind was being drawn out and was being replaced by a white energy that made me feel light and weightless. My head began to clear and regain focus, allowing my attention to be turned to the sensation of someone squeezing my arms. When I looked, I saw the sleeping man, who was now very much awake, holding me as he looked closely into my eyes. His turquoise blue eyes bore into mine almost as if he was willing his own energy to take over my body like a helping hand pulling me out of the blackness.

It was in that moment that I felt myself letting go and allowed this strange feeling to consume me. I felt myself lighten as our two energies entwined. Then, as if this entire situation couldn't get any weirder, he spoke to me. But he didn't speak with his mouth, I heard him speak inside my head. Our eyes remained focused on each other as he began to hum a song inside of me immediately making me feel relaxed and peaceful.

"What are you doing? How is this happening?" I asked him out loud, baffled.

'We are two halves of one whole my love. Our paths have been heading toward this moment since the day we were born,' he said silently as his forehead touched mine. 'We are stronger together.'

Lifting his forehead off of mine, he leaned his head back to face the ceiling while continuing to rub my arm. I felt as if I couldn't take my eyes off of him, mesmerized by what was happening inside my body. I felt almost effervescent. While the worry lines between my eyes began to release, I noticed a single tear run down the side of his face, and somehow I knew that he too was feeling the same relief I was.

"What the fuck is going on?" I whispered.

5

My thoughts were not my own anymore. I heard his thoughts and felt his emotions in my own body and mind. It was all incredibly disorienting. I continued to feel his warmth run up my arms and through my body as if I were submerging in warm water. The emotional pain and suffering that I had been enduring for so long now seemed to be a distant memory. A new sense of relief and joy flowed into my body like a slow drifting stream beginning at my arms and then moving up to spread to the rest of my body. He was somehow gently pushing these feelings into me. And instinctively, I knew that all I had to do was passively accept them into myself and allow them to take over my innate darkness.

With a clearer mind I began to feel more animated sensing that my anguish had been at the very least oppressed for now. As our eyes remained connected, he withdrew his hands from my arms and pulled himself to sit on the bed beside me.

"I have been waiting for the right moment to come for you. I could sense that the time was near but I didn't think you would really try again," he said in a sad whisper.

"Who are you?" I gasped.

"My name is Jonas. You and I have been living our lives separately but intertwined since our birth. All of our choices have led us to this one outcome...to this moment where we came back together," he said as he stood.

"What...?" I asked seemingly losing the rest of my words as I tried to make sense of what was happening.

He began to pace in front of the bed while I remained seated under the stark white covers and my blindingly white hospital gown. I watched him pace back and forth, feeling completely transfixed, sensing that he was carefully weighing what he would say to me next.

"Where am I Jonas?" I asked glancing around almost fearful of the answer.

"You are safe Lily. You are in a hospital about an hour north of the city," he paused. "I have been following you for quite some time now... We belong with one another you see," he said after a pause, "two halves of one whole, born at the exact moment, having known great loss in our lives. Our journey, as painful as it has been, has led us to this moment. Where our lives intersect and our energies can reunite."

It is difficult to explain his tone as he explained this to me. Because as joyous as I felt his energy to be, I could also feel a deeply buried sadness and longing. After a few minutes, he finally sat beside me on the bed and reached for my arms. Again ensuring that our eye contact was never broken, I began to feel a tingling sensation and then a zing, as he somehow was able to push his energy into me again along with his thoughts. Allowing myself to sink into his mind and explore these new feelings. Through the chaos of these confusing sensations, I saw the face of a man with dark eyes and dark hair. I felt deep love for him, almost as if my heart beat for him alone. I somehow knew that this man was named Jack and that he is the source of Jonas' greatest love and also his greatest pain.

As the image began to gain more and more clarity, Jonas suddenly let go of my arms and almost jumped away from me to resume his pacing of the room.

"Jonas! What the hell is going on? How did you do that? What is happening? Who was that man? And how do I know that his name is Jack?" I yelled frantically.

"Yes," he breathed, "that was Jack. He was the love of my life."

He continued to pace and I could see it in his face that I had unintentionally seen something very private. My mind began to spin as the number of questions continued to build in my mind.

"Jonas what is happening to me?" I paused for a moment, hoping for a response. "How is it that I can see these images in my mind? Was that you in my bathroom? How did you get into my apartment? How did you know what I was trying to do to myself?" I asked him as my lungs felt as if it were running out of air and my exasperation shook in the bed. "Who are you Jonas? How are we connected?" I asked, "What kind of hospital is this? What is going to happen...? What the fuck is going on?"

The door suddenly and loudly swung open interrupting my rant forcing Jonas to stop his incessant pacing. In walked two very large men who looked like they spend way too much time in the gym followed by a petite woman with long pin straight mousey blonde hair wearing a lab coat. The two men who hovered over the little blond as if they were her bodyguards, were surprisingly wearing white scrubs and white sneakers. Their tight scrub tops seemed to be way too small for their large physiques making them look very uncomfortable in their very unattractive outfits. The blonde lady wore black patent leather heels high enough that I would have twisted my ankles the moment I tried to walk in them. Her slim bare legs peeked beneath the hem of her lab coat. Her beauty and style made me suddenly feel very self-conscious about my own appearance as I shyly tugged at my white hospital gown while attempting to conceal my bandaged wrists.

"Hello Lily. My name is Naomi and I am here to answer as many questions as I can. I am certain you have many right now. Please try to control yourself. I would hate for Marc and Jeff to have to jump in here," she said with a smirk, almost wanting me to challenge her so that her two brutes could contain me.

I looked down at my body to make sure I hadn't morphed into

Wolverine or something. What was she talking about...control myself? What the hell was I supposed to do in my hospital gown with my bare ass hanging out? That's not even taking into consideration that I was hooked up to an IV, which in and of itself limits my mobility.

"I'm just fine Naomi. I think I can contain myself. Please go ahead and begin explaining to me what is going on here and where the fuck I am?" I said gritting my teeth angrily.

"Lily, you and Jonas have known each other since you were children, infants really. You were raised in our children's facility in the mid-west," she began to explain, "the two of you became quite close as children, which we encouraged by enrolling you in a special program that links two bodies, minds and we think maybe even souls, if one were to believe in souls. The two individuals can continue to experience their own separate lives but are never complete without the other." She finished her sentence with a bright but almost sinister smile.

I grimaced as my mind continued racing with questions and confusion as all eyes remained fixed on me. Is this a joke? What the hell is going on? I'm not sure if I should laugh at their prank or cry because I have legitimately lost my mind or if I should be angry because these people just kidnapped me. I kept staring at Naomi open mouthed just waiting for her to say, 'Oh you silly psycho, I'm just kidding.' But I could tell that wasn't coming. I could feel a buzzing in my ears as Jonas fixed his gaze on mine and then suddenly, I could 'hear' him speaking in my mind again.

'I know this is a lot to take in darling. Believe me, it was hard for me too. But I am here with you, we are bound together my. We will get through this.'

Jonas then outstretched his hand as he walked to the opposite side of the bed, in an effort to get me to unclench my hands as they held the blanket tightly in my fists. Releasing my grip, he held my hands reassuringly and as I continued to watch him tears began to fall from his eyes. "I have missed you so much. I have needed you. I have been so lost," he said as he rubbed my hands on his cheeks.

I then looked at Naomi with obvious confusion on my face. Almost pleading for help with the crazy man on my bed.

"Lily, infants come to us from time to time, from different places. We search for links between two bodies and sometimes we get lucky. The scientists were very lucky to have found you and Jonas simultaneously, both with a genetic predisposition to link to one another. It's quite rare. You're very lucky," Naomi explained with a fake joviality.

Gawking at her open mouthed, I finally spoke after a short pause. "What the fuck are you talking about? What the hell is going on here?" I shouted. "I grew up in Virginia. I have parents. I went to school and college. I have a husband and children and friends that I grew up with. I have known them my entire life. I have a job and a home. I wasn't raised in a home for children. You have the wrong person lady. I want you to call the police. You have kidnapped me and are holding me against my will!" Now I could feel the tears streaking down my hot cheeks. Jonas reached up to wipe them away but before he touched me, I hit his hand away from me as I looked at him with fury.

'Lily, you can hear me can't you?' Jonas said this in my mind. I just looked at him without responding.

"Lily, I know you can hear Jonas. He is part of the puzzle that makes you, you." She paused, took in a deep breath and then let it out slowly almost as if she were counting. "It is late and you are upset. Let's resume in the morning." Without another word she turned and headed to the door turning just before she was completely out of the room. Looking at Jonas she asked, "Are you coming with us?"

Without taking his eyes off of me he replied to her in an almost whisper, "No. I can't be away from her again."

As he reached forward to take my hand, I let go of the breath I hadn't realized I had been holding, feeling a sense of relief that he wasn't leaving me. As I caught myself thinking this, I began making peace with the fact that I had obviously had a psychotic episode. But before I could begin my barrage of questions again, a female nurse in white scrubs walked into the room unannounced. Without looking at

Jonas and I, she walked to my IV and plunged a medication into my vein without ever saying a word.

"What are you giving me?" I asked just before suddenly becoming exhausted. Unable to keep my eyes open for another moment, I laid my head down and fell asleep instantly, while still very much aware that Jonas held me tightly as he lay beside me.

6

I was dreaming that I was flying again. In a building this time with the same stark white walls, white flooring and white everything similar to the Birches. I rose to the ceiling until my head touched the fluorescent lights. As I looked around the windowless room I glanced down to the floor and noticed that I was wearing a white jump suit and that my small feet were bare as they floated beneath me. The air was moving around me making my long brown hair sway around me softly. As I pressed my hands above my head up against the ceiling, the wind continued to push me up as if it were trying to get my body past the solid barrier. I began fighting the strength of the wind as it encircled my body and penetrated my skin, pushing its way through muscle and sinews all of the way to my bones. Feeling the pressure and sensation of air beneath my skin, I focused on its power after realizing that the wind was not coming into my body but actually leaving it. I was the source of the wind and I was the one pushing it out.

This dream did not fill me with joy and wonder as my other dreams of flying had previously done. This time what I felt was fear. I was scared that if I didn't concentrate had enough I would lose control and would be unable to keep my body together. I had to draw on all of my strength to not allow myself to break apart and turn into the air itself. What scared me the most *was the possibility of breaking apart to only then pass through the ceiling and then to continue ascending into the atmosphere in a million pieces. I feared that I would be unable to pull myself back together if I did?*

A woman's voice below me said, "Lily come back down please."

Not having noticed anyone below me before as I pondered these new sensations and abilities, I startled slightly before looking down to discover that directly beneath me stood a kind and tidy looking woman with her brown hair up in a tight bun, her wide brown eyes watched me through her small cat-eyeglasses as she wore a neatly pressed lab coat. She looked so familiar and I somehow knew that she liked me very much. Immediately doing what was requested of me, I closed my eyes and grabbed onto gravity as if it had hands reaching up to me, welcoming me back. I drifted down slowly, landing as I looked up at the nice lady. She stared at me with obvious annoyance before saying, "I told you Lily, today is not flying day. There are other things that you need to work on. Now, let's go find Jonas shall we?" She firmly but kindly took my hand in hers.

The moment her cold hand wrapped around mine, I felt my body jolt awake while sweating and panting, in the same sterile hospital room I had fallen asleep in. The unease I felt in the dream seemed to have followed me out of the dream as I lay in the hospital bed. With the sensations from the dream still vivid in my mind, I examined the hand that the scientist had held and was surprised to discover Jonas sleeping beside me. It was very likely that he had slept there all night, curled up in the chair with his head down on my arm while clutching my hand. As I stared at his peaceful face, I relaxed my body and stilled my breath hoping to not waken him.

The strangeness of my present situation began to consume me as my mind raced with a million questions. Who is this man that can't seem to be able to leave my side? I can't deny the pull I feel toward him. He feels so familiar and his energy felt so welcoming. What the hell was I thinking? His energy felt welcoming! What the fuck? I shouted in my head.

Most surprising though, and despite all of the trepidation I felt about this unknown situation, I couldn't help but feel curious about how his words seemed to me have made sense in a strange way. I wanted to believe him, but did that make me crazy? Or crazier perhaps? Was it just my loneliness talking?

I closed my eyes and tried to replicate the sensation I had experienced before, where I could see his thoughts. After taking in a deep breath, I tried to push my feelings out of myself, beyond the boundaries of my body. After a few distracted attempts where I tried to channel Yoda by saying silently in my mind, "Stretch out your feelings." I was very much surprised when I successfully made contact. It was astoundingly easy actually, for my mind to connect with his sleeping mind. The moment my energy touched his, it felt as if a vacuum pulled me in. Startled by the sensation, I shut my eyes and allowed myself to slide in while anchoring myself with the sound of his breathing, its depth and rhythm. I could feel the warmth and energy flowing in his blood vessels as his heart beat strongly in his chest while my own breathing pattern subconsciously, instinctively altered to match his. Startled, I let out a small gasp when my heart began to beat erratically as if it were about to jump out of my chest until suddenly slowing as its rhythm also synched with his. This was an incredibly peaceful sensation, unlike anything I had ever experienced. I felt joy, acceptance and openness where I felt not only connected to Jonas but also fulfilled by him.

In a bright flash I began to see what Jonas had been seeing in his dreaming mind. The sun was shining brightly and the warm breeze gently kissed my skin. Jonas was calmly walking on a beach wearing nothing but swimming trunks, revealing his tanned skin as the soft waves kissed the shore over and over again. Feeling the suns warmth on my own skin sent me into a euphoric bliss. I closed my eyes, drawing the sounds and sensations of my surroundings into my body so that it could flow through me, filling me with light. I was startled out of my brief meditation, suddenly opening my eyes as I realized that the wind had been calling to me in a whisper. The experience was mesmerizing. The happiness and peace in this space was all consuming. Instinctively I knew that the sensations I had been experiencing were the same as Jonas had been feeling.

In a whisper I heard him say, "I love you," as he reached and caressed the face of a slim dark haired, dark eyed man that I had known from before to be Jack. I could feel the pace of my heartbeat quicken with the sensation of their emotions flowing through me. My body was filled by their love and admiration as it enveloped them in their private protective cocoon. As they continued to speak lovingly and kiss softly, I felt guilt for intruding on such a very private moment.

Unaware of how I achieved it, I somehow pushed myself out of Jonas' dream. When I opened my eyes in my stark white hospital room, I discovered that he remained peacefully asleep despite the bright sun shining through the sheer white curtains. I began to cry silently as I processed what I had just experienced. Somehow I had invaded Jonas' privacy and witnessed something very sacred to his heart. His purest and deepest love had filled him with purpose along with a drive to be a better man. But somehow, it had all come to an abrupt ending. This had caused those feelings and desires to morph into a source of deep loss and sadness for Jonas. Jack was gone, of that I was certain, but how I did not yet know.

Feeling sadness for his loss I instinctively began to caress his curly brown hair and by doing so I somehow began to pull his pain into myself. As I stroked his hair the palm of my hand and my fingers seemed to become electrified as a subtle glow emanated from my hand. The sensations and the ability itself felt like second nature, as if I had done this a million times before. My body buzzed with the electricity that flooded into me making my entire body hummed as my muscles like they had been filled with strength. Once the sensation of negativity disappeared from Jonas' subconscious and it flooded my body, I glanced down at him and saw a look of tenderness as a small smile slid onto his lips. I couldn't help but smile as I covered my mouth with my hands in an attempt to hold in any sounds that might escape from the sheer curiousness of what I had just achieved and experienced.

Our peaceful moment was suddenly interrupted as the door slammed open loudly as Naomi and her two brutes walked in. Jonas jumped from his chair, startled awake into a protective stance.

"Good morning, I believe it is time to begin our day. Lily, please have a shower and I will have breakfast sent to your room. Jonas, please go shower and then come join Lily for breakfast. Lily you will find all you need in the bathroom including clothes. I will return in one hour, so please move along," Naomi said authoritatively before leaving the room as her two goons trailed behind just as quickly as they had come in.

"Why does she have bodyguards?" I asked in a whisper to myself.

"She can be difficult sometimes," Jonas responded as he relaxed his stance.

I turned to him and smiled, feeling our connection holding strong as if we had just shared a deep and personal secret. I climbed out of bed and made my way to the bathroom surprised to discover that I was no longer connected to any medical devices. Someone must have disconnected my IV fluids as I slept, I thought to myself. My confidence was abruptly halted as I was forced to stop walking when I became overwhelmingly dizzy. Jonas rushed to stand in front of me so that he could hold my shoulders in place to help me steady myself.

As we stood there for a few moments while Jonas continued to hold me he said, "Thank you Lily. I haven't had such a peaceful moment with Jack since he was still here. That was a true gift." He reached up and stroked my face tenderly.

"I don't know how I did that," I stated with a pause. "I have so many questions...I could feel the joy and love you shared with him. Along with the pain you feel from his loss. I feel sadness for you." Instinctively, I pulled him into a tight hug which he accepted with relief on his face.

"Don't feel sad darling. You just gave me an incredible gift, as brief as it was. You have given me a reprieve from the sadness involving Jack. I love you Lily and I have missed you so. You will soon remember all of this, I promise. It will all make sense. Please remember that I will be here to help you get through the memories.

Much of it will be difficult, but you are not alone. I will always be here. We are two halves of one whole. Where you go I will follow." He smiled sadly with his piercing turquoise eyes before bending down to kiss my forehead.

"Somehow, deep down, I know that that's true. I don't understand what is happening to me. How is all of this possible? Why do we have this connection? How is it that I can see... well actually be in your dreams? How did I do that with my hands? It was so instinctual, as if I had done that so many times before," I explained while looking into his eyes before examining my hands.

He nodded and smiled, "I know this is all very disorienting. But I promise, all will become clear. Now, I'm going to shower and I suggest you shower as well because you kind of stink," he said as he winked at me.

Feigning shock, I watched him leave my room with amusement, turning to smile at me just before shutting the door.

"I'm in the Twilight Zone," I whispered to myself.

"You're not in the Twilight Zone Lily. Go shower!" Jonas said from the other side of the door.

7

The water pressure in the Birches shower was amazing. I lingered in beneath the hot water for as long as I could while examining the wounds on my arms and admiring their expert suturing. There must have been 30 sutures per wound. I traced the lines that started at my wrists and ran almost all of the way to my elbows. Two lines per arm, four arteries in total. It was amazing to recall my level of intoxication when I expertly cut into myself the way that I had. Most amazing of all was that Jonas had gotten to me when he did.

After quickly dressing, I dumped my white hospital gown in the hamper and put on a white jump suit that was identical to what I had worn in my dream. I brushed my long brown hair and then French braided it down my back while looking at myself in the mirror. Much to my surprise my cheeks looked pink making me wonder if they had given me a blood transfusion. I had lost quite a bit of blood in the tub.

I rolled my sleeves up to get a look at my arms flinching at how angry and red the lines were out of the shower. After making a valiant attempt to re-bandage my arms, I gave up after repeatedly failing miserably. Once I had given up, I decided to just pull my sleeves back down past my wrists so that my arms would remain covered. Stepping out of the bathroom I was quite startled to find Jonas coming into my room while pushing a breakfast cart. I was instantly relieved that I had covered my arms before coming out of the bathroom. I didn't want Jonas to have to see that mess again.

"Come here, I'll redress those," he said as he glanced at my covered arms.

I raised my eyebrows in alarm, realizing that my lack of privacy both physically and mentally had suddenly become my current reality. Jonas left me pondering this as he walked into the bathroom and then quickly returned with the necessary supplies. Expertly, he wrapped my arms in silence as his pain became palpable in my own body and his words of aguish screamed loudly in my head as he looked at the severity of my self-inflicted wounds.

Once he was finished and seemed satisfied with his handiwork he smiled and said, "It's time to eat. We have a long day ahead of us. There is much to do."

The mere mentioning of food made me realize how famished I had been. I sat down at the food cart not bothering to move anything to the table and began removing the tops off of the plates to see what my options were. Eggs, bacon, biscuits, home fries and pancakes, it was carb city. I gulped my coffee and shoveled food into my mouth in silence while Jonas contentedly watched me eat making me feel very self-conscious. When he realized that I had noticed what he was doing he began eating as well. But the small smile remained on his face that seemed to reach all the way to his eyes.

"What are you smirking at?" I asked.

"I'm happy that's all," he said.

"Jonas, where are we?" I asked softly, remembering I had just about a million questions.

"This is a military medical facility," he explained, "it's called The Birches."

"I've never heard of it. Why was I brought here instead of a hospital near my apartment? I'm not military," I asked.

"But you are military Lily," he paused, took in a deep breath and closed his eyes for a moment, "Lily, this story can be difficult to hear.

But, nonetheless it is your story, our story actually, and so you must hear it," he explained with a sad tone as he reached across the food cart to grasp my hand. "I know that to you think we have just met. And you are discovering that we have this strange connection. You are also discovering that you are able to do some things that you have not been able to do before coming here. Please believe me when I say that I know exactly what you are feeling, the confusion is all consuming. We will get through this together," he explained.

"What the hell are you talking about? Spit it out! The suspense is killing me!" I spoke more forcefully than I had intended pulling my hand away.

He nodded slowly and let out a deep breath. As his gaze remained fixed on mine, he began to tell the story of how we came to be.

"WE WERE both born to women who did not want us," he started with a morose tone. "On the same day and at the same time, separated by an entire country. The Birches scientists were taking as many infants like us as they could find. They raised and modified unwanted children so that they would grow up to be perfect soldiers, perfect fighters and strategists. They would experiment on us, examining our DNA, looking for ways to make each of us better. One day they learned that a small group of us had mirror like DNA structures. Sometimes even completing a component of one another's genome that had previously been almost half formed. Like two pieces of a puzzle locking together. You and I were one of these children. We were identified when we were infants. We were raised together as if we were one person and not individuals. We spent night and days together, linking our minds and bodies to the point where we would move as one. We knew what the other was feeling and thinking and we were able to speak without uttering a word. We did everything together. Sleep, bathe, eat, play...all of it," he said with a small smile.

"Why is it that you know all of this and I do not? Why do I not have any memory of any of this? We were raised here...in this hospital?" I paused for a moment looking around me. "I must say Jonas, I think that I have lost my mind. We are in a psych ward aren't we...and you're one of the other patients just fucking with me. Isn't that right?" I began to laugh, "I think I was hallucinating this morning, I could see light coming out of my hands. I mean really. What the hell is happening to me? I think that that Naomi chick gave me some heavy-duty drugs in my IV and now I'm seeing things. I mean really, I'm actually listening to you and really wanting to believe that what you're saying is true. I actually want to believe this ludicrous story," I said wide-eyed.

That's when I just started laughing to the point where my side began cramping and tears rolled down your cheeks. I had lost my mind and was now in a lock down psychiatric unit. Either that or I did die. Maybe I had been successful in my suicide attempt after all and was in some weird in-between place where I was being secretly evaluated to determine what the hell should happen to me next.

As my hysterical laughter continued, I glanced up at Jonas and noticed that he had started laughing as well which made me laugh even harder. He began belly laughing as he watched me. We laughed hard until I could no longer breathe. We sat there panting until he reached across our meal, our food long forgotten, as he grabbed my hand and held it tightly, he closed his eyes as he spoke in my mind, *"You are not insane my darling. I did not realize how much I had missed your laughter. It's always been so contagious."*

He was smiling at me with his eyes again. "What I tell you is true my love. I was like you not that long ago. I too had no memory of any of this. Then one day they found me, brought me back here...and they helped me remember."

"How did they help you remember?" I asked still out of breath.

"They have their ways...they have medicines that will help you," he said with sadness in his eyes.

"Then why did they bring you in first, why not bring us in together?" I asked.

"Because they need me to maintain the stability. To be sure that you receive all of the information well," he took a deep breath before continuing, "this is quite the journey you are about to embark upon and I am part of you as you are part of me. Together we are balanced. We are weaker and more out of control apart. I am needed to help you achieve your memories and regain your potential."

"What balance are you talking about? Keep what stable? Me? Keep me stable? I am not following. I mean what do people think I will do?" I asked curiously.

"You must understand darling, there are other Duals. Others like us. In each Dual there is always the balancer, the strategist, the one who ensures stability in the union. The fighter is the other half. They are stronger in all ways. My role as you learn of your beginnings is to ensure that you maintain a clear head and allow yourself to relearn the control over your abilities as you were once able to," he explained.

"Oh my god, this is pure insanity!" I said with a smirk as I looked out the window. "How old was I when I left here? Wait, I had a mother. I went to school and had friends. I was married with two children for god's sake. How could this have been completely elimi-nated from my mind?" I asked.

"You were seventeen when you left the Homestead. When we were separated," he said sadly, "we both had lives in between..."

"The Homestead?" I asked.

"Yes, The Birches, where we are now is just a hospital. We were moved to The Homestead to live. To foster our new found abilities and to continue to learn what other potential we held within us," he explained.

"Where is The Homestead?"

"It's in Iowa."

I turned to look out the window before saying. "How is this possi-ble?" I asked myself in disbelief.

"I know this is a lot to process. It will all make sense. I promise."

"You had Jack?" I said looking at him again.

"Yes, I had Jack. And then I lost him," he said as his eyes began to moisten.

It was then that the door was abruptly opened and in walked

tweedle-dee and tweedle-dum with Naomi in tow. I jumped, startled by their pace and intrusion, rolling my eyes at their drama.

"This is a good point to stop," Naomi said. "Let's get started shall we?" she ordered.

Jonas tightened his grip on my hand and winked at me while speaking in my mind, *"I'm always with you. Don't be scared darling."*

Keeping a tight hold of his hand I stood and followed Naomi out of the room. I couldn't help but freak out a little inside as I wondered what the hell it was I had gotten myself into? Do I actually believe this crap?

8

As we walked down a completely nondescript hallway with its stark white walls and blinding white floor with not a door or window in site, no natural light at all, where the only sounds I could hear were the buzzing fluorescent lights and the echoes from our foot steps. Jonas squeezed my hand softly, trying to reassure me after seeing my obvious nervousness on my face.

Continuing on down the hall, we took several turns until finally reaching a set of double metal doors. As Naomi approached the doors, an opening appeared on the wall allowing access to a glass identification pad. After placing her hand on the security device and her identification confirmed through her finger prints, she then entered a lengthy code into the keypad. With a slight click the doors slowly opened, revealing a large scientific lab composed of multiple stations with glass jars and vials, microscopes and other mechanical contraptions I was unfamiliar with. Along with the devices, each station also held its very own scientist. Each appeared focused on their tasks until as if all sound had been suddenly sucked out of the room, all eyes turned to us as they remained sitting motionlessly while watching us following behind Naomi. Their eyes could not hide their curiosity and dismay as their gazes remained fixed on our movements. I tightened my grip on Jonas' hand and he reciprocated the squeeze.

Suddenly becoming self-conscious about my appearance, I stroked the stray hairs back away from my face while remembering that I wasn't wearing any shoes. Not that that should have bothered me. After all I was wearing a white jump suit, which I'm sure, was not doing my figure any favors. I turned to Jonas and tried to throw my mind open so that I could speak to him in his mind.

"Am I not allowed to have shoes? What's the deal?" I asked him.

He barely perceptibly shook his head and said, *"It's all part of your sensory awakening."* I caught myself frowning at him a little before looking straight ahead again.

"I request that you both keep your non-vocal conversations to a minimum please," Naomi instructed. "I am glad to see that you are beginning to relearn that skill Lily. It's one less thing we will need to address."

Silently, we made our way to a much smaller lab located within this larger space. The smaller room had clear glass windows on two of its four walls to allow for easy visualization of all of the scientists as they continued to gawk at us. Naomi gestured for me sit on an examination table located in the middle of the room. As I scooted up onto the table with it's crinkling paper I looked out of the window and noticed that all eyes had remained on me even as I sat on the table. Naomi noticed all of the scrutiny I was getting and that my attention had also remained fixed on the spectators outside of the examination room. Silently she looked at her two bodyguards and made a silent gesture that presumably indicated, 'go deal with that would you.' One of the men turned and pushed a button by one of the windows, instantly making the glass turn an opaque black. The other bodyguard walked out of the room and shut the door.

"Well, that was interesting," I said sarcastically.

"I apologize for that. There is much curiosity about the both of you. They wonder how you will fare after I awaken you," Naomi said.

"Awaken me?" I asked.

"Once I reverse your amnesia, yes," Naomi said matter-of-fact.

"And how exactly are you planning to reverse my so called amnesia?" I asked her sarcastically as I glance at Jonas who is sitting on the edge of the examination table on the other side of Naomi, while still holding my hand tightly.

"With this," she said as she held up a very large syringe filled with a milky green liquid. "Lay back please," she ordered firmly.

"What is that?" I asked as I slowly began to recline.

Without saying a word, she turned to duffus number one, who had remained in the room with us and gave him a slight nod. Silently, he made his way to the door, cracked it open slightly and then whispered to his buddy who had been guarding the room from the outside. Once their conversation is done, the door is closed again without a sound. Not long after that a very soft alarm is sounded as lights flash. The sound of chairs scrapping against the concrete floor erupt and the echo of footsteps fade away as the scientists made their way out of the large space, this was followed by the loud slamming of the double metal doors that we had entered through. All that remained was complete silence with the exception of the humming fluorescent lights overhead.

"They have all left Lily. This entire space is now ours. You are safe. Please lay back, I need to place an IV in your arm so that I can begin your infusion," Naomi ordered as she turned to gather supplies from the counter behind her. "It will take several hours for the medication to infuse fully. We will need to monitor you the entire time and Jonas will remain in the room with you. He will be connected to our monitoring equipment as well," she explained.

"Hold on a second. What is that first of all? Before you come anywhere near me with a needle you need to tell me what the fuck you're injecting me with," I said angrily while pointing to the syringe she wielded like a knife.

Naomi turned to Jonas and gave him a knowing smile.

"Lily, this is a serum that we use to help reunite Duals. We have used it many times, all with great success at reversing the amnesia. It will all make sense, I promise," Naomi explained stiffly. "Now lay back please. We need to get started."

THE IV WAS PLACED EXPERTLY and smoothly while carefully avoiding my wounds. EKG leads were then placed on my chest and head before the monitors were turned on. A hospital bed was brought in for Jonas so that he could lay right beside me with our beds touching. Naomi placed the same leads on Jonas' body while never letting go of my hand. Once he was connected and the monitors were turned on, Jonas looked at me lovingly and expectantly as he squeezed my hand reassuringly. His presence and touch created a sense of calmness that ran through my body like electricity.

Naomi walked up along the other side of the bed and connected the serum to my IV, programmed the IV pump and started the infusion. I watched as the milky green liquid began to make its way through the tubing toward my arm. Naomi ran her fingers through my hair softly and tucked a strand of hair behind my ear.

"This will take approximately eleven hours to infuse completely. The serum also has a sedative component, so your discomfort from the infusion should be minimal. You should hopefully sleep through all of it," she explained with a cold smile. "You will both be monitored during this process," she said, "the darker of the Duals must have a guide to re-engage the part of the brain that has been placed into dormancy. That is why Jonas is here and that is why we need to track him as well."

The darker one...what the hell was she talking about? I asked myself. Turning to Jonas with a questioning look, he gives me a small smile and a wink but says nothing. Before I could ask him what it was Naomi had meant, everything quickly faded to black.

9

My body felt as light as a feather floating in a soft spring breeze. I could feel the wind twisting and turning around my body as my arms and legs hung limply, completely at its mercy. These sensations were familiar. I had certainly experienced this before. As if the warm air hugged and comforting me. Almost as if it were welcoming back an old friend. My eye lids felt heavy and as I slowly peeked through my barely open eyes I could see my long brown hair whipping around my body. I began to stretch and extend my limbs feeling as if I were coming out of a prolonged hibernation. I engaged my limp extremities, extending my arms over my head as I straightened my legs all the way to my toes locking my joints back into alertness, moving the sluggish blood in my veins.

When I widened my gaze and tried t shake my mind out of the pharmaceutical induced fog, after some moments I was able to process my surroundings and see what was happening around my body. With striking alarm, I discovered that my body was in fact levitating off of the bed as a vortex of wind spun around, cocooning my body. With a loud gasp, I jumped within the windy enclosure and became even more startled when I discovered that the spinning wind mimicked and followed my movements, no matter how small or subtle they were. As the sensation of shock began to dissipate, I looked at body and was relieved to discover that I was still wearing the white jumper from when I had started this process. It was all so beautiful and it made me feel so welcomed and relaxed, I began to contemplate whether I was in a narcotic induced hallucination or perhaps even a dream.

'You are not dreaming my darling,' Jonas said in my mind. *'The vortex is of your own creation. You command it. Move your hands and will it to move in the manner and direction in which you desire.'*

Floating higher and higher until I was inches away from the ceiling, I turned my head as much as I could before fear of the possibility of turning the full 180 degrees struck me. I could feel the electrodes still connected to my head and chest as I moved my hands in front of my body and pushed against the vortex so that it would turn me instead of me turning inside of it.

When my eyes finally found Jonas', he smiled brightly and said, "Well hello darling. Look at what you can do."

Instinctively, I moved my legs just so, making the vortex begin to bring my body closer to the floor as if I were, but without breaking the barriers around me so that my bare feet remained several inches away from making contact with the white linoleum. With my fingers extended in front of my upright body, I calmed the speed at which the vortex spun around me until it became barely perceptible. The ability and knowledge to do this felt completely natural. As if the wind were an extension of my body and that I had been controlling it my entire life.

"Is the infusion complete?" I asked Jonas as he continued to lie on the bed watching me with his leads still firmly in place.

"No darling, it's only been about two hours," he said with a small smile, unable to hide the concern in his tone.

I glanced down at my arm and traced the tubing all of the way to the syringe noticing that it was empty.

"Am I done? The syringe is empty. The infusion is complete," I stated with a tinge of joy. Certainly this means I'm done. I mean the syringe is empty and look at what I can do, I thought to myself.

But Jonas could not hide his fears. "What is happening Jonas? Why is it that I sense worry from you? Is there something wrong? How is it that I can move the air around me like this? You said that it comes from me... but how? Where is it coming from there are no windows in here?" I asked as I moved my arms up and delighted to see the spinning wind continue to follow my arms. "The syringe is empty, I must be done right?"

Naomi entered the room cooly and silently with another syringe in her hand.

"I apologize Lily but you are not finished yet. It seems that your body is actually drawing out the serum from the syringe. As if your body is pulling it into itself. The syringe is programmed to deliver the medication over a period of time but you somehow bypassed the mechanics of the pump and drew it all into yourself," she cleared her throat before continuing. "During the past few amnesia reversals, the initial introduction to the serum has actually been quite lengthy. We infuse it slowly intentionally so that we can detect undesirable side effects and stop the infusion early if we need to. Are you feeling well? Your body temperature is much higher than when we started. Your heart and breathing rates are normal however, so I believe there isn't anything to be concerned with. Do you feel like you can continue?" she asked.

"I feel fine. I do feel quite warm now that you mention it. Is a second syringe dangerous? What does it mean that my body is drawing in the serum? I don't understand what is happening. Is this all a hallucination?" I asked pointing to the vortex.

"You are not hallucinating I promise. This is all in fact really happening. Your body is just different, that's all. It's almost as if your mind is ready to remember and it is doing what it needs to do to make that happen," Naomi explained. "We normally have a break of 3 or so days before introducing more medication to the body. This is after the initial dose I mean. But do you want to go ahead and begin the second dose now? Or do you wish to stop?" She asked me this as if she really didn't care what my answer was because her intention was clear, she was going to connect that second syringe no matter what I said.

After a short pause I said, "No. I'm not sure how this can get any weirder. Let's get this over with. Jonas are you OK? What do you think?" I asked looking at his concerned face.

"Is this safe Naomi? She can't be harmed. Please," Jonas said pleadingly.

"I am watching both of you very closely. I believe it is safe to proceed. Her body is pulling this in almost as it is parched for it. It's just soaking it in," she said with guarded elation and astonishment.

"Let's get started," I said firmly, "I want this done and over with."

Before I could change my mind, Naomi connected the new syringe, much larger syringe almost double the volume of the first infusion. Once she had pushed start on the pump, I watched my arm with anticipation just waiting for the fluid to begin moving in the tubing so that it could flow into my body. As the medication made it's way into my vein, I turned to Jonas clearly sensing his reticence. He watched me as his eyes began to fill to the point where one small tear escaped and slid down his cheek. With a small smile he silently mouthed, 'I love you. Please remember me.'

Returning his smile, I gave him a small nod before instinctively moving my arms to thicken and tighten the vortex's embrace so that it would cradle my body, protecting it as I sank into blackness again.

I could tell that I was dreaming again. I knew for certain this time. But this was unlike any other dream I had before. There was a boy with curly brown hair and turquoise blue eyes. We were running in a field of wild flowers as we held each others hands and laughed while chasing butterflies. I suddenly tripped on a rock and fell, painfully scrapping my knee. Without hesitation, he bent down and kissed the cut, visibly getting my blood on his lips. With the arms of a small boy, he carried me to the house where a very

kind and familiar looking woman cleaned up my knee as the boy sat beside me, holding my hand. I knew that we were inseparable.

Bathing, eating, reading even sleeping as we held one another was done together. He brought me joy and comfort. Even during the many tests and medications.

We would lie beside each other holding hands while the needles pierced our skin. I would whisper reassurances in his ear in my little girl voice as he screamed from the pain. I would sing him songs and brush his hair away from his forehead as his muscles clenched and sweat ran down his brow from the agony he felt.

I loved and needed him so much. Until the day he was ripped out of burning arms as I screamed and fought, but still lost him.

I BEGAN to regain consciousness with the sounds of my own screaming in my ears and the feeling of an earthquake around me. It took a few moments for me to realize that the shaking that was I feeling was coming from within my body. My clothes and hair stuck to my sweat dripping drenched skin. I held my knees tightly to my chest as I lay in fetal position...I pulled my knees even tighter, hoping to stop the shaking. My breath escaped through my dry lips in a rhythmic pattern as if I were grunting. When I opened my eyes, I discovered that I was still floating inside of my wind tunnel, but the air around me seemed different this time. The spinning air was now red where before it had just been a white cocoon around me. As I began to closely examine it, I noticed that every once in a while there were red flickers resembling little explosions or sparks of energy. It took a bit of exertion to straighten out my arms and legs this time, in order for me to uncurl my body, stretching my arms and legs so that I could push the air away from my floating form. Once my body was free from my own grip, moving and controlling the vortex was surprisingly much simpler than it had been before. It seemed as though the movements of my body didn't really matter because I was now controlling the vortex with my mind so that the wind anticipated my movements.

The bursts of energy curiously increased in frequency and it wasn't until after I had fully stretched myself out that I noticed where the sparks were originating from. They were in fact drops of my blood. The wounds on my arms had opened slightly as I slept and were now oozing crimson droplets of fire that sparked when they came in contact with the speeding vortex. I became hypnotized by the beauty of what was happening around me. Thoughtlessly, I reached my hand to touch the flickers of light and was met with an intense rush of power that made my toes curl. The loud gasp I involuntarily released startled my hand away from the wind while still holding a drop of my burning blood on my fingers. I desperately tried to contain my shock when the small red droplet ignited into a small fire. Without much thought, I instinctively pressed my palms together and when I pulled them apart I discovered that the burning droplet had turned into a spinning sphere of fire between my hands. With simple motions of my hands I widened and shrunk the sphere at will, somehow knowing that this power resides in my core and that I had complete control over it.

When I brought my hands back together the heat flowed back into my body bringing along with it the energy that had built up inside the sphere as it had spun in my hands. I could hear the rushing of energy in my veins as my heart beat intensified it's pumping so that the power would kiss every cell in my body with this newfound and most welcoming source of energy. I felt invigorated and alive, newly born even, as my blood ebbed through me.

I closed my eyes and squeezed my hands together in prayer in front of my chest and willed the sphere of fire to come out again and to my surprise, it did. Silently commanding the vortex to turn me to stand so that I could again descend closer to the floor, I held the burning ball as I slowed the wind. After thinning the vortex wall, I searched for Jonas excitedly, eager to show him what I was now able to do. I was startled to discover that he was not where I had expected to find him. I was even more alarmed when I noticed that we were now in a completely different room.

"Jonas!" I shouted.

"I am here my darling," he said from behind me.

Turning towards the sound of his voice, I found Jonas sitting on is bed with his knees drawn to his chest as if he were trying to make himself as small as possible. His eyes were tightly shut as beads of sweat soaked through his clothes.

Hovering closely above him, I whispered, "Jonas, are you alright?"

When there was no response, I pulled the wind and the fire ball completely into myself, so that my bare feet could stand on the floor. Bloodied, I slowly sat beside him and began caressing his sweaty hair away from his face while inadvertently getting some blood on his cheeks. His skin felt like ice, which was concerning especially with all of the sweat he was producing.

"Jonas, please open your eyes. You're scaring me. Please look at me," I begged.

He opened his eyes slowly and once he registered that I was standing next to him, he pulled me down into his chest and squeezed me tightly until I was sitting on his lap.

"Oh my God, I was so scared," he said with a shaking voice as he pressed his ice-cold cheek up against mine.

He kissed my head and face with what felt like desperation, inexplicably filling my body with love. And as his arms embraced me, it felt as though there was an awakening inside of me. The memory of his arms wrapped around my body was familiar and welcoming. The tightness of his hold and the way his lips felt on my skin and how it felt to be loved by him came rushing back in a flash. I was suddenly able to remember it all. Once I realized that the little boy from my dream was him, I was instantaneously consumed with joy at having found him again, that loud sobs burst out of me as I cried into his chest.

"I remember this feeling. I remember your arms and how they felt when they held me. How could I have forgotten this? I didn't know how much I had missed you," I said sobbing loudly into his neck as I squeezed him to me. I could feel his body shaking with emotion as he cried tears along with me.

"I have missed you so much my darling. I have been so alone, just waiting for you to come back to me," he said through sobs.

We stayed on the bed, holding each other for a long while until I finally pulled away from his embrace and caressed his face as I gazed into his turquoise eyes.

"Look at your face. You're a man now...still so handsome. I've missed these eyes," I said as I kissed them. "Where are we Jonas? This room looks different. What is happening? Why were we made to forget?"

"Your vortex was getting too large and strong for the other room. We had to move you to a safer place," he explained while caressing my hair away from my tear and blood stained face. "You are a bit stronger than they had anticipated you would be this early on in the process."

"How many hours has it been?" I asked.

"Naomi has given you five times the normal amount of serum. Your body just keeps pulling it into itself. It's like you have an insatiable thirst for it," he explained with a sad smile.

"How long has it been? How many hours?" I asked.

"It has been 13 hours my darling," he said in a kind voice. "The vortex became so powerful that your leads were all torn away from your skin. We had no way to monitor you."

"But your leads are still on, why?" I asked.

"Because I am the only one who can reach you. They were trying to monitor you through me. Which is fine because I wasn't going to leave your side anyway," he said with a slight chuckle, "you and I are never separating again, you understand? You are my everything," he said as he leaned forward and kissed my bloody cheek.

"How was I moved though? Have I not been floating this entire time? I don't understand how I could just be moved with all of that around me," I asked.

"It was a very delicate process. But we managed. Your little wind trick kind of destroyed the other lab, so we had no option but to move you actually," he explained with a chuckle.

"I destroyed the lab?" I asked with a grin.

Uh-hum, he hummed and nodded while delicately placing a strand of hair behind my ear.

Naomi opened the door quickly, startling us out of our bubble of re-acquaintance with her two duds following close behind.

"Hello Lily. How are you feeling?" she asked.

Before she was even done asking the question I began to search the room for the IV pump and syringe. I followed the IV tubing that was still connected to my arm and saw the pump was now connected to a very empty medication bag and not a syringe anymore. The bag looked as if it had been sucked dry.

"You have managed to process more serum than we had anticipated. How do you feel?" she asked with a fake smile.

"I feel fine. I'm hungry and tired. But otherwise, I feel like I'm remembering a lot," I said while looking at Jonas.

I began to laugh and cry while reaching for his face again. All of the loneliness and emptiness I had felt for so long was now clearly explained. The mere thought of being away from him made my body ache. My dream of us as children replayed in my mind as we continued to look at one another. We had found so much love and support in each other as children. All of those memories and feelings were at the forefront of my mind making me feel as if we hadn't been apart at all.

While still holding me tightly, he whispered softly in my ear, "It will all be OK now. We're together again and that's all that matters. Never again, I promise. "

We both cried tears of relief as we held each others loving gaze.

"Well, I am glad to hear that the memories are returning," Naomi said dryly. "We must leave at once. There is a plane waiting for us. Marc and Jeff will take you both back to your rooms. Please change into civilian clothing after a quick shower. Jonas please help Lily redress her wounds. I will suture them back up when we get to where we are going," she ordered. "I need to make an additional stop. I will meet you at our next location, but Marc and Jeff will escort you both there."

Glad to hear that I would be free of Naomi for a bit, but was doubly excited to discover that the duds had names. Marc and Jeff... "Where are we going? Why do we have to leave right now?" I asked her.

"We need to be in a more secure location. More secluded. The work that we have ahead of us requires privacy and confidentiality. There are some delicate discoveries ahead and I would prefer to be prepared," Naomi explained.

I frowned and looked at Jonas to silently say, '*Well that was clear as mud.*'

He responded with a wink as he began to stand while I remained in his arms. It wasn't until that moment that I noticed how positively thin and weak he appeared. I gasped, "Oh my God. Are you ok?" I asked as I pushed away from him a bit.

"I'm just fine darling. Nothing a strong cup of coffee and some sweet pastries can't fix," he said while smiling falsely trying to reassure me.

We followed behind Marc and Jeff with my bare feet on the cold tiles as we made our way to our rooms. Holding Jonas' cold pale hand in mine, I instinctively began to force heat up his arm and into his body. Sensing what it was I had been doing, he lifted our joined hands and pressed his lips to my fingers as his cheeks began to regain some color.

With a slight head nod, Marc indicated that I should follow him so that he could escort me to my room, while Jeff led Jonas to his. As soon as I opened the door, I discovered a pair of jeans, a long sleeve white t-shirt and a thick black sweater laying on my bed, along with a pair of thick socks and sneakers.

After collecting the clothes, I made my way into the bathroom and removed my bloody clothes as I stood in front of the mirror. I stared at my naked reflection in shock at my appearance. I had so much blood on my hair and body that I resembled Sissy Spacek in the movie Carrie after she had pig blood dropped on her. It was not an attractive look. Standing beneath scalding hot water, I scrubbed the dried blood off of my body and hair until the water ran clear. After carefully drying myself, paying especially close attention to not rub the towel on my arms, dressed in my crisp new clothes. Examining my wounds closely, I was surprised to see that they were closing up again without the need for additional sutures which seemed curious especially since I had essentially just hemorrhaged in the vortex because some of the sutures had loosened, causing some splits in some parts of the wounds.

After brushing my grotesquely knotted hair, I braided it down my back again before pulling on the knitted black hat that I had also found on the bed. As soon as I felt presentable, I took one last look at my reflection and was pleasantly surprised to discover that my usually lifeless brown eyes had regained the semblance of a tiny sparkle in them again. It had been several years since the last time I had seen that.

I walked through the bedroom and just as I was about to open the door, I was startled back as Marc opened it suddenly.

"Excuse me, I could tell you were finished," Marc said.

"Oh yeah, how?" I asked.

"I am also a Dual," he said matter of fact.

"Is Jeff your half?" I frowned, still finding it hard to believe that I was uttering these crazy questions.

"He is. And for the record we are not duds, duffuses or tweedle's of any sort," he said with a serious tone.

I was a bit taken aback by his comment which forced me to have an involuntary nervous giggle. "I apologize Marc. I'm sure you are both very competent and I am lucky to have you around me," I said with a smile, desperately trying to contain my laughter.

He nodded his head and began to lead me down another hallway. "Where is Jonas? We have to wait for him," I urge with panic in my voice.

"Jonas and Jeff are on the plane waiting for us," he said dryly as he continued to lead me away from my room.

It wasn't until we had made it down the hall that something

dawned on me, "Hey Marc, how did you know that I was calling you and Jeff those names?" I asked.

"You will learn how to block others from hearing your thoughts and you will also learn how to have private conversations when you desire to." This he said with a ghost of a smile.

I think I'm going to like this guy I thought.

"Don't count your chickens before they hatch," he said in response to my thoughts with a smirk.

I just looked at him and laughed.

10

Jonas and I sat next to each other on the plane. We were in the air for several hours and in that time we noticed our movements becoming more and more synchronized with one another. The sun had set and the dark earth below made it impossible for us to determine where it was we were headed. It was even difficult to know our general direction. We were not flying over water, that was about the only thing I was certain of.

"Marc was telling me that there's a way to learn how to block your thoughts and how to have private conversations with each other without others overhearing," I asked quietly.

"There is darling," he said while stroking my hair. "We have plenty of time for that."

"Where do you think we're going?" I whispered.

"I'm not sure." I detected some concern is his tone. "But if I were to guess, I would say we are headed to The Homestead," he said.

"This is all so strange. I don't know who I am anymore. I don't know which life was real and which one was a dream. I mean this is crazy! I'm 43 years old for God sakes. This is stuff of fiction... always happening to some unsuspecting teenager." After a brief pause I continued with my banter, "I know that I lived a life with a husband

and children. That life almost killed me...I have the scars to prove it. But where was this life we had together. You and I. Where were we? Where did it all go? I remember large portions of so vividly now. I remember us as small children together. I just don't understand how could I have forgotten all of that? We were teenagers when we were separated correct?" I asked Jonas.

"Yes, we were 17 years old when they cleared our memories and placed us in homes with our handlers. The people who would care for us until we were ready to be brought back," Jonas explained.

"But I have memories of elementary school. I had a mother, friends and a husband. Was that all dreamed?" I continued. "How do I know that the memories I now have of us aren't the planted memories and the memories I have from before all of this aren't the real memories?"

"The memories you have prior to the age of 17 were planted memories. They didn't really happen to you. The woman you called your mother was a scientist for the agency. She raised you and made sure that the protocols continued after you left the Homestead," he explained. "Your husband and children were real. The love and life you had with them were real. That part was all real," Jonas reassured sullenly. "We were also real. All you remember of us is real...I promise. The memories of elementary school and the people you knew then were not real."

After a few minutes of contemplation I finally said, "I think the weirdest part for me is that despite the confusion and...pretty much everything, I do believe it. What my body did back there...is indescribable. And the bond and love that I feel for you, I simply know is real. I can feel it so profoundly," I explained, "I was so ready to die. I had let go of everything. In hindsight its like I was so lost because you were lost to me...Does that make any sense?"

"It makes absolute sense my darling. It will all begin to make even more sense as your memories are restored and you regain your abilities," he said gently. "We are together. We are going through all of this together. Nothing is going to keep me away from you again. I promise."

We sat beside one another holding each other's hand tightly as I linked the lines and grooves on the face of the grown man that sat beside me to the memories I had of the boy from my visions. "When did they bring you back Jonas? How is it that you know all of this already?" I asked finally.

"A little over a month ago, Jeff and Marc showed up at my door. They have been good friends to me," he explained. "You can trust them. They're like us," he whispered.

"I feel like I have just had an amputated arm sutured back on after having lived without it for decades. It feels so good to have you back. I didn't know that you were what had been missing all of this time," I explained. "I'm overflowing with so many emotions...I'm worried about what else there is that I am going to remember. I have a feeling deep inside that I am only at the very tip of the iceberg of this stuff." I took a long pause as Jonas squeezed my hand before continuing. "Naomi called me the dark one. What did she mean by that? Is it the sadness inside of me? Is that what she meant?" I asked.

Jonas began to rub my hand between both of his hands before he said, "Each Dual is composed of a light and a dark half. Much like the yin and yang symbol. Where there is hot, there is also cold. We balance these two extremes. But one will always lean to one extreme more so than the other. This is why you heat up when you begin tapping into your abilities. You hold the fire within your body. It resides within you my darling. You can call on it at will. You are the fire and I am the ice," Jonas explained. "Your sadness is your darkness. But it isn't a source of weakness it is a source of strength. Just as the light is mine."

We kept looking at one another until a military version of a flight attendant approached us. She was wearing an impeccably pressed military uniform with not a hair out of place and ruby red lips to boot. "Dinner should be out in about five minutes. May I interest you in a non-alcoholic drink?" she asked politely with a pearly white smile.

"I'll take a seltzer water please," I requested.

"I'll have the same," Jonas replied.

She nodded her head and turned back towards the galley. That was when we noticed her firearm in a holster attached to her belt on the back of her skirt.

Jonas and I just looked at each other.

"We all carry," Marc said from two rows ahead of us while turning his closely shaved brown hair in our direction, as if knowing what we were just thinking. I'm actually certain he did know what we had been thinking.

"Why is that?" I asked. "Are we just preparing for a potential attack or are you protecting yourselves from us?"

"Both," Marc replied with a grin as he turned a bit more in his seat to get a better look at us from across the isle.

"Wow, Okay. Which one is more likely to cause trouble? Us or the outsiders?" I asked.

This time Jeff's red head popped up over his seat to responded, "Hard to say. You have not completed your full transition yet Lily. Until you do and you gain control of your abilities we have to be prepared to stop you from harming anyone." It was just then that I noticed that he was sitting beside Marc.

His response silenced me immediately. The possibility of my injuring someone had not crossed my mind. This sudden realization made me panic. Could I possibly hurt Jonas unintentionally?

As I sat there contemplating this while staring out the window at the darkness outside, Jonas continued to stroke my hair softly, trying to reassure me that all would be well.

Finally I asked, "had I reached my full potential before I was sent away?"

"No," Jonas replied flatly. "We were both sent away before that. Before either one of us could reach our full potentials. Pushing us to the edge of our abilities requires a great deal of discipline. It requires maturity, self-awareness and control," he explained.

"Were Marc and Jeff sent away?" I asked while turning to look at the both of them.

"Only for a short time," Jeff replied, "we were older when we started the program."

"So you remembered it all while you were away? Were you sent away together?" I asked full of curiosity. "Did you have partners or spouses when you were out?" I continued without giving them a chance to respond.

"We were separated," Jeff answered as his face reddened beneath Marc's burning stare. "Our memories were temporarily erased just as yours have been. We did try to live life as one does under normal circumstances. We both had jobs and tried to be good contributing members of society. We had lovers but after a few years it became clear that our needs could only be fulfilled with one another. I mean that in every sense, not just physically." He paused and looked at Marc briefly. "The Agency had to intervene when we were both overwhelmingly incapable of living anymore. We were on a very self-destructive path. I began to use heroin as a means to cope with the gnawing emptiness inside. We got to a point where our reunion became mandatory. I had become erratic and dangerous with only one path ahead of me. We had both become incapable of functioning in the manner the Agency needed us to function without the other," Jeff answered in a sad tone. "I was lost and much like you was trying to end my life."

"We were both dying slowly without the other. The Agency pulled us back in as a means to preserve us. We are two halves of one whole much like you and Jonas are," Marc explained as he held Jeff's hand, repeating Jonas' words to me. "It will return to you Lily. But be aware that with the good memories come the bad. You must prepare for that. Our upbringing and ultimate separations were very painful experiences for all of us."

Jonas continued to hold my hand tightly as I listened intently. It was then that I recognized the energy pulsing in my hand, almost like a flow of electricity running from my fingertips, up my arm, down my chest and then ultimately collecting in my abdomen. The power inside of me intensified stirring the dormant tempest that had been sitting quietly.

Relishing in this newfound feeling and the exchange of power between Jonas and myself, I watched Jeff and Marc reassuring one another as they told me their story. I watched them with fascination and admiration as I silently reprimanded myself for judging them so harshly initially. They genuinely were really great guys who obviously cared intensely for one another. It was then that it dawned on me that I had actually never seen them not making contact with one another in some way. The nonchalant elbow-to-elbow or brushing of a hand on a wrist, there was always some form of contact.

Their need for proximity was exactly like the compulsion I felt to always be in physical contact with Jonas. The sensation and reassurance that I feel when Jonas is beside me has limited words to explain the effect that it has on my body and psyche. But I began to think about it like a spiritual fulfillment, a lifting of the fog that had lingered around me for so many years.

As I held Jonas' hand seemingly able to watch the blood flow through his veins, I wondered how this entire situation could possibly make any sense to a sane person. How could I have lived an entire life with a husband and children while not having a single memory of any of this? How could this bond that I feel for Jonas, as profound as it is, simply be erased.

Unexpectedly, I began to experience a sudden surge of energy that erupted in my abdomen. With this sensation came the flashes of memories. There were catheters, infusions and other medications. There was pain and sadness. But through it all, there was always Jonas beside me bringing me strength and love. But unlike Marc and Jeff, our deep connection and love had never taken us down the path to become lovers. As I thought more about this, I remembered the advice that Marc had given me about others being able to read my thoughts. I quickly glanced up making brief eye contact with Marc, who had been watching me begin to put the puzzle pieces together. He gave me a very subtle nod before looking back at Jeff.

I lay my head on Jonas' shoulder and just as I began to drift off into sleep I decided then and there that the four us would be great friends. And that even though I have no memory of it, I could feel that the four of us had been inseparable before our forced separation. My job now was to try to remember it.

I WAS RUNNING GLEEFULLY *through thick woods as someone playfully chased after me. I could feel deep inside my body that the person running behind me was someone that I loved deeply with my entire being. This was a game we often played, him chasing me as I ran away in giggles. Searching for a few squirrels with my mind as I continued to run, I told them to jump on him from their overhead branches in an effort to slow his pace down. His screeching as the furry little beasts jumped on him made me giggle even louder. I could hear in my mind his disgust at the animals calling them rats with puffy tails.*

I kept running until I reached the clearing around the lake. It had become our lake. This was our place of refuge, away from our responsibilities and regiments. As we ran, our feet loudly crushed branches and dry leaves, breaking the silence in the forest that we ran through. But I could also hear in the distance, a bird's wings flapping overhead.

Slowing down for a moment, I turned to see if the boy was still rushing up behind me, halting suddenly when I saw no trace of him and thought that I was alone. I could hear no sounds from human feet as I stood perfectly still, listening while trying to breathe as quietly as I could. Anxiously, I made my way to the rocky shore and waited for him to jump out from behind a tree as he always did. Despite knowing his tricks, I still jumped and screamed with laughter as he suddenly grabbed my arms and embraced me tightly as he leaned down to kiss me passionately on the lips.

My body filled with elation and joy to the point where I thought I would burst. I could not contain my smile as he continued to kiss me on our private shore. Making me feel as if we were the only people on earth.

I WOKE up panting and crying wile repeating a name over and over in a pained whisper, Peter. Peter. Peter.

Jonas stroked my sweat-laden hair off of my forehead and smiled sadly nodding in acknowledgement, "I know darling. I know. All will be explained soon."

THE HOMESTEAD

11

I woke up with a jolt as the plane touched down. Instinctively Jonas and I tightened our hold on one another until the plane came to a full stop. A large black SUV awaited us at the bottom of the steps as we disembarked the plane on the tarmac. There was no fanfare. There was no one there to welcome us. Not even the pilots and flight attendant said goodbye as they remained safely sealed in the cockpit, barely even making eye contact with us through the planes window, making me feel like a dangerous criminal.

The weather outside was cold and crisp with clear skies. Snow could be seen in the distance in tall piles where it had been plowed from the runway. A light shone on the tarmac but beyond that there was little light, natural or man made.

Jeff took the drivers seat with Marc sitting beside him in the front passenger seat, while Jonas and I sat in the back. We drove through the empty darkness for what felt like hours, through flat nondescript terrain until finally reaching our destination. A few feet after turning into the driveway, we were stopped at a well-guarded gate. The awaiting armed guard approached the vehicle cautiously but was unable to conceal his reaction when he recognized the driver and passenger of the vehicle. There was a second guard that stood at the station door carefully watching while a third paced on the opposite side of the SUV.

"Good evening sir, welcome back," the guard said to Jeff before nodding at Marc in the passenger seat.

"Good evening," Jeff responded authoritatively.

"How many are entering sir?" the guard asked Jeff.

"There are four in the vehicle," Jeff said drily.

Before the gate was lifted, all of guards turned and looked curiously into the back of the car where Jonas and I sat.

Without further acknowledgement Jeff closed his window as the gate lifted in front of us. With a heavy foot, Jeff forced the car quickly into action propelling us forward while dirt and rocks went flying behind us. We drove for another ten or so minutes down a dark tree lined road before finally reaching a very large white farmhouse with a welcoming wrap around porch in the middle of a forest clearing. The house seemed to glow as the snow shimmered in the fading moonlight as the sky began to lighten from the approaching sun rise.

The air felt crisp and the air smelled clean and fresh as we jumped out of the SUV. As we made our way up the shoveled walkway heading to the front door, I couldn't help but feel a certain sense of familiarity filling me with excitement about increasing my remembrance of this place. Sadly, my balloon of wonder was suddenly burst by the sight of Naomi standing on the porch waiting for us with arms tightly crossed at her chest. She welcomed us with a grunt as she opened the front door for us to enter. As soon as I stepped into the welcoming warmth my mouth began to water and my stomach grumble as my sense of smell was bombarded by the delicious aroma of fried onions and garlic. The microwave meal we had consumed on the plane had been less than desirable.

A roaring fire burned in the hearth of the large living room, welcoming us with its warmth. The room had walls covered in wood paneling and various leather seating options. The combination of scented candles burning on the mantle smelling of roses and the melancholy voice of Edith Piaf playing on the stereo made this feel like an alternate universe. I tightened my hold of Jonas' hand, seeking reassurance that this wasn't a dream since it was so hard to believe this was a government run facility with its military presence at the front gate.

"Marcus! They're here," Naomi shouted over the music. "Marcus, for the love of God. Where the hell is the volume to make this wretched music stop? Marcus!" Naomi said in a huff.

A tall, very attractive bearded blond man with tattoos covering both of his arms walked out of the kitchen and began making his way towards us while wiping his hands on a kitchen towel.

"Hello there. Excuse the loud music," he said as he strode over to the stereo to lower the volume.

Once we no longer had to shout over the music, Naomi said with an annoyed tone, "Jonas and Lily, this is Marcus."

Marcus walked over to stand in front of Jonas and I before saying, "Lovely to see you, Lily and Jonas. It has been some time hasn't it?" He had an easy smile and his tone was friendly and warm.

I returned his warm greeting before turning slightly to Jonas to as him silently, *'Do we know this guy?'*

Marcus frowned slightly and then said, "Apologies. I didn't realize you had not fully recovered yet."

With that Jonas extended his free hand and said with a smile, "Good to see you again Marcus. You look well. Lily has not been fully reversed yet. But she has done amazingly well so far," Jonas explained as he stroked my hair back as my cheeks reddened from embarrassment at forgetting that my thoughts were not private.

"Well, I look forward to having you back fully Lily. I have certainly missed you. I can imagine Jonas has missed you most of all," Marcus said warmly as he looked at Jonas.

"Well, I certainly hope you are all hungry. I assumed the food on the plane had not been improved upon since my last company trip," Marcus blurted out excitedly after a short pause. "I have been slaving away all morning," he proclaimed sarcastically. "No seriously, I have made a juevos rancheros dish that is absolutely divine if I do say so myself."

"That sounds really good Marcus. Thank you," I said bashfully.

"Thank you Marcus. Let's all eat quickly. We have a very busy day ahead of us and we need to get started," Naomi commanded.

THE MEAL WAS unbelievable and by the end of it, I could barely keep my eyes open despite the three cups of coffee I had consumed. It was clear for me to see and sense that Jonas felt the same way. After cleaning up a bit, Marcus showed us to our separate rooms so that we could get ourselves cleaned up before our day with Naomi started. The colors of my room were less than desirable with it's varying shades of brown and pinks. The New Mexico desert flower theme was horrendous. Their designer needed to be fired immediately. The bathroom was covered from floor to ceiling in a dusty rose color, which included the sink and toilet. "Oh my God," I whispered in horrified shock.

Despite my insulted esthetics, I took a scalding hot shower and was pleasantly surprised to discover clean clothes in my size in the closet. I tried not to think about how creepy it was that that was someone out there shopping just for me who knew my size. As soon as I was dressed, I slowly and quietly snuck under the bed covers, telling myself that I just needed to rest my eyes for a few minutes. As my muscles began to relax, I let out a slow exhale I said to myself, "Just a 5 minute power nap. That's all I need."

Just as my body was slowly melting into the mattress, Jonas spoke to me silently from outside my room. *'Can I come in?'* he asked. I hummed a yes in response not bothering to open my eyes.

Silently, he made his way into my room and turned off the light just before sliding into bed beside me.

"Do you mind if I lay down with you?" he asked after he had already pulled the covers over his body and pulled my body tightly up against his.

I smiled at the timing of his question and how he was essentially already asleep before I even had a chance to answer. "Come in," I whispered with a sluggish smile.

We lay on our sides with our bodies tightly fitting together as I held his hand against my chest. His warm breath on the back of my head relaxed me further as our breathing pattern synchronized with one another. The familiarity of how this felt was a bit alarming and wonderful all at once. And just as fear had begun to rear its ugly head, reminding me that at any moment I could wake up to discover that this had indeed been a strange dream. I pushed those thoughts aside, not caring about what the end result of this moment would be. I needed to feel this love right now. I needed Jonas beside me. And before I could obsess any further, my mind drifted into a deep deep sleep feeling comfortable and safe.

I WAS DREAMING of flying again. I was headed toward a forest filled with thick, lush and verdant trees as I floated over a clearing of grass. A male voice shouted up at me and said, "Hey! Take me with you." I smiled and saw that it was that boy Peter again. He was standing directly below me in the clearing, reaching up to me as he jumped and smiled.

I gestured my hand slightly, sending the wind down to wrap itself around him as I reached for him with my mind. He lifted off of the ground gingerly, up to my waiting extended hand. Once we were face to face, he smiled broadly with his gleaming white teeth and big bright green eyes. He reached forward and caressed my cheek pulling me closer so that he could kiss me delicately on the lips as we continued to float in the still warm spring air. When he pulled away, we continued to hold each others gaze while the feel of his delicate lips lingered on mine, creating a whirlwind of energy to expand in my abdomen.

Peter was so good at triggering this response within my body. His eyes watched me tenderly as he whispered, "I love you Lily with all that I am, forever." His smile began to fade from his lips elevating the seriousness of his words.

As I opened my mouth to respond, the sound of a crow cawing as it circled over our heads made me jump. The feeling of panic rushed into my body as the crow whispered with a raspy voice in my mind, 'Caution! He is watching Lily.'

I looked down and was startled to discover that a man in a white lab coat stood below us watching with a stern look on his face. I gasped loudly as I pulled Peter's body closer to mine.

I WOKE up in a state of panic as I sobbed and panted for air. I opened my eyes and found Jonas leaning on his elbow facing me while stroking my hair away from my sweaty face. Once I had regained control of myself and all that remained was a lingering tremor, Jonas looked at me and said, "You're safe my darling. It looks like you're remembering more and more through your dreams," he said with a sad and worried look.

"Who is Peter?" I asked him.

"Someone from your past, someone you loved very deeply," he said with a morose tone.

Our eyes remained locked on one another until I asked through silent tears, "I lost him didn't I?"

"Yes," he whispered sadly.

I turned my body away from him so that I could continue to weep silently while the image of Peter's face lingered in my minds eye. Jonas lay behind me again and pulled me into his body tightly as he tried to reassure me that everything would be okay. We laid there for a long while with our racing thoughts just waiting for the knock on the door to come, to pull us away from our own little private moment of remembrance and comfort.

12

I woke up from our nap slowly with the warm sun shining on my face. Jonas remained asleep beside me, his arm still holding me tightly. Keeping as still and as quiet as I could, I relaxed into the mattress relishing in the peace and quiet. Hoping to prolong this moment for as long as I possibly could before the confusion of my new life returned.

Pulling Jonas' arm closer to my body as he reflexively squeezed me in response, I reached for him with my mind and slowly entered his dream. I knew that this was probably inappropriate and a complete invasion of his privacy, but my curiosity at whether I could do it again got the better of me. Maybe that would help me believe that this new life of mine was really happening.

I FOUND myself standing in a bedroom with crisp early spring air pouring in through the open windows. The billowing sheer white curtains swayed softly around a beautiful bed as two bodies moved in unison with heavy breath. It took only a moment to realize that it was Jonas and Jack, kissing as they made love while caressing and whispering desires. My heart swelled with emotions as their love and desire seared my skin, as I felt within myself what Jonas had been feeling.

OH JACK...WHERE did you go? I thought before quickly leaving this very private and intimate moment, instantly feeling guilty at my selfish intrusion. Jonas' dream had filled me with the need to comfort him. To hold him tightly so that I could soothe him from the loss he felt in his heart. I caressed his hair and kissed his closed eyes before slowly peeling myself out of bed. After quietly brushing my teeth I made my way to the door but before I turned the doorknob to leave the bedroom, I looked back at Jonas and noticed that he now seemed to be having a nightmare. Tears streamed down the sides of his face landing on the white pillows as he shook his head slightly from side to side. Unable to leave him in such a state, I quickly returned to the bed and held his arm as I sat beside him. The moment that we made contact I was hit with a sudden vision that flashed me out of my taupe bedroom.

I saw Jonas as a teenager struggling beneath the strong hold of two adult men in green military uniform as they held him from running away as he cried and screamed my name. I could feel his panic and fear knowing instantly that this was the moment of our separation. Turning my head to look in the direction he screamed I could see myself as a teen struggling beneath the strong hold of four uniform clad men as a fifth injected something into my neck. As the clear liquid was plunged into my body my struggling slowly began to diminish until I was finally unconscious. Two of the men lifted me and threw my limp body into the trunk of a black SUV before driving away as Jonas continued to scream and claw at his captors. Then appeared a third man who without hesitation injected him in the neck as well, instantly incapacitating.

FEELING MYSELF JUMP AND GASP, I returned to the present to find myself still sitting beside Jonas on the bed and still squeezing his arm tightly. My heart raced as my chest heaved with every difficult breath I took. Jonas panted as well while beads of sweat collected on his forehead as he stared at me wide eyed. He looked just as confused as I did as he pulled me down to lie beside him again so that we could embrace one another until our breathing normalized.

Once we were calm, I sat up while holding his fixed gaze and said as I shook my head, "Never again."

He nodded and stroked my cheek before saying, "Never again." It was our promise to one another. A pact to never be separated like that again.

He then closed his eyes after taking in a few deep breaths and began speaking in my mind, *'There's a lot that we are both still learning about our pasts.'*

With a nod, I pushed off from the bed and made my way out of the bedroom, silently pulling the door shut behind me. But before I could walk away from the bedroom door, I took a few deep breaths in an effort to release the tension I had rebuilt in my muscles. Realizing this journey would be long and difficult for both of us. I had to be strong for him just as he was trying to be strong for me. Our past experiences would bring back many long lost traumas along with their potential for re-injuries as we experienced them over and over again in our minds. With a silent vow, I promised myself to be strong and to stand by his side through all of the challenges we were about to face.

I began making my way down the old wooden steps, stopping when the loud creaking announced my descent. With a small smile I closed my eyes and with the energy that always seemed to be present in my abdomen, I reached for the air molecules floating around my body in the hope that they would respond to my call and lift my socked feet off the floor. My smile broadened as the sense of lightness began to slowly encompass me until my feet no longer touched the steps. Filled with a sense of accomplishment, I floated down to the main floor in absolute silence. Just as I reached the kitchen, I released my invisible hold on the air and gently set my feet back on the floor by the kitchen sink with its window overlooking the clearing in the back of the house.

"Well, looks like someone is remembering their abilities," Marcus said from behind me startling me into a jump.

"Yes," I said shaking.

"Not to worry Lily. This is a safe place. We are all here to help you both get back to where you had been before you left and to push you forward so that you can reach your full potential," Marcus said with a smile.

"What do you mean push us forward?" I asked.

"Well, you were both not finished when you were separated. The Agency people say that only age and maturity can give you the self-awareness and control you need to continue with your cell advancement," he explained with a smile. "Certainly this has been explained to you?"

After a short pause I shook my head slightly and said, "I know we were separated so that we could have these life experiences and gain maturity. Naomi did explain that much. I was also told that I needed to have the amnesia reversed so that I could reclaim my abilities. But I was not aware that there was going to be additional 'advancement' of my genes as you say." I couldn't hold back the concern in my tone as I said this.

"My apologies, I did not mean to give you concerning information. I was under the impression that this had all been discussed with you and Jonas already. This is why you were brought here, to the Homestead," Marcus explained.

"The famous Homestead, the place where it all started," I said with a sarcastic joy as I looked around. "Are you one of us Marcus?" I asked.

" Yes, this is the infamous Homestead," he responded with a wink. "This is where it all started. This is where we grew up together. There were five successful Duals created. There are now only three. You are the last of the Duals needing advancement," he explained as he reached for his cup of coffee.

"Where are the other two Duals?" I asked as I opened cabinet doors, searching for coffee mug. Without a word, he opened one of the doors and handed me a coffee mug. I gave him a small nod in gratitude and proceeded to make myself a nice cup of coffee in silence. I was grateful that he was allowing me some time to process this new information. I made my way to the bar stools on the other side of the island and sat down facing him while he stood across from me.

"Well, you have met Marc and Jeff." I nodded in response. "The other Dual pair is out in the field."

"What field?"

"The top secret field," he replied with a bright white toothy smile.

"Interesting... Is that what will happen to us when we advance fully? Will we go out in the field?" I asked.

"Yes, it is. This is a scientific military operation. That is the purpose of the program. The gene modification had initially been attempted on fully grown adults. All willing subjects of course. All highly trained soldiers at the peak of their physical prowess. The scientists had assumed that their physical strength and formal training would help them withstand the uncomfortable changes associated with the process of conversion. But they were only partially successful. It wasn't until one of the founding scientists injected a slightly modified serum into a child that he realized that the response to the modifications would be better received by younger cells. Once he got clearance from his superiors, he moved to testing on infants." His voice sounded slightly pained as he explained. "These children developed impressive abilities as they grew. But the project didn't really peak until they discovered Duals. It happened accidentally of course, like most scientific discoveries are made. See, the way it works is that the serums that we were injected with targeted a slight gene variation in our DNA. These variances were different in each child, but what they discovered is that the Duals tended to have variances on either of two distinct chromosomes. These variances were susceptibilities really, that would then allow for an almost complete modification of every gene. The more fascinating thing is that Dual infants had gene sequences that mirrored another infants genome. The serums were able to modify these variances so that these genes could be bound within each Dual child, effectively uniting the two separate bodies in a way that had not been predicted. The two individual children became stronger together physically and emotionally to the point where they very much needed each other in order to sustain themselves psychically. There was an exchange and sharing of energy, that was in constant motion. It's fascinating really and quite rare. We are the unique of the unique," he paused to give me a wink. "And that my friend was how you and Jonas came to be." Finally able to take a sip of his coffee, he watched me in silence ponder this information for a bit before he continued.

"You for example were born to a drug addicted woman who left you in the hospital shortly after birth. Scientists in the field were alerted of your circumstances, retrieved you from the birthing facility and brought you to the Homestead. My understanding of this process is that the scientists felt that the absence of family connections was important. They wanted it to be a clean process with no interference from people wanting to claim their infant relatives," he explained somberly.

"My favorite story about you is that interestingly enough, when the two scientists were dispatched to your location, a second pair of scientists were sent to another location for another orphaned infant across the country. This child was born at the exact time that you were born. The teams initially thought it was all a fortunate coincidence. It wasn't until you were both here at the Homestead that they discovered in your blood work you were a perfect match for Jonas," he explained very animatedly.

"Each child was assigned a scientist who became responsible for their upbringing while they remained here at the Homestead. Trusting bonds were formed between the children and their handlers. This became especially necessary when painful tests were needed and also when infusions were due. It helped reduce the protests as we grew and became cognizant enough to know that there was often pain involved with all of the testing and infusions. But they also learned that even though our handlers were important, there was nothing like the Dual bond. Once that was discovered, the Duals were never to be separated. The separations would cause such internal disarray that our bodies would reject the modifications. There were a lot of kids that became gravely ill because they were separated from their Duals during the infusions. We were stronger together. It's that simple," he paused while examining my face.

I tried to keep the disdain and anger secretly contained beneath my skin as I listened in shock and awe at what I was hearing. Holy shit, they experimented on infants! We were all lab rats. I squeezed my hands into fists and tightened every muscle in my body just so I could keep the ball of energy contained in my body as I sensed my body temperature rising.

"Please don't be upset Lily. We were all very loved and well cared for. Yes, there was a little testing here and there, but all in all it was probably a better future than we would have had out there in the world. Jumping from foster home to foster home, hoping to be adopted someday," he explained sullenly. "Well, that's what I tell myself anyway."

"You consider experimenting on infants loving and kind?" I spoke as calmly as I could while gritting my teeth painfully.

"It's all about perspective I guess," he spoke softly with obvious sadness in his eyes.

"So what happened later? How does the decision get made to separate pairs and release them into the world to gain this oh so needed experience and maturity," I asked with a sarcastic tone.

"Seventeen...that was the age that was chosen." Now his sadness was plain as day to see. "The scientist handler assigned to each child was responsible for raising them on the outside. In a home where they could experience the outside world, develop relationships, find community. New memories were...let's say programed while all memories involving The Homestead were removed. This included our Duals of course, as you are now well aware. Every memory that they planted in us involved things that happened in regular lives including family and friends, schools and lovers, relationships and life in general. It was learned that all of those experiences helped foster the abilities development later on," he continued. "At least that's what we're told. I guess we'll never really know for sure if the separations were really necessary."

"And so here we are. You and Jonas back together. Preparing for that final push," he said with forced joy as he gestured with his hands.

"What about you Marcus? What's your story?" I asked.

"Me? Same as you I guess. Memory erased, sent to live in the great big world and then brought back here."

"So you're a Dual? Where's your other...what do I call them? Half? Partner? Ball and chain?" I said with a fake chuckle.

"I am...I was...a Dual. Luna is my half. We were separated. She's... missing," Marcus responded with a sad tone.

"Missing?" I asked. "But how? What happened to her handler? When did she go missing?"

"I don't know much really. I was brought back about a year ago. The Agency was hoping that I could help locate her through our Dual connection, but I can't go through the completion phase without her. So I haven't been successful at finding her," he explained.

"I'm sorry. I can feel your pain inside of my body," I said as I squeezed his hand.

"You and Jonas are the last of the Duals to be brought back. Jeff and Marc have been back for some time now. We will all work together from here on out...The Five of us. I am told that the remaining Duals have all been deemed to be very advantageous to the Agency," he said this while waving his hand in the air.

After a pause I asked, "Do you think that pain is necessary for maturing to the level they deem necessary?"

"What do you mean?"

"Well, I think it's interesting that both Jonas and myself suffered a severe personal loss while on the outside and were emotionally devastated before being brought back here. You continue to suffer now... Did you experience loss while you were out?" I pondered.

"Yes, I did. I've been in pain for a long time Lily," he said while nodding his head several times with a morose look on his face as he looked down at the floor.

"Is it by design you think? Intentionally made to suffer. We suffered as children, then as adults. Are they at the root of all of our pain?" I asked in a whisper.

Just as he opened his mouth to respond, Naomi entered the kitchen silently and said, "Good morning. Thank you Marcus for helping Lily learn our histories," she said as she turned to me and gave me a forced smile.

Sensing Jonas opening the bedroom door I closed my eyes as the rush of his approaching energy began to flow through my blood stream.

As the squeaking on the stairs announced his descent, Naomi began to exclaim in a louder tone, "Since you and Jonas decided that you needed to sleep our first day back away, we do have quite a bit of catching up to do. We have a long day ahead of us. Let's eat some breakfast quickly and then begin shall we?"

I could feel my face involuntarily grimacing as I thought, 'What a bitch.'

Naomi snapped her head back to look at me with a huff.

Jonas walked into the kitchen and rested his hands on my shoulders as he stood behind me. The contact instantly calmed and reassured me. I turned and smiled warmly at him.

"Ok then, let's eat," Marcus declared triumphantly as he flexed his tattooed biceps .

As I watched Marcus prepare our breakfast, I became overwhelmed by the care and love I felt for him. It was as though I had known him all of my life. I guess I probably had even though in my mind we had just met. He gave me a subtle wink presumably sensing my emotions. I could feel deep down that we had been close as children. And that he needed our help right now.

13

After breakfast, Naomi led Jonas and I to a windowless room located in the basement of the home. The room had surprisingly high ceilings along with its mandatory white walls and white flooring. The far wall had what looked to be a floor to ceiling two-way mirror, presumably for watching the subjects from a safe location. There were two hospital beds located on the wall opposite the mirrors. The beds were separated by at most three inches. They were covered with white linens with an IV pole and an IV pump beside each bed. It all felt very sterile. Would a little art kill someone? I asked myself. Jonas let out a short giggle at that.

'I need to learn how to have some private thoughts moving forward,' I thought as Jonas shrugged.

"Ready to get started Lily?" Naomi asked.

Jonas and I stood facing one another holding each other's hands tightly. He looked a bit nervous as I nodded at him. "I'm ready Naomi," I said while turning to face her.

"Great, both of you lay on a bed please. You both need IV's today," Naomi stated.

"Jonas needs an IV as well?" I asked.

"He does. His full transition needs to occur when yours does. He is close but not complete."

My body tensed as I looked at him with fear of experiencing more loss.

"Don't be afraid darling. It will all be fine. We are together. I will help you and you will help me," he explained while kissing my hand. "Right?"

I nodded and smiled before we walked over to the beds so that we could lie down. Once we were settled, I reached for his hand as fear began to course through my body. Naomi expertly placed the IV in Jonas and then promptly began his serum infusion. Our eyes were locked on one another until his eyelids became heavy and he drifted off into his drug-induced sleep. I tightened my hold of his hand as it became limp and slowly began turning blue and ice cold. I sat up in a panic to search for a pulse as panic spread through me.

Noticing my alarm, Naomi interrupted my thoughts by saying, "He's fine. Cold is his ability, it's just manifesting with the serum. He has done a really good job of keeping it in check lately. The anesthesia has taken effect, so he is no longer in control which is why the cold is coming through."

With some trepidation, I lay back on the bed so that she could place my IV and then without wasting any more time she began my infusion. My eyes widened when I saw her hang a liter bag filled with the now familiar milky green serum.

"Is this a normal dose for the stage that I'm in? A liter bag is quite a bit more than the 50 milliliter syringes that were used before," I asked with moderate concern.

"No, it isn't. It's a much higher dose. But you've shown me that your body is ready." Naomi's statement shocked me a little but by the time I had formulated a response in my mind, the serum had already begun to take effect and I drifted off to sleep.

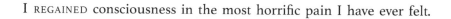

I REGAINED consciousness in the most horrific pain I have ever felt.

Like every other time, I regained consciousness while floating many feet off the floor as the red vortex enveloped my body. I was lying on my side in fetal position with my knees tightly drawn up to my chest while sweat poured out of every possible pore. It felt as if my skin was being punctured by a small thin spike repeatedly. My body was again covered in blood with a majority of it originating from my bleeding arms. Just like before, the blood droplets were causing little sparks of fire to ignite as they came in contact with the spinning wind. I tried to stop the bleeding by applying pressure to my wounds but found the change in my position only intensified the excruciating pain even more.

Realizing that Jonas was likely in pain as well, I attempted to turn to look for him but had to stop when the painful misery I was in made me lose my breath as the stabbing pain intensified making my exhalations tremulous.

After some serious concentration, I was able to build up my mental strength enough to be able to thin the vortex just as I had done before while struggling through the pain, until I was able to turn myself enough to see Jonas laying motionlessly in fetal position. The serum continued to move through the IV tubing and into his pale blue body that was now blanketed by a thin layer of ice.

With a hoarse voice I said, "Jonas. Jonas, wake up darling. Look at me." When there was no response, I raised my voice as tears began to pour out of my eyes and get engulfed by the spinning wind, "Jonas please open your eyes. Look at me."

With still no response, by body began to shake uncontrollably, making the wind tunnel increase its speed which in turn made the air feel almost aggressive as it responded to my emotions. Pushing through the pain, I straightened my body and moved myself to be upright within the spinning cocoon. Instinctively, I slowly floated to where Jonas lay and with a small movement of my hand, I was able to create an opening in my enclosure so that I could reach out and touch his cold blue cheek. It wasn't until my hand had already made contact with his skin that I noticed that it was glowing red. As if the fire that they told me burned inside of me could be seen through my skin. Jonas remained unresponsive as the ice around him began to melt.

"Jonas?" I whispered. "Can you hear me?"

As the intensity of my fear increased and I continued to melt the ice that encased him, I noticed that his syringe of serum had only infused about half of its volume. Tracing my own IV line to the source of the infusion, I was only but so surprised to discover that my medication bag was completely empty. Confused, I looked at Jonas before Naomi's voice very suddenly boomed through a speaker in the ceiling.

"Lily...your treatments are finished. How do you feel?" she asked formally.

"Why isn't Jonas responding me?" I asked in a panic, ignoring her question. "Why won't he look at me? Is it the anesthesia?" I screech.

"Yes, it is probably the anesthesia," she responded unconvincingly after a brief hesitation.

"What do you mean probably? Is this still his first infusion?" I asked in a panicked tone as the wind speed around me intensified as it responded to my emotions.

"It is still his first infusion. He is much slower at receiving the serum than you are. We changed your medication bag seven times," she stated matter-of-factly.

"What? Seven times!" I responded in a shock.

I pulled the IV tubing out of my arm, barely holding pressure as the puncture site began bleeding. After a moment had passed, I felt myself fill with rage instigated by my fear. I rushed to the two-way mirror so that Naomi could see my anger which in turn unintentionally intensified the vortex even further. Only pausing briefly when my reflection revealed glowing red eyes as my long brown hair floated neatly around my head as if it were floating in water. I felt powerful and indestructible as I shouted, "Naomi! Turn his fucking infusion off now or I will pull the IV out of his arm."

"Lily, you must control yourself. Do not stop his infusion! His body is controlling the speed at which it draws the serum in. It doesn't matter how much time I program the infusion to deliver over. It's him!" Naomi explained through the speakers.

"Lily, you need to go to him. Reach down inside and pull him out," Marcus advised over the speakers.

As I remained suspended in front of the mirror, processing what I had just been instructed to do, I discovered that I could see both of their hearts beating behind the glass despite not being able to see Marcus' nor Naomi's body. It was as if I was being drawn to the heat contained in their chest.

With much concentration, I am able to pull myself away from the hypnotic rhythm of their beating hearts and heed Marcus' advice. In an instant, I am hovering over Jonas' balled up body and with closed eyes and a focused mind, I draw the vortex into myself while still maintaining enough of a hold on the air around me so that I remain airborne.

Suspended over Jonas, I leaned down close to his ear and whispered, "I'm right here and I am not leaving you. We will get through this together. It's my turn to help you."

With fiery strength I reach into his thoughts until my mind gets pulled into his.

I FOUND myself engulfed by a freezing cold darkness, an almost black water that tosses my body with each wave that passes, forcing me hold my breath every time it crashes over my head. After a few moments, I dive beneath the surface as a gigantic wave threatens to pound into my body. While submerged, I opened my eyes and am panicked to discover Jonas' limp motionless body floating in the darkness a few feet from mine.

After fighting the current, I am able to swim to him and grab his shoulders in my tight fists. With the slightest smile, he slowly opened his eyes and said in a sweet sweet voice in my mind, 'See darling. We both have darkness within us.'

'What's happening Jonas? Why are we here?' I asked him silently.

'This is where my struggle is. Moving past the darkness. I am the light

and you are the dark. I must be rid of this before I can evolve fully and be the half that you need me to be,' he responded sadly.

'You're wrong. We must have a balance within ourselves. With the dark comes the light. That is the only way that we will balance ourselves and each other,' I said as I take his hands into mine. 'It's not your job to be there for me. We are there for each other. We must be the balance that the other needs. When you are light, then I will be dark. As I will be the light in your dark. Let me be your light at this moment. Please my love. Only we know what it is we need, it should never be dictated to us.'

After some hesitation, he nodded his head and closed his eyes as his mind accepted my words. With a sudden pull from above, our bodies rush out from beneath the water and pushed high into the cool starry night sky, propelled by as a cold wind that instantly envelopes our bodies. With a smile full of joy, Jonas faces me as I will the air to set us down on a small stretch of beach, shinning brightly from the warm sun overhead as the waves softly crash onto the sand. While holding each others gaze I tighten my grip on his hands realizing what beach it is that we now stand upon. With a subtle nod he turned his gaze to the dunes that lie behind him, knowing exactly who he will discover embracing in the soft warm sand.

Jonas and Jack walk hand in hand as they smile and laugh in the endless loop of this sweet summer day. Where after every few steps, they stop to kiss with carefree minds and full hearts. They had not a care in the world and as far as they were concerned, they were the only two people on the planet and nobody else mattered.

"I can't seem to leave this memory here. I can't seem to let it go. Its like a skipping record, always bouncing back to this one memory. He was and always will be in my heart. I don't know how to leave him here...how to let him go," he said sadly as he watched his past self joyfully holding his loves hand.

I wrap my arms around his waist and leaned my head onto his chest before asking, "This is a happy memory to hold onto. Why let it go? This is a memory of when you were carefree, full of love and life. You should hold onto it and never let it go. It is a good reminder of who you once were. It will help you find the light. Use it to pull yourself out of the darkness."

With realization dawning in his eyes, he tightened his hold on my waist *and after a long period of silence he finally said, "Thank you. This is why I need you."*

Tilting my head up to look at him, he continued to watch the two lovers kiss longingly before he let go of me and dove into the ocean.

"This is why we need each other," I shouted after him, correcting his words just before I jump in the waves after him.

While treading the beautiful warm blue water, he turns to me with conviction and says, "I'm ready. Let's be done with this."

With a nod I say with a proud smile, "See you on the other side babe."

In a flash, I pulled myself back to where my body had remained floating over Jonas' cold form. With wide eyes I leaned down closer to his face until he opened his eyes. Reaching down, I caress his face and smile, noticing that his serum infusion was finally complete.

"Thank you," he whispered.

"We are in this together," was the truest response I could give him.

14

J onas and I dragged ourselves up the steps to our bedrooms with our hands tightly clasped together, almost pulling one another up each step as exhaustion claimed our bodies. Our newfound abilities demanded engagement and flexion from every possible muscle in our bodies. In addition, there was also a higher need for emotional and psychological functioning which seemed to make the physical exhaustion feel greater than it perhaps was.

I stood beneath the scalding hot shower for what felt like three hours before my body felt relaxed enough. After drying myself in a butter soft towel, I stared at my naked body in the bathroom mirror, fixated by what I saw. It seemed as if my skin had a crimson glow and my muscles seemed more defined in my ever slimming body. Sadly, it appeared as if my small breasts had grown even smaller over the past few days from the increased metabolic rate that my abilities demanded. I was grateful for the curves I still had, if not for those I would have looked like a fifteen year old prepubescent boy. My caloric intake definitely had to increase, I told myself.

After dressing in a pair of jeans and a soft white T-shirt, I made my way down to the kitchen for some much needed supper. I could feel a change in my gate with every step I took. It was as if I had to concentrate on keeping my bare feet firmly planted on the floor, otherwise I could easily float away like a helium balloon in the hands of a toddler. One small maneuver and off I would go. As I approached the kitchen, the smell of sautéing onions, garlic and butter, the most heavenly of culinary triads, filled my nostrils instantly making my mouth water.

"What's for dinner? It smells amazing," I asked Marcus as I walked up to the kitchen island, plopping myself down into one of the bar stools. Marcus stood over the stove as he stirred his magical pot of goodness.

With a smile he turned to me and asked, "Would you like a glass of wine?"

"Yes, thank you," I said as I floated slightly off of the bar stool so that I could make my way to the front door without putting my feet down. Silently, I opened the door and was immediately blanketed by the cold winter chill as it draped on my hot skin. The euphoric feeling drew me out of the house and onto the front porch where I continued to hover so that I could watch the silent snow fall. As my senses became consumed by the silence, the feel of the snow as if instantly melted on my skin and the crispness of the air, I hovered down the front steps, over the walkway and all of the way down to the driveway in an almost hypnotized state. Without much thought or concentration, I reached for the sphere of energy that resided in my core, pulling out a layer of heat to instinctively create an invisible heat shield around myself. The heat felt wonderful as it enveloped my body.

Looking around myself in wonder at what I had been able to achieve, I looked up at the trees that surrounded the homestead and willed the wind to lift me up to their tops. I continued to ascend into the winter sky, watching the snow continue to silently float around my protected body. With a broad smile on my face, I turned 360 degrees curious to know how far the property extended and if there were additional buildings or neighbors nearby. But as I had suspected, we were all alone in our little oasis.

Relishing in the freedom I felt, I willed the wind to move me away from the house while maintaining my body low over the treetops. I silently floated further away from the house as I gently grazed the trees with my hands in complete amazement of what I was capable of doing this. I could feel myself morphing into someone else as my strength changed and grew within me.

I didn't stop until I had drifted far enough away from the house that it was no longer visible behind the trees. I began to breathe in deeply and slowly with my eyes closed in meditation and was immediately bombarded the memory of Peter's face and the way he made me feel as we floated over these very trees all of those years before. I could still feel the way he caressed my face along with the love that I had felt for him. His contagious smile as he gazed at me with his deep green eyes made my heartbeat race.

The world around me seemed to melt away as these memories consumed me making me never want to leave. The cawing of a crow rudely brought out of my peaceful little reverie. When I opened my eyes, I found a very large black bird, quickly flying straight at me while cawing frantically.

"What the...?" I gasped before quickly turning to head back to the house. As the farmhouse came into view, I looked back and was surprised to discover that the bird had been following me. Fascinated by this response, I stopped midair and quietly watched it approach, feeling my muscles begin to tense slightly as I prepared myself for the possibility that I would have to somehow engage it physically. The bird was not any old standard crow as I had assumed it was when I first noticed it. This fella was huge, almost as big as an eagle. When it was within a foot away from me, it set down on a branch and just silently stared at me. It felt incredibly awkward, almost as if I was being spied on. It wasn't until after a few moments that I realized that the bird looked familiar and remembered that the same bird had actually been in my dream just the other night.

'Lily, come down to me please,' Jonas reached out to me in my mind, startling me with his sudden intrusion. With a jump I turned and saw him standing on the front porch looking up at me with his hand extended out to me, beckoning me to join him.

Before I set off for the porch, I turned to the mammoth crow and whispered, "Goodbye old friend. Whoever you are. I hope to see you again soon. I just need a little more time to remember who you are."

As I slowly began making my way back to Jonas, I heard a raspy whisper in my mind, *'Lily my old friend. I am Raven. Remember me.'*

With a small shriek, I turned back to see if the bird had been the source of the ghostly voice I heard, but he had already taken off and was quickly flying away from me.

Once I reached Jonas, he lifted his index finger to his lips, indicating that I should remain quiet as I continued to hover in front of him. With a barely perceptible nod, I held his hand as he pulled my hovering body through the front door and back into the house.

"I have a glass of wine waiting for you darling," Jonas said loudly.

"Well, thank you love," I responded with a bright smile.

"Would you mind returning to earth please?" Jonas asked me jovially. With a smile I sank my feet down to the floor while simultaneously pulling the heat shield I had created back into my body.

"Your drink my dear." Marcus approached with his hand extended, handing me my wine glass. "Welcome back. Was it nice up there?" he asked.

"It was quiet and beautiful," I answered with a big smile.

"Well, good! How are your memories doing Lily? Anything coming back?" Marcus asked just as Naomi was entering the room.

"My memories are slowly returning, thank you," I replied politely while tightly holding onto Jonas' hand.

Silently, we all made our way to the dining room where the table had already been informally set and a large bowel of steaming pasta along with a big plate of meatballs and warm rolls awaited us. My mouth began to water immediately.

"Are Jeff and Marc joining us?" Jonas asked.

"They are away for a few days. They'll be back soon," Naomi responded.

"I'm starving," I said. "I didn't realize how hungry I was until just now."

"I'm not surprised, you haven't eaten in quite some time," Naomi said.

"Yes, it's been at least 10 hours," I said sarcastically with a wink as I responded.

She turned to Jonas with a confused look on her face and said as she looked back at me, "No Lily. You have both been down in the lab for four days."

I turned to Jonas stunned. "What?" I asked Naomi. "How could that be? What happened down there? Four days...really?"

"Yes, you were both regenerating your cells and your abilities while reinforcing your Dual connection. It took about 96 hours," Naomi answered in a slightly annoyed tone. "It was impressive to watch and I was able to gather really great data from your energy transferences." She paused to take a sip of her wine while Jonas and I stared at her in obvious stunned shock. "I was able to take blood samples from you and was able to analyze your cells under a microscope. It was interesting to see first hand that when your individual blood is placed in the same petri dish on opposite ends of the dish, the cells will always migrate towards each other. This happened even when the blood was placed in separate dishes, it would immediately move to the side of the Petri dish where it could be close to each other. I've never seen anything like it. I've heard about it of course, from the other scientists. Your strong connection as children was well documented and studied. It's still the strongest seen to date, but this, what I've been seeing for the last few days is on an entirely new level than what had been previously seen," she spoke with excitement in her voice.

"How did you get blood from us? Lily was floating 30 feet in the air," Jonas asked.

"Oh, that was easy. She had an IV. I could just draw the blood back into the tubing," Naomi answered with a tone that conveyed annoyance at his ignorance. "What was difficult was actually entering the room. Lily's heat increased the ambient temperature to about 190 degrees Fahrenheit. Luckily, Jonas' ability subconsciously protected him by creating a layer of ice over his unconscious body. But the most fascinating thing about that, is that no matter how hot it got in the room, the ice would not melt," Naomi explained wide-eyed with a chuckle.

Jonas and I listened to her in silent fascination while processing her words. This was all very exciting from an intellectual and nerdy perspective. I mean how amazing was it that our blood reacted that way to each other? But despite that, I couldn't help by feel uncomfortable by how excited Naomi was when she spoke about it. It was very clear that we were very much her science project, her lab subjects and not actual people. That moment seemed to solidify the feeling that I had been having. Naomi was definitely not someone I could drop my guard around.

"So Marcus, you are quite the chef. Is cooking one of your genetically modified abilities?" I asked him in jest, trying to change the subject.

Jonas and Marcus both chuckled as Naomi glared at me.

"Just a hobby really. It helps me keep my mind off of certain things," Marcus said.

Nodding in understanding, I asked, "Marcus what do you think happened to Luna?"

After a few moments of silence he finally said, "I am told she just disappeared and that nobody has been able to find her."

Jonas and I held hands under the table as we listened to Marcus. Naomi began eating in silence seemingly unfazed by Marcus' words.

"Do you not sense her Marcus?" Jonas asked softly.

He shook his head and said morosely, "I have occasional glimpses but nothing of any real use."

Marcus looked down at his plate while a wave of fear and sadness exuded from his body, abruptly hitting Jonas and I. His emotions were so palpable that my eyes began to water involuntarily as I began to blink quickly. Sensing my emotional change, Jonas squeezed my tightly hand as he brought it closer to his abdomen.

"How can we help you find her?" I asked Marcus with concern.

"I need you to remember everything," Marcus responded firmly.

15

Once we had finished devouring our amazing pasta dinner with plenty of wine to wash it all down, we all helped with clean up before Jonas and I bid everyone goodnight and made our way upstairs to our rooms. He held my hand tightly to keep my feet firmly planted as we climbed up the steps, knowing full well that I wanted to float my way up. We just smiled at one another as we took each step in unison, just the old fashioned way.

Without saying a word, he followed me into my room, turned down the sheets, dressed in our pajamas and then brushed our teeth in complete unison as we stood over the bathroom sink.

After climbing into bed, I turned to face and whispered, "How do I close off my mind so I can have private conversations with you?"

"You know the heat shield you created around yourself while you were outside?" he asked. I just shook my head in response.

"That's how. You create a shield just around your mind. Seal it up tight and then reach out for my mind, a link will be created," Jonas explained. "That's how we would sneak off and go on our adventures when we were children."

"Where would we go?" I asked with a smile.

"Oh lots of places. We would mainly explore the forest. There's a lake with a small river feeding it not far from here," he said.

"I've seen that lake in my dreams. But I wonder why I can't remember it as clearly as you can. I get snippets in my dreams but that's it. I must admit though, the clearing and the line of trees outside are definitely familiar. And that bird, did you see that crow? He spoke to me Jonas," I said with amazement.

He lifted his head slightly off the pillow so that he could look at me intently and ask, "What did he say Lily?"

"How do you know it's a he?" I asked.

"His name is Raven. You were very close friends when we were children. You always would say that he could speak to you. He would always sit outside of our bedroom window just watching us sleep. He was like your watchdog... and mine actually by default. Sometimes we would fly to the river to play on the rocks. We didn't always get permission to go, Raven would warn us when the caretakers were approaching. He always gave us enough time to sneak back to the house before getting officially caught. All of the adults knew where we were of course, they just couldn't catch us in the act." He gave a small giggle. "Its good to see him. I'm glad he's still around. He loved you very much, that was always very clear."

"I hope I dream about him tonight. I want to remember him," I said. "Why do you think I don't dream about my husband and children? Like you dream about Jack I mean. I've dreamed about Peter... well snapshots of Peter and my feelings involving him. My dreams have done nothing to shed any real light onto who we were or who he was. But there's been nothing about my family, just nothing. I don't understand why. Is it the stress of it all?" I asked in a fluster. "It makes me sad that I don't dream about them. I feel like a horrible person for it," I continue with a sad tone.

"You will remember when you need to... but most importantly, when you're ready. Your mind is in self-preservation mode right now. It will only feed you memories you can handle and process effectively," he explained while kissing the top of my head.

"What happened to Peter?" I asked.

Jonas took in a deep breath before responding. "He was one of the subjects, like we were. But he wasn't the same as us. He didn't have a Dual he was a Solo. His abilities were different, more tactical and geared to military mentality. Where our abilities were geared more to protect, his was to attack. I am not sure where they took him...after we were all taken I mean. You both had snuck off to the lake that day, as usual. You were 17 and he was 18. You were caught together and things got bad. He was immediately shipped off to who knows where, probably some highly classified military base somewhere. I'm certain he had his memories wiped as well, just like us. Old memories wiped, new memories implanted and then off he went." Jonas took a long pause and then said, "That day...when we were all separated...I could feel you shattering. I could feel you struggle against them as I watched you and then suddenly I felt nothing from you. You just vanished into thin air like you had never been there. The emptiness left behind would have killed me if they hadn't erased you from me."

I began to sob uncontrollably as the rush of memories hit me in the gut. The feeling of deep debilitating loss hit me all of a sudden as the memories came flooding back. I remembered the military men tying me down in my drug induced stupor, while I subconsciously knew exactly what was about to be done to me. On that day, the scientists ended who I had been. They put out the light that had burned so brightly inside of me leaving behind someone that would be full of emptiness, darkness and misery. Someone who was only capable of seeing glimpses of light.

As soon as I was able to reel my emotions back in, I noticed that standing outside on the window sill stood Raven, watching me. He began to caw like he did on that horrible day when he was warning us. Things may have turned out differently if only we had heeded his warning.

Wiping my cheeks dry, I stood and opened the window. Raven remained immobile as I spoke, "I remember that day. I remember you trying to warn us."

He cawed while moving his head back and forth, '*A sad day for all of us. Our Lily. We will have many more flights together in the future,'* he whispered in his raspy voice in my mind.

I nodded as tears began to flow again. Jonas stood behind me holding my shoulders. "Let's get some sleep darling. We have had a long and exhausting few days. We need rest. Goodnight Raven," he said while giving the crow a short bow before shutting the window.

Silently, I allowed him to steer me to bed and once we had crawled beneath the covers, Jonas curled up around me, holding me tightly. As I lay there motionless my mind began to wander, replaying these new memories over and over again. Remembering the pain that all of us felt, the loss of our lives and loves. But most importantly the loss at the ability to have choices, something that we didn't know had eluded us our entire lives. I could feel myself becoming enraged. My body began to tremble while I instinctively fisted my hands in an attempt to control myself.

I could feel Jonas reach out to me in my mind, *'Be calm my darling. Let me be your calm'.* After giving him a short nod, I could instantly feel the calm unfurling inside of me like flower petals opening and stretching to reach every part of me. It was an intense sensation that I welcomed openly allowing it to consume me until peacefully I drifted off to sleep.

QUIETLY I SAT in the classroom with the other children. The teacher who spoke in the front of the room reminded me of my mother when she was young. She spoke softly and sweetly as she explained mathematical principles as she wrote on the blackboard enthusiastically. I sat at my desk frantically writing with my right hand while my left held onto Jonas' right arm. We all looked to be around 10 years old. All of us sitting in pairs, two per desk, much like Jonas and I. Jonas' bright turquoise eyes were wide and his face was of a sweet little boy, watching me take notes.

With a smile and a little boy voice he said to me, 'Don't worry, I'll show you how to do this later.' Our ability to speak privately had obviously started at a very young age along with our ability to feel one another's emotions.

With a sense of relief, I looked around the room and saw five desks with two children per desk. Each child holding onto its partner in one-way or another. The comfort we found from our Dual connection was obviously something we all shared. It was easy to spot Jeff with his puffy red hair and Marc with his slick brown hair and bruised knees. They were both toned and muscular, even as children. But nothing could compare to Marcus' physique, with rope like muscles on his arms. He sat beside a girl with short blonde hair, with their hands clasped on the desk. The other two pairs were certainly familiar but I could not recall their names.

Suddenly the location in the dream changed and we were all in the basement lab at the Homestead. This time, instead of an empty room with two beds, the room was filled with scientific devices and machines scattered about the room. All ten of us children stood in a circle wearing our white jump suits with our bare feet on the cold white linoleum floor.

There was a woman that stood in the middle of the circle watching each of us closely. She said, "Ok children, you have all been doing a wonderful job practicing on your own, now let's take turns showing the group how far we have come with our abilities."

The first person to come forward was Marcus' blonde half. She amazingly was able to lift up into the air and then become invisible. "Well done Luna," the woman said as the almost white blond haired girl returned to the ground and solidified her form. 'Amazing,' Jonas and I thought to each other.

With his Dual back by his side, Marcus then stepped to the center of the circle, closed his eyes tightly, held his arms out with his hands open, palms up and fingers splayed. Loud rattling began to vibrate from the walls as the entire room began to shake violently to the point where ceiling tiles began to dust overhead, ready to crush us all. As the dust began to thicken around our feet, he began to run around the circle in a blinding speed until his feet began sparking and a black line appeared around our small group while also creating a whirlwind at the center of the circle, lifting the dust into the air forming a small tornado. We all watched with amazement as the spinning dust continued to grow until the woman cleared her throat and thanks Marcus for his demonstration.

Jeff and Marc were next to enter the circle, walking in together. After a quick moment to concentrate, they began to make slight movements in complete unison, until the equipment around the room began to rattle slightly. As the sounds began to grow and their movements a bit more pronounce, the scientific equipment around the circle began to be disassembled by invisible hands as Marc and Jeff manipulated the pieces with their minds. From the pieces they gathered they were able to create guns that could shoot plastic bullets. With their weapons in hand, they moved at blinding speed running, jumping and hiding all while hitting the bull's-eye targets that had been set-up on the walls around the room. They were 100% accurate with every shot they took.

"Nicely done boys, very impressive what you have been able to achieve. Any chance you could reassemble my computers now?" the woman asked with a smirk. Without wasting a moment, Jeff and Marc gave each other a nod and suddenly their guns floated back toward the workstations where they were invisibly disassembled and returned to their rightful place on the scientist's desks. "Thank you gentlemen," the woman said with a smile.

"Lucius and Amber, you're next. Please step forward," the woman said while gesturing with her hands. The children walked to the center of the circle together and then while facing each other, they raised their hands in front of their bodies with their palms facing each other. Nothing seemed to be happening until suddenly the air began to smell of electricity and a blue ball of energy appeared, sparking and moving as it grew between their bodies. Lucius and Amber lifted their hands slowly over their heads in turn making the ball also lift into the air high above our heads. I felt exhilarated watching the brilliant glow and couldn't help but smile. With prompting from the teacher, they moved their hands back down bringing the ball back between their bodies so that they could pull the energy back into their bodies. With a smile of approval from the teacher, they silently walked hand in hand back to their spot in the circle.

"Delilah and Rebecca, you're up next please," the teacher said. The two girls looked at each other with mischievous smiles as they walked to the center of the circle. With their gazes fixed on one another, they ran their hands through their long brown hair and were instantly transformed into the teacher. There were suddenly three identically looking teachers in the

room. *Everything was perfect, down to the small rip in the beige stockings and the missing button on the white lab coat.*

With obvious annoyance, the teacher walked in front of them and began to reprimand them while shaking her finger in their faces, "That is not funny girls. You are not permitted to impersonate anyone while you are at the Homestead. Is that understood?"

Delilah and Rebecca returned to their former 10 year old bodies with their long brown hair and nervous big round brown eyes. Softly they said in unison, "Yes Mrs. Simmon."

Once the girls had returned to their place in the circle, Mrs. Simmon turned to look at Jonas and I with her cat shaped glasses and salt and pepper hair expertly twirled into a bun at the top of her head. "Jonas and Lily you're up next. No funny business this time please," she cautioned with a frown.

Jonas and I responded simultaneously, "Yes Mrs. Simmon."

Together, we walked to the center of the circle. Jonas turned to me with a smile while nodding. I felt calm but very shy as all eyes intently watched us. Silently, I kept repeating to myself that this was a safe place and that Jonas was right here with me. I knew that I needed to hold back a bit and not reveal everything I could to anyone, except for Jonas. When the butterflies had stopped flapping their wings in my belly, I closed my eyes and conjured the air around me to move and lift me off the floor as I simultaneously pulled the fire that resided in my belly out in front of my body and into my extended hands, willing the flames to form a floating sphere of fire. Once I felt as if I had demonstrated long enough, I pulled the flames back inside of me and slowly descended back to the floor.

"Nicely done Lily, good control," Mrs. Simmons said. "Jonas, it's your turn now."

Jonas lifted his hands over his head and stood as still as he could until suddenly it began to snow in the room while a cold wind blew through the lab that lifted him up in the air, over our heads as the snow swirled around his body. His smile broadened as he visibly savored the chill he had created. I smiled as my body felt a rush of pride at what my Dual had achieved.

"Very nice Jonas, well done. Now, please come down Jonas. Good work all of you. Keep it up. Now, its time for supper," Mrs. Simmons said.

Jonas landed beside me and immediately grasped my hand tightly. I loved how his cool hand felt in the heat of mine.

I AWOKE with a jump as the memory of that incredible dream remained fresh in my minds eye. It felt as if I had been dreaming for 10 hours, but the clock revealed that I had slept for a mere 2 hours. Jonas stirred a bit but remained wrapped around my body as he continued to snore slightly. Stealthily I peeled myself away and climbed out of bed without waking him. I quietly opened the bedroom door and floated down the stairs noiselessly. Silently, making my way out of the front door and outside into the cool night winter air, I continued floating well above the snow in the hopes of keeping my feet dry while building a warm shield around myself. Rising up above the treetops, I began reaching for Raven with my mind. It wasn't long before I heard a loud caw in the distance. As his mind touched mine I was able to locate him easily. Swiftly, I turned and made my way over a tight grouping of evergreen trees where I knew I would find him, hidden in the boughs of a mighty pine.

'Hello my fire angel. I have missed you,' he said silently as he shuffled towards me. I could sense his attraction to the heat my body excuded.

"I had a dream of all five Duals tonight. We all grew up together, here," I said as I pointed at the Homestead house. "We were all very powerful children. Do you know what happened to all of them?" I asked.

'Once you were grown you were all sent away. But I knew that I would see you again. When the singleton returned, I knew the others would follow,' Raven rasped.

"Do you mean Marcus? Why is he a singleton, do you know? His mates name was Luna. Do you know what happened to her?" I asked in a whisper.

'She wasn't sent away when the rest of you were. She stayed here.

Terrible time for her, much screaming. She left with the soldier boys,' he said.

"Soldier boys? Was Peter a soldier boy? Did she go away with him?" I asked.

'Very angry and unpredictable without her partner. She needed many drugs to stay calm. Not smart what they did, separating a Dual. Sending her with soldiers. All a mess!' he cawed.

"Where were they sent? I need to find them Raven," I pleaded.

'Many years ago. Lives have been lived, this changes people. Boys are now men. All are still soldiers. I do not know where they went,' he explained.

"How is it that I can talk to you and understand you Raven? And you can talk to me for that matter," I asked a bit frazzled.

'It is one of your abilities and one of mine. They tested on animals before testing on the humans. I was in the lab when they brought you in as an infant. They started your medications very early. Your mate as well, Jonas. Just babies,' he explained, *'I calmed you when you would cry. It was very easy to love you,'* he said as he nudged his head into my arm.

There were glimpses in my mind of flying with him, sleeping in the trees as he watched over me. I somehow knew that I loved this bird, very much because the feelings seemed to return to me as I instinctively reached my arm around him and pulled him closer to my body.

16

I fell asleep leaning up against the main trunk of the tree while Raven slept beside me. I woke up to find Jonas hovering over us smiling, "You would do this all of the time when we were kids. You gave me quite a fright this morning though," he said with a fading smile. Raven stood and stretched his wings wide-open showing off his very large wingspan.

'Sleep well?' I asked him.

'Best sleep I've had in years. Thank you my lady. I'm so glad you're back,' he said as he lifted off into flight.

"How was your night you sneaky girl?" Jonas asked smiling at me as we both ascended over the treetops.

"I had an amazing dream about the five Duals. I remember their names and their abilities. I also realized that our teacher, Mrs. Simmon, was my 'mom' when she was younger. It was so crazy to see her so young. She was a really loving mother to me." My voice caught in my throat as memories of her funeral came alive in my mind. "She died a month before Philip, Gemma and Sam had their accident," I said, feeling my eyes begin to fill with tears. It was the first time I had said their names in weeks. The sadness felt all consuming, bringing me right back to how I felt as I was preparing for my last suicide attempt. It felt as if I was suffocating in blanket of melancholy. The many losses I experienced in a short period of time took a big bite out of spirit, leaving me in complete shreds. Everyone I encountered after the incidents understood my loss of sanity.

Jonas pulled me to him and held me tightly. "Those days are behind you. This is a new beginning my darling," he said knowing exactly what it was I had just vividly recalled.

As the tears silently ran down my cheeks I said in a whispered voice full of shame and regret. "I'm a horrid person. All of this time and this is the first time I am mentioning their names. And here you are dreaming about Jack every night."

"Now you stop this. You have made peace with this while I still have a long road ahead before that happens for me. I'm quite envious to be honest. I wish I could move forward and let go. I wish I didn't have the same recurrent dreams every night," he said sadly.

We floated over the trees holding one another tightly as I continued to sob silently until it felt as though there was not a drop of liquid left in my body.

With a deep sigh, I lifted my eyes to Jonas' and said, "Let's go in, I have a killer headache from all of this crying."

He laughed and said, "OK. Let's go find ibuprofen and a cup of coffee."

After a moment, as we descended I asked, "I wonder where my friends think I have gone. I just up and disappeared. I'm sure they went into my apartment and thought I was murdered with all of that blood. That or I was finally successful and they just hadn't been contacted by the authorities to identify my body."

Jonas halted our descent and turned to me as he tightly held my shoulders. "You were successful as far as they are concerned my darling. The Agency had a funeral service and everything. For all intents and purposes you are dead. As am I. This is our life now. There is nothing out there waiting for us."

"Oh my God, are you serious? That's intense... I'm dead? My poor friends, I have put them through so much...." I said. "How long have you known this Jonas? Why didn't you tell me before now?"

"I was told the day after you came back to me. I was asked to tell you when I thought you were ready. I'm sorry I delayed so much it's just that you have been through so much lately. I wanted to protect you for as long as I could," he explained while hugging tenderly and kissing me on the cheek.

I was in silent shock. "Please don't ever keep anything from me again Okay? Never. We will never be as strong as we can be if there are secrets. Got it?" I asked firmly.

"Yes, my darling. I'm sorry and I do promise," he said while stroking my hair behind my ears. "I was only trying to protect you. You're my life."

"As crazy as this all still seems to me, you are mine as well. But I need you to trust that I can handle whatever it is that is thrown at me as long as you are beside me," I explained. "I love you. I take care of you and you take care of me. Remember that. Please."

"I promise," he said as he kissed my hand.

"Okay, now let's go get me some pain killers and caffeine," I said as I winked at him.

17

Marcus had created an incredible breakfast for us as usual. As we ate our meal and discussed the logistics of our day, we were happily surprised to see that Jeff and Marc had returned from their expedition.

"Just in time for breakfast," Jeff said jovially as he walked into the house. "I could smell that bacon from outside."

Marcus smiled and said, "Well hello boys. Good to have you back. Come join us, plenty of food."

Jeff and Marc pulled up chairs and began to pile food onto their plates.

"Your journey was successful?" Naomi asked in a professional tone.

All eyes turned to the pair. It seemed I was not the only one in the dark about where they had been.

"There have been a few sightings reported, but no legitimate leads. But we will continue to look every chance we get," Marc responded while looking at Naomi intently.

"Good." Was the only response Naomi before she continued drinking her coffee.

Jonas and I remained still, watching everyone eat, just waiting to see if there would be further elaboration on the topic at hand until Marcus spoke up and asked, "Who or what are you looking for? Are we allowed to know?" he asked as he looked around the table.

Jeff and Marc turned to Naomi silently asking clarifying if they should divulge this information to the group. Once she gave them a barely perceptible nod, Jeff began to speak. "We have been searching for Becca and Delilah."

Marcus' mouth fell open. Jonas reached for my left hand and held it tightly. I looked at him and then at Marcus wondering what was going on. When nobody asked any other questions I spoke up, "I dreamt of all Five Duals last night. My memories are slowly returning to me. Rebecca and Delilah were shape shifters. I could feel their strength and power in my dream. They were very strong as children. I can only imagine how powerful they are now. They've disappeared?" I asked.

Jeff nodded and said, "Yes. They were sent on a mission to Egypt. We lost contact with them about a week after they arrived at their destination. That was 2 years ago."

You could hear a pin drop in the seemingly silent vacuum we sat. Finally Jonas asked, "What was the mission?"

This time it was Naomi that spoke, "The Agency sends out Duals to covert missions. A majority of these are military missions. This is your purpose and why you were brought back now. You were the last of the Duals to be brought back. My superiors determined that your particular abilities are needed to help our brothers in arms be successful. Becca and Delilah were sent on a mission. They were successful in the first component of the mission. They were able to help destroy many enemy military strongholds and for that we are grateful. The second component of their mission was unsuccessful and that is when we lost contact with them. We have been searching for the girls since. We have reason to believe that they were not killed during the mission but rather they are doing everything in their power to not be found. As you recently remembered Lily, this will make it incredibly difficult to find them."

"Shape shifters..." I whispered as I nodded in agreement.

"Exactly," Naomi replied. "If they don't want to be found then the chances of finding them are quite small. But we have to keep trying."

"What was the second part of their mission? The one they disappeared during?" Marcus asked.

Naomi leaned forward and looked Marcus in the eyes and said just one word, "Luna."

The color immediately left Marcus' cheeks. I could see his breathing pattern change as he sat unmoving. I reached my right hand for his as it sat motionless on the tabletop. I closed my eyes and sent him an image of what Luna looked like in my dream as a child with her small features and short almost white blond hair. His body quivered before turning to me startled. I began to speak to him in his mind *Remember who she was. She loved you very much. She was made to stay behind. We can find her again.*

Jonas squeezed my hand and began to speak with both of us in our minds, *We will help find her. She had much sadness and anger when she was taken away from you. We need to help her remember you and who you both were together.*

"Okay that's enough of that," Naomi said in a curt tone. "It is rude to have private conversations when you're in a group." She cleared her throat and looked at Jonas and I as she spoke, "We should take this opportunity to discuss how we will continue with your training. Jonas and Lily, from here on out we will allow the memories to return on their own. Your physical training needs to begin immediately. Your services are needed elsewhere but we cannot send you out until you are ready. Marc, Jeff and Marcus will become your trainers from here on out. They can help you become physically stronger and help you harness your abilities. We need you all at your strongest for this next mission."

"What is the next mission?" Jonas asked.

"You won't know until you are at the necessary location," Naomi answered.

"Who goes on this mission?" I asked.

"The Five," she responded.

After a few moments of quiet I asked the burning question. "Why wasn't Luna kept with Marcus, Naomi? Duals are stronger together. Why would your team jeopardize that? And who was the male scientist I saw in my dream? Dark brown hair and large rimmed, really thick glasses. He also had a mustache. I sensed he was a leader of sorts."

She sat motionless looking at me debating her response. "Luna had a mission she needed to conduct on her own. The scientist you speak of was called Richard. It was his decision to separate Luna and Marcus. He was a brilliant man that was able to achieve amazing scientific feats. But some of his decisions were not well received nor accepted by his colleagues in the end. It was his decision to separate you all for the purposes of maturation and gaining life experiences. Teenagers can be reactive and impulsive, not to mention hormonal. He wanted to be careful with each one of you and your abilities. It was a way to protect you from accidentally doing harm. I am not sure how I feel about his decision to separate some of the Duals yet. We'll see how your training progresses." She had a silent threat buried in its cadence.

She sat still, smiling dryly at me, expecting me to smile back excitedly about our potential training and what it would yield in terms of our abilities. Needless to say I did not have any pleasantness in me to return her smile. With that I asked, "Where is Peter, Naomi? Was Peter sent on the same mission as Luna?"

Her smile quickly faded and I could see her appearance begin to turn to frustration and anger. She slammed her fist on the table as she stood abruptly, her chair slamming into the wall behind her. She leaned over the table and said, "Peter was not my priority. He was a soldier and soldiers go where the fighting is. Luna did get sent with his platoon. Her mission was for her to achieve on her own. I am sorry about Peter. Nobody could have foreseen that," she said yelling at me.

I could feel my blood rushing to my feet, leaving me feeling faint as my breath became hitched in my throat. "Foreseen what Naomi? What happened to Peter?" I asked her with a shaky voice as I tried to hold back tears.

She seemed to actively calm herself down as she sat back in her seat. "I'm sorry Lily. He was killed in action 10 years ago. He was in the Middle East with his platoon. He was very strong and very brave and his actions saved many lives. I'm sorry. We all saw how deeply you both felt for one another."

The room suddenly began to spin as the shock of her statement hit me hard in the chest. The shock quickly translated into sadness, leading to uncontrollable tears. I could feel Jonas begin to shake beside me as he held my hand. I remained in my chair shaking as Jonas jumped out of his chair and slammed both of his fists in front of Naomi.

"You bitch!" he yelled in her face. "How could you tell her like that? You know how deep their connection was. You are cold and heartless." And with that she began to shiver as ice crystals began to form on her skin. Her lips turned blue as mists of condensation escaped her mouth with each breath.

I could feel Jonas' rage. I reached for his hand, which remained fisted on the table and as our skin touched I pulled his rage into myself. Feeling the heat in my body begin to rise as Jonas took his seat beside me and said, "Lil, look at me. Please darling. Look at me."

The temperature in the room continued to climb as the rage took over my body. My vision began to change much like it had during the infusion until I was suddenly able to see inside Naomi's chest. I could see the blood flowing in her arteries as her heart pumped the blood with every steady beat. My breathing became deep and intense as my body began to rise out of my seat until it hovered over the table. Marcus yelled, "Naomi, get out of here!"

As she began to move out of the chair, I held her in place with my mind while she pointlessly struggled against my invisible restraints. The tears continued to flow silently out of me as the glasses filled with water on the table beneath me began to boil. With my minds fist, I wrapped my invisible fingers around her heart and began to squeeze while watching it shrink in her chest. I would have continued clenching it if Jonas hadn't started blasting my face with cold subzero wind.

"Stop it! Control it! Look at me!" he said fiercely.

As soon as I released Naomi's heart and the blood began to flow freely again she fell to the floor as she lost consciousness. Jeff and Marc ran to her side and carried her to the sofa.

"Darling, look at me. Please. Please look at me." I could feel the sadness and desperation in his mind as he spoke. "I'm so sorry this is how we had to learn about Peter. Please come back to me. I need you my darling."

As I lowered my feet back to the floor, I looked at Jonas and without a moment of hesitation he took hold of my body and squeezed me tightly. "I'm so sorry Lily. I know how this feels." Was all he could say over and over again.

It wasn't until I felt pain in my throat that I realized that I had been screaming and crying like an injured animal slowly dying on the side of the road after being hit by a car. Marcus came over and began to rub my shoulder and arm. "I'm so sorry Lily," Marcus said softly.

Without much warning, my eyelids became heavy as my body began to slide to the floor with a sudden loss of muscle control. Jonas lifted me into his arms, cradling me as he floated us upstairs to our bedroom. Not a moment after he laid me on the bed, my mind shut down in a self-preservation maneuver, seeking refuge from this new world I found myself in.

18

I was flying over the pine trees again. I could feel the breeze holding me up in the air, like a warm hand pushing up against my abdomen propelling and lifting my body into the sky. I was holding Peters hand, keeping him in the sky beside me. We smiled at one another full of excitement as we snuck away secretly to the lake, our lake which I could now see in the distance. Raven's wings beat beside us as he followed us along on our journey cawing with excitement.

We landed on a large rock beside the waters edge. I ran my fingers through his short blonde hair looking like spun gold in the bright sun as he pulled my body into his and kissed me passionately.

"I love you to the point of madness. Be with me today, tomorrow and forever," he whispered as he held my face gently. His clear green eyes pierced my heart with its pure love and radiating joy. I smiled as a happy tear drifted down my cheek.

I nodded my head and said, "Forever."

I woke up startled. Sad to leave such a lovely dream but reassured to find myself safely bundled in Jonas' arms. I pulled his hand closer to my body and he responded by squeezing me back. "It's OK my darling. I'm here. Get some more sleep," he whispered.

I closed my eyes and tried to bring back the feelings I had just experienced in my dream to the present. The feeling of Peter's lips, his breath on my face, how his hands felt as they caressed and held me, the lightness of his green eyes as they sparkled in the sun. I silently began to cry wishing hungrily that I could remember all of it. As I began to spiral into sadness, overwhelmed with the knowledge that all he would ever be to me were memories of a distant past. Just like Philip and the kids. I missed them all so much. Philip was a good husband and father. He deserved someone better than me. In hindsight it all made sense of course, my inability to love him completely and to allow our relationship to truly take root. Unknowingly to both of us, my heart had been lost to someone else a long time before we had even met. All of them were lost to me forever.

As I lay in the bed listening to Jonas breathe beside me, I also began to miss my mother despite having learned that our lives together had been a lie. Remembering her hugs and the way we would laugh at the same things. I could feel deep inside that her love for me had not been false. At least I hoped that it wasn't.

My thoughts then brought me to my three best girlfriends. They had been so supportive through all of the tragedies in my life. I had caused them so much pain through my own suffering. I prayed that since the burden of caring for me now eliminated from their lives, that they were able to find peace in my death and that they did not mourn for me long. I loved them dearly and wished them nothing but peace.

Allowing myself to actually feel these emotions, I found myself remembering my children. Gemma with her long brown hair that she refused to brush, always wearing crazy patterns. My little artist with her grand imagination giving voices and lives to the animals she would see in the park on the pages of her sketch book. She was always so grandiose with her stories with her big round brown eyes, adamant that she could speak with the squirrels and that they would speak with her.

My breath hitched in my throat for a moment with the realization that she could have been telling me the truth. The similarities between the both of us had always been remarkable. People always commented on how she could have been my clone. Could I have passed that ability on to her I wondered?

As my mind raced, I began to remember my golden haired sweet boy Sam. Only five years old when he was killed in the car accident. He had such a gentle spirit with his easy smile. I searched my memories that linked him to possibly having inherited abilities as well but all I kept coming back to were his blue turquoise eyes that always watched me lovingly. They were both so young, filled with so much life that still needed living...five years old and my Gemma only nine. My God why did this happen to them?

Everything and everyone that I had ever loved were taken from me. I prayed that their lives were not cut short because of me, and who I had been forced to become. I wished that I had appreciated all of them more. That I had been more in the moment every time we were together, with eyes wide open and a heart overflowing with love for them. Jonas was now my touchstone, my last remaining link to life. He was the only thing keeping me from trying to end it all again.

Suddenly feeling overwhelmed, I slowly climbed out of bed, desperately trying to not wake Jonas in the process. I walked to the window and silently opened it and instinctively called to the wind until it gently lifted me out into the cold winter darkness. The quiet snow was falling again welcoming me into its simplicity and silence. I floated outside turning back to make sure Jonas had remained asleep. Drifting away from the building for a few minutes in no particular direction, I closed my eyes and relished in the feeling of the snowflakes giving me their icy kisses before evaporating from my hot skin. My yearning for solitude and silence suddenly became overwhelming.

With a mental push, I propelled myself through the night sky, zipping over the treetops, welcoming the feeling of the cold winter air on my skin as the snow drifted around me. I didn't bother to create a shield around myself. I wanted to feel the cold, I wanted to wake up, and I wanted my body to feel as much discomfort as possible.

As soon as I reached the lake I discovered that a layer of snow and ice had formed on the waters surface. Slowly landing in the center of it, I stood there for a moment before starting to shout and roar into the night sky, purging the anger, frustration and sadness that I held inside my tightly wound body. I continued to scream until the tension in my muscles dissipated and I was able stand on firm legs again. Flinging my arms open, I pushed a ball of energy out of myself, controlling and willing it to grow until it was the size of three basketballs with a bright red glowing core. Closing my arms forcefully in front of my body I propelled it across the large frozen lake stopping only as it came crashing into a collection of mature pine trees that lined the edge of the water. Six tree trunks were smashed into splinters, severing the tops from its bases. The sound of the explosion could be heard for miles and after a brief moment of quiet, the tops came crashing down onto the icy layer of the lake, creating a large fissure on its frozen surface. I lifted myself into the air, watching the split in the ice lengthen and travel beneath me in a thunderous roar that reached all of the way across the frozen water and to the opposite edge of the lake.

Once the lakes surface had been split into two, I pushed my body higher into the air pausing briefly before driving myself through the large fissure to then plunge into the freezing cold black water below the ice. The coldness of the water felt deliciously painful as the darkness and silence swallowed me whole. I wanted it all to consume me, to seep into my flesh as it pushed its way into my organs.

After a few moments, my lungs began to struggle for air and a I fought the urge to rise to the surface and breathe, I submerged myself even further almost challenging my body, holding it below the surface until it began to twitch uncontrollably. My mind began drifting into darkness until I felt a sudden explosion in my brain. The pain seared through me violently causing my minds eye to see flashes of blindingly bright red and white light. It was then that what I had wished for began to happen. My mind seemed to blossom, opening its many hidden corners to allow for the memories to flood back into awareness in flashes like an old movie projector with its jumpy images.

I remembered growing up at the Homestead with Jonas always by my side. Our sibling like love was always strong as we held each other through all of the training, experiments and injections. The scientists pushed us everyday to develop our abilities, forcing us to learn how to control them and harness the power within our bodies to the point where I would collapse from exhaustion. And through it all Jonas had always been there to carry me to bed.

As we aged, the scientists forced all of the children to train together and sometimes spar one another. I remember how strong Luna was, often beating me in these mock battles. I knew that I was powerful and could have subdued her if I wanted to but fear always seemed to hold me back. Jonas and I would always be stronger together, mirroring each other's abilities and often sharing our strength.

In a sudden flash, I remembered the first day Peter and I met. His small body weak, dirty and neglected. He was brought to the Homestead at the tender age of six. I was five years old on that fateful day and I loved him from the very moment he told me his name in his soft little boy voice. All of our private moments growing up together flooded back to me in a flash, filling me with warmth and comfort until a painfully horrid memory came flooding back. The dread I felt on the day we were all separated poured into my body like melted lava. When all of us were forcibly sent away, told we were too old to remain at the Homestead and that it was time to live a normal life on the outside. The day I was sent away was filled with fear and anguish. The memory of it seemed to make my body heavier, forcing me to sink further in the dark water.

As my lungs continued to fight its instinct to breathe, I continued to remember it all. Pulling the memories out of all of the hiding places also came the voices of the scientists promising that we would be brought back to the Homestead when we were ready. That memory seemed to be blended with the pain from that last injection that ultimately created the large emptiness in my mind and spirit. I recalled that it wasn't just an injection that I received on that day. The memory loss had been further induced by electroshock therapy that was then followed by the long hours necessary to create new memories. I remembered repeating Jonas' and Peter's name over and over again in my mind in an ultimately failed attempt to keep them present within me. Fighting the process worsened the pain I felt, forcing me to ultimately give up the fight and accept my new fate.

These returned memories filled me with rage at the unfairness of it all. We had been children forced to experience unbelievable physical and emotional suffering. And behind it all stood Richard. I swore at that moment that I would find him and terminate him just as he had done me and the ones I loved.

With this final promise, the remembering completed and as I opened my eyes, I was startled to discover a pair of eyes watching me in the darkness. They were Jonas' eyes and I would know them anywhere. Urgently propelling my body back through the black water, I took his hand and pulled us through the icy fissure and up into the night sky high above. After allowing me to catch my breath, Jonas pulled me into his arms as we continued to float above the frozen lake.

"Don't you ever do that again do you hear me! I was so scared." He shook me angrily before saying in a shocked tone, "You remembered everything...I can feel it."

"Yes," I said as I pushed myself away to look into his eyes. "I remember it all."

Placing my cold wet hands on either side of his face, I pushed all of my new knowledge and visions into his mind, sharing all of it with him. His eyes flickered as the images played in his mind. Until finally he slowly opened his eyes and said, "My God."

19

The two of us held hands as we quickly flew back to the house. Upon reaching the front door, we simultaneously lifted our hands pushing energy out of our bodies to throw the heavy wooden door off of its hinges, sending it crashing onto the floor in a loud thunderous boom. After drifting inside we yelled in unison, "NAOMI!"

Immediately the house began to stir with Marc and Jeff running down the stairs in nothing but boxers and a Glock in their hands. Marcus followed closely behind with his own weapon drawn. He at least was wearing pajama bottoms. They lowered their weapons after quickly assessing the situation and realizing that we were not in any danger. They stared at Jonas and I with quizzical looks.

"Where is she?" I asked angrily through gritted teeth.

"Your eyes Lily..." Marcus began, "they're glowing red."

Focusing my gaze on him I said, "I'm a bit upset. Where is she? I can feel her fear in this house."

"Naomi, come down please. We will not harm you. We just have questions that need addressing," Jonas said with a raised voice.

"Speak for yourself, we're not gonna harm her...huh!" I spit out quietly.

I turned towards the stairs as the sensation of her body heat reached me. She stood at the top landing watching us before she began to make her way down. The squeaking sound from the old wooden steps reverberated through the house as we all watched her in silence.

When she finally reached the ground floor, I focused my vision on her body, zeroing in on her heart again. I could see it beating quickly in her chest as her lungs filled and emptied with each breath. It would be so easy for me to finish her retched little life that I caught myself maliciously smiling. Jonas and I turned to each other sensing each others menacing thoughts while we continued to hover over the collapsed door, still dripping lake water from our clothes.

I looked at Naomi and asked her in a sweet voice, "Where is Richard, Naomi?"

I could see her cheeks flush as she looked at me, presumably debating what her response should be. I reached into her mind and shouted, *'Where is he?'*

She jumped at the invasion and said, "Get out of my head. You are not welcome."

Everyone turned to look at me having heard my mental yell. They watched me with wonder as my eyes continued their fiery glow.

"I will continue to probe your mind until you answer us," I said. I could see Jonas smiling from the corner of my eye as he spoke to me privately, *'She doesn't know where he is.'*

I turned to look at him with a questioning look. *'He left everything including her behind. She doesn't know where he is. She wants to find him as well. Your yelling distracted her.... I reached into her mind,'* he said.

Slowly moving to hover over the hard wood floor, we lowered ourselves down. I concentrated my thoughts to contain my rage so that I could push the fire back down into my body. Turning to Marcus, I waited for a response to know if my eyes were back to their basic brown. He looked at me and nodded slightly.

"He left you behind as well," Jonas stated to Naomi. She nodded her head in agreement.

"He disappeared after you were all cleared of your memories and placed in your handlers homes," she said. "He has not been seen from since then."

"No sign of him anywhere? This was his life's work and he walked away from it?" I replied in disbelief. Naomi shrugged and nodded her head.

"I know how upsetting all of this is to you. I was abandoned here as well. Just waiting for the right timing to begin calling you back. Waiting for him to come back," Naomi said and began to shake her head again, "I don't know how he could walk away from all of this. But on the day that Peter and Luna were sent away, he travelled with them to their destination. We lost contact with him right around the same time we lost contact with Luna."

I looked at Marcus as this last revelation came to light. He stared at Naomi with a slack jaw for a few moments until finally he turned to me and said, "We need to find them."

I nodded and said firmly, "Yes. We do...we will!"

"You need to complete your mission before you can go. The military has invested a lot in this project and I will be held accountable if you don't succeed. Please. Let's finish your training so that we can get this done. Understand that your freedom means my freedom as well," Naomi explained.

I turned to Jonas as Marc, Jeff and Marcus walked over to stand beside us.

"Are we all in this together?" Jonas asked as he turned to look at everyone.

We each took each other's hands as we stood in a circle nodding in agreement to Jonas. The feeling of unity between the five of us was an incredibly glorifying moment that united us as a team and it was in this act where we officially became "The Five" all on our own, without anyone telling us we had to.

We all turned to Naomi as Marcus spoke to her, "Let's finish Naomi. We have work to do."

She nodded with a serious look and said, "Alright."

20

T he next few weeks were spent remembering and training. Between the two, the memories were the most difficult and overwhelming to manage at times. They would come back to me unannounced in bright flashes of light and heat. They would even make me lose consciousness sometimes only to later wake up in my bed with Jonas lying beside me. Naomi explained that I was especially susceptible to these memory bursts because I fought the hardest when they were taking them away. This was a theory of course, but could be well founded since the men were having a much easier go at it. Maybe they were just better at hiding the pain.

Physically, the men were definitely further in their training than I was. Mentally, their memories seemed to have been almost fully recovered. Naomi continued to give Jonas and I infusions daily. She explained that they would help us reach our full transition. The infusions were very painful but much shorter than the initial doses, lasting approximately 30 minutes each time. Jonas always stayed by my side for these, holding my hand reassuringly. I tried to remain strong for him but would often lose the battle with a scream.

My days again became filled with routines. Only this time, it was very different. I was thriving in the discoveries. Our days would start after breakfast, where Jonas and I would go to the lab for our infusions, then rest for a few minutes until we were well enough to proceed to the gym for strength training led by Marcus. After our ass kicking, we had weapons training with Marc and Jeff, only to then end the day with ability development. That we did all together.

Despite the routines and the schedules, my days continued to surprise me with each new discovery made that ranged from new memories recollected to new abilities surfacing. The more I called on the flames and willed the wind to do my bidding, the stronger I felt and the stronger my abilities became. I was beginning to learn how to control these new skills so efficiently and accurately that it took little to no effort to put up a force field or set a pile of wood on fire. I learned to levitate objects by using my ability to control the air. But my most exciting discovery was when I figured out how to block my mind from the others. Being able to have private thoughts or conversations was a big relief to me in this new world that thrived on connections.

I was also becoming more familiar with the ability to feel and see the heat that radiated from the blood pumping through each vessel, pushed through the body by with each squeeze of the muscular hearts I was so easily able to see pumping in my friends chests. This was the ability that scared me the most. The ease with which I could constrict and prevent the blood from flowing made me feel dangerous. Even more so than the fire made me feel. When I had accidentally discovered this new potential, driven by rage at Naomi, I feared what I would have done if it were not for Jonas stopping me. I focused on controlling this ability more than any other until I was able to harness its power at will. It made me hyperaware of the heat sources that radiated from the bodies that pulled at my core. I instinctively knew that manipulation of these heat sources, if I so desired, would be only too simple for me to do. It tempted me and dared me to unleash the tight grasp I had around it. Curious to know if I could go through with ending the beating of someones heart with nothing but a twinge in my mind.

Whenever the temptation to experiment became too overwhelming, I would stop what I was doing and watch Jonas knowing that I would be distracted by the awe of his abilities that always took my breath away. He could create a winter wonderland in the most profound heat that I could muster. He would create snowy blizzards with gusting winds that would carry him to the very edges of the property. It was incredible to witness how our opposite abilities complimented one another. I would remember some of the first words Jonas said to me at The Birches, he said we fit together like yin and yang...fire and ice. My heart overflowed with love and tenderness for him as I watched his graceful form manipulate the elements like a dancer on an invisible suspended stage. It was in those moments that I would wonder how we were able to survive without one another for so long.

Marcus had also become markedly stronger since we had all started training together. His determination to get Luna back was palpably fierce, driving his desire for strength and control of his ability to escalate to new heights. Marcus' ability to cause seismic movements around himself had become so strong that he even scared himself when he tore a 2-feet wide and 10-feet deep crevice in the earth outside the Homesteads back door. Which forced him to learn how to really focus his ability until he was able to reverse his energy in order to repair the fissure he had inadvertently created.

But Marcus was most excited to learn that his earth moving ability helped him become airborne, where he would will the earth to push him up into the air appearing as if he were doing nothing but jump on a trampoline that just so happened propel him hundreds of feet away at a time. His first few attempts were remarkably unsuccessful since he flung himself up instead of forward. We all laughed heartily watching his big muscular, very masculine, half naked tattooed man fly high above our heads only to then be violently sucked back down to earth. After the first couple of times watching him so demeaningly do this to himself, I began sending the wind to catch him as he plummeted back down, hoping to prevent him from injuring himself too badly. Only once did I almost let him crash down because I was laughing so hard. He did not find any of it amusing of course. But as the days progressed, his ability strengthened and he learned to control it. Once he had figured that out, it allowed him to travel great distances in a single jump, allowing him to cover one mile in the blink of an eye.

Marc and Jeff were instrumental in helping the three of us hone our abilities and become physically stronger. Their extensive military skills made them our teachers in hand-to-hand combat along with extensive weapons training. It almost seemed silly to be trained on how to shoot a gun or wield a knife when I could explode someones heart in their chest or set their bodies on fire with little to no effort. Regardless, M&J took great pride in teaching us their craft and for that I admired them, making me remember how much I loved them when we were young. Marcus was a natural, obviously having had training in the past. Jonas was startlingly precise with his gun, almost as good as Marc and Jeff. Almost...

Naomi kept her word. She helped guide us and encouraged us during this time. I would sometimes catch glimpses of her memories that would burst through her defenses. She had abilities of her own, of this I was certain of but what they were I had been unsuccessful in discovering. She could clearly shield her mind and would get very upset when she would catch me prying for information. There was more to her than what she was revealing. She looked to be about our age, early to mid forties, making me wonder if she had been a child of the Homestead as well. But then it begged the question of how it was that she came to be in her current position. She had such extensive knowledge of the histories and experiments that were conducted on the hundreds of children that I wondered who had mentored her. My mind raced with questions for her but I knew that she did not welcome my prying. All I had to do was remain patient until the right time presented itself.

Each day our new self-discoveries drew us closer together as a team. We pushed each other to learn to control our abilities while strengthening our bodies. We each suffered many injuries that were mainly self-inflicted as we learned focus and control. But despite the pain, we laughed often even when tears were shed, mainly by me.

Our bond and love for one another strengthened with each passing day. And before we realized it was happening, we became our own little family.

In the evenings, we would spend hours eating our meal, drinking wine and talking. We would laugh and sometimes cry, but most importantly we would accept. We accepted each other as individuals and who we were in our little community. I loved these men and I knew that they loved me.

Naomi on the other hand remained a challenge for me. No matter how kind she attempted to be, I remained full of distrust for her. It was plain to see that she was keeping some pretty big secrets making us all feel as if we were walking on eggshells around her.

Through the highs and lows, my love and adoration for Jonas also grew during this time. We were never separated, our movements always mirroring one another's. Our challenges and successes would be meaningless if the other was not there, which never actually happened. More of our childhood memories returned to us, we would talk late into the night reminiscing about our experiences. We would hold each other tightly as we laugh at some of our mischief. Despite this, there were some memories I kept to myself, feeling that the moments that poured into the forefront of my mind were for me only. To hold them, guard them, protect them as if they were fragile things that could be shattered into dust, never to be held in my mind again. All of these remembrances were made up by one single thread, one common denominator that made my hands shake and my heart beat faster when I remembered his face. The one face I longed to have seen one last time. The face of a boy who would live only in my mind, haunting me everyday, with his warm eyes and loving arms. I knew irrevocably that I would miss him from my soul for the rest of my life.

NIGHTS REMAINED the most difficult for me to manage. The recurrent lake dreams and memory flashes of Peter seemed to debilitate me for hours after opening my eyes. I would wake up in a tearful state of panic wanting to jump out of bed to search for him. More often than not Jonas would continue to sleep despite his arm tightening around me reflexively.

As sweat ran down my panicked skin, I would silently make my way outside to search for Raven, who always happened to be waiting for me to appear outside of my window, in the hopes for a nightly flight together. I loved our time together. He had so many memories and stories to share with me about all of us growing up here. He was especially fond of stories about Marc and Jeff, because they were the naughtiest of us all. He had been such an important part of my life at The Homestead.

But my favorite stories that Raven would share were of course about Peter. I learned that he had received many doses of the serum but that it had never helped him develop his abilities further like it had done to the rest of us. Raven called him an enhanced human.

'He had unusual strength and speed. He was incredible with guns. He could shoot a fly out of the sky a mile away on a windy day,' Raven explained while fluffing his feathers. I smiled as that image popped into my mind.

As he spoke, I couldn't help but close my eyes as the memory of what Peter's skin smelled like after a day in the sun returned to me. 'I have to find out what happened to him. I need to at least know where he's been interred Raven. I have to see where he is now for me to get closure. I need a proper goodbye so that I can move forward or I don't know what will happen to me,' I said silently.

'Stay with the program,' Raven encouraged, 'Complete the mission that you will be tasked with. You will then find yourselves with a bit more freedom. But understand that you will forever belong to them. No matter what they say.'

Once I had digested what Raven had said I turned to him, fully comprehending the seriousness and severity of his advice along with the reality of his words. Knowing that moving forward, any feeling of liberty would always simply be an illusion.

I MADE my way back into bed just as the sun had begun its daily ascent in the horizon. Jonas welcomed me with open arms pulling me into his warm sleepy body where I had left him. As I snuggled up against him, he fell back to sleep almost instantaneously. Before I myself could fall asleep, I reached into his mind to make sure that he was all right, only slightly berating for my shameless invasion of his privacy but proceeded anyway.

I FOUND myself standing beside Jonas as we faced Jack on that same fateful beach. It was the same dream he had been having since we reunited. The emotions and love forever present in the air. Where the warm breeze moved slowly, carrying the sounds of the ocean while the soft waves lovingly kissed the shore.

After a moment of realizing that nothing had changed, I walked away from them, turning to watch from a distance as I remained in the dream for just a little bit longer. Hoping that Jonas would turn to me. When he finally did, I was immediately flooded with his sadness and despair.

"Come on darling." Was all I could say to him as I took his hand and pulled him back to consciousness and away from this recurrent nightly pain.

21

It took us a total of six months to feel as if we weren't walking disasters with the potential to cause some serious destruction on our surroundings and scariest of all, each other. My abilities became such a part of my being that it required little effort to engage them. A simple lift of a finger or flick of the wrist could create a windstorm carrying with it an inferno of flames. Jonas' abilities came in very handy during these early learning stages for me since he was often the person who would extinguish any accidental blazes I would create. This did however work both ways for us, as I was made responsible for rewarming items before they shattered into frozen shards.

The weather had become warm and all of the snow had melted, revealing new growth and greenery in the landscape of the Homestead. Naomi had started taking frequent overnight trips, leaving late at night and returning in the early afternoon the next day. Her excuse was always that The Agency had summoned all of the scientists so that they could debrief the chiefs on our progress. It felt very violating to know that she was always documenting our achievements and then reporting on them. Talk about big brother watching...

"How was your trip Naomi?" I asked sarcastically as she walked into the house after her third trip. We were all sitting at the dining table eating our lunches when she walked in.

"It was quick thankfully. But I must tell you all that my supervisors don't share my same sentiments when it comes to all of you. They would like for you to be sent on your first mission immediately. They think that you are ready. They are of the opinion that your abilities will only strengthen with real life experiences. I tend to agree with them to a certain extent. So I think that the next training exercises should be off the Homestead grounds. You need to be exposed to civilians," Naomi explained as she sat down at the table.

We remained silent as she bit into of sandwich and began to chew. Jonas reached to take my hand reassuringly. "We haven't been around...normal people," I said nervously looking around the table. "What if I lose control and blow up a building?" I glance nervously to Jonas.

Jonas squeezed my hand and nodded in agreement with me. I could feel he was nervous as well as Marc and Jeff watched us with big smirks.

"We will all be together when we go out. You'll both be just fine. We have to know how you will be around un-enhanced people," Naomi explained as she ate a potato chip.

"I don't think you will blow up a building," Marc said while winking at me, "the thing that you will both need to focus on is closing your minds off. You have to really work on building that shield around yourselves because once you're out there you will be filtering through every thought, every emotion and every past experience in the minds you come close to. It's very disorienting and to be honest you may really want to hurt some people after you learn who they are and all the shit they've done in their lives."

"You both have been in a very safe place here with us. Protected. I know you can each build shields, but they must be strengthened and this is as perfect a time as ever," Jeff explained reassuringly.

"To be honest, we could all use the practice. We have all been in this fucking house for too long," Marcus said contemptuously while looking at Naomi, who responded with a nod.

"Okay, how about we go into town and get some groceries for the house," Naomi said with a clap while leaning back from the table.

Jonas and I exchanged a concerned look, *'Holy shit!'* I said to him privately.

'We'll be Okay. We have to do this,' he answered while taking in a deep breath and standing. He then tugged at my hand so that I would stand as well.

I went into my closet in my bedroom to find actual clothes I could wear in public instead of the stupid white jumpsuit. Thankfully there were jeans, a shirt and a sweater that I could wear since the spring days were still a bit chilly. While rummaging in the closet I saw something shimmer on the carpet out of the corner of my eye. Leaning down to get a closer look, I found a gold necklace with a tiny gold feather pendant. I picked it up and took a closer look at the feather. Suddenly, something seemed to snap inside of me and I could feel the blood draining from my head only to then pool in my feet as a cold chill ran through me. This was my necklace. I was wearing it in the tub that night. But most shockingly, I remembered Peter had been the one to give it me.

WE WERE AT THE LAKE, sitting on the large rock in the sun. He reached into his pocket as he held my gaze with a sweet smile before leaning forward to place the necklace over my head. I held the feather pendant in my hand and watched it shimmer in the sunshine. He brushed my hair away from my face and kissed me softly on the lips. "I love you," he whispered.

JONAS STARTLED me out of my reverie by abruptly coming into the bedroom and saying, "You ready darling? Everyone is waiting," he paused with a gasp. "Are you Okay, I felt a little something as I was walking here." He looked around the room searching for me before discovering me sitting in the closet while holding the necklace in the palm of my hand. He gently kneeled in front of me with eyes fixed on my hand as it held the necklace before instinctively reaching for it with a sad knowing look.

He held the necklace in his hand for a moment before saying, "I remember when he gave you this. We had to keep it secret of course. Nobody could know you were together and God forbid cared for one another more than friends." He paused, took in a deep breath and then sullenly said, "You were wearing this when I found you that night."

I looked at him startled by the memories that came flooding back to me about that dreadful event in my apartment and all that transpired after. "I've had this with me all of this time. Oh my God. I would never take it off. I had told Philip my mom had given it to me. I thought that she had actually," I said as I raised my eyebrows.

Taking the necklace back from Jonas, I put it around my neck and held the pendant in my hand to take a closer look at the feather. I raised my eyes when I discovered tiny bits of blood embedded in the small crevices. There were so many reminders of my past in this one little piece of gold.

Jonas kept watching me with worry in his eyes, "I tried to clean it while you were still in the hospital. I'm sorry, I guess I didn't do a very good job."

I shook my head and said, "No, I like having this just as it is. It adds to its power for me." I tucked the necklace under my shirt and pressed the pendant up against my skin over my heart. After a quick pause I looked up at Jonas before taking his outstretched hand so that he could pull up on my feet.

"Let's go," I said determined to keep myself composed.

IT WAS strange to be traveling in a car after so many months of not leaving the compound. We drove in the same large black SUV that had originally brought us here. The windows were tinted a very dark black making it impossible for anyone to see the passengers in the back. Jeff sat behind the wheel and Marc rode shotgun beside him. Marcus and Naomi rode in the middle row while Jonas and I sat in the far back. We sped down the tree-lined road thick with low hanging branches making it feel as though we were driving in a tunnel. During one of my solo flights, I had flown to what I believed were the edges of the property but was just now feeling how complete isolated actually had been. We drove for about 5 minutes before finally reaching the main gate. Remembering the fully armed uniformed guards from our first night made our second encounter with them not as shocking. When we pulled up beside the gatehouse, Jeff opened his window and greeted the guard in the same manner with which he had done on that very first night.

"Good afternoon sir," the guard said to Jeff, "How many are leaving the property today?"

"Six," Jeff answered. The guard subtly lifted an eyebrow in surprise but gave no other outward reaction as he documented this in his paperwork.

"Have a nice day sir," he said before turning to a second guard who had remained in the guardhouse, motioning for him to open the gates.

As we began to drive away, I looked at Naomi sitting in front of me and asked, "Naomi, where do the guards go when they're off duty? Do they live in the town?"

She was silent for a few moments before responding presumably thinking about how she should answer.

"The property is composed of various bunkers that are all subterranean, connected by tunnels. The Homestead is the only above ground building on the compound. Much of our work with the Duals Project has been conducted in the subterranean labs. They kept you children in the above ground house because you all seemed to do better if you had a somewhat normal life surrounded by nature, where you were able to run in the meadow, hide in the trees and breathe in fresh air."

"The house doesn't seem very big and there were many children here. The children who were not Duals, where did they go at night?" I asked.

"Children who were unlinked are called Solos," she explained with an annoyed tone. "They were kept with the soldier's underground. Their focus and training was very different from yours. Only the Duals stayed in the house," Naomi answered dryly. "The Solos would come out for training exercises daily and were allowed a period of free play, however the interactions between the two groups were intentionally limited."

I could feel the anger building up inside of me as the fire pushed against my skin. Jonas reached over and took my hand, forcing cold into my body while I glared at the back of Naomi's head imagining what it would feel like to smash it up against a wall.

She finally turned to me and said, "I can feel that you know. Your rage and desire to hurt me. You can't change the past but you can create a peaceful future for yourselves if you play your cards right."

"You know what... I try to tell myself that beneath that Barbie doll façade of yours there's an actual human being in there somewhere, but then I'm reminded of what you and your people have done and it shatters the little hope I have for you. The Agency stole our lives and led innocent children to war and their deaths just to be able to learn how to kill other people more efficiently. We are all nothing but your fucking lab rats, your pawns. And stop telling us that we can make a peaceful future for ourselves once this mission is over. You know as well as I do that none of us will ever be truly free from this," I raged. "Tell us your story Naomi. How is that you have abilities and yet we find you fighting for the other team?"

"I know what you're feeling. I went through the same experiments you all went through. Only I was a failure. I was unable to fully make a link. They tried to match me, to create another Dual," Naomi said and was then stopped by Marcus.

"Stop it Naomi. She isn't ready," Marcus commanded in a low tone.

"She wants to know. No, she needs to know. She needs to understand that we were all forced into this. Including me," she said to

Marcus fitfully. Turning back to look at me she said, "I was meant to be a Dual with Peter."

Her words seemed to physically knock the air out of my lungs and the fire rush through my veins. I could feel my vision begin to change again as my eyes began to moistened with rage, "You are not allowed to say his name. Ever! Do you understand me?" I yelled in her face as I slammed my fist into the back of her seat.

She turned around to face the front of the vehicle again before saying, "This is all very difficult for me as well you know. Growing up feeling like a failure. Being treated like I'm less than everyone else just because my genes kept me a Solo. Peter and I were very close growing up, you have to know that. But I was no match when it came to you. He would always leave me behind because of you. You were his whole world and I hated you for it." She paused to formulate her next sentence. "We shared a strong mind connection, which was about the extent of our linking. I felt every emotion and heard every thought he had. Which really pissed me off because they were always about you," she said through gritted teeth, "you were everything I wanted to be. You were a Dual with strength the scientists had not seen before, you had Jonas and you also had Peter. I was alone. Left to face the facts of my circumstances on my own."

Jonas squeezed my hand while she spoke. I could do nothing but stare out the window in silence, watching the world outside zip passed us as we sped down the road. The tree filled landscape that had surrounded us seemed to be an island in a land composed of farmland that overflowed with corn crops that filled every available square inch, as far as the eye could see. I cried silently and wished that I was able to go somewhere to be alone. Jonas put his arm around my shoulder and held me tightly.

"Did you feel him when he died?" I finally asked her.

"No," she said quickly.

"Do you know where he was when...when it happened?" I asked.

"No."

In silence, we made our way to the city as I pressed my gold feather over my heart.

22

The city was much bigger than I had expected. There were shopping centers and large grocery stores with people bustling about. As we drove, I was able to determine that we were in the state of Iowa based on the majority of license plates that drove by us. We made our way through town until pulling into a parking space in front of an outdoor clothing store.

"We need to buy clothes for our mission. They are sending us out to the Middle East somewhere. All you really need to know is that it's sandy and hot during the day and that it can get cold at night. Marcus, please help Jonas and Lily in there," Naomi said motioning to the store authoritatively.

Before we jumped out of the car Marcus turned to both Jonas and I and said, "Work on your shields while you're in there. It doesn't look too crowded from out here so it's a good spot to practice."

I was in no mood to shop or be around people for that matter. I felt emotionally drained, angry and sad. All I wanted to do was crawl into a dark closet and sit in stillness for a few hours after hearing these most recent revelations.

"Come on darling," Jonas said as he gently tugged on my hand after climbing out of the SUV.

I jumped out and followed him into the store with Marcus walking behind us. "Okay, Lily you're going to need a few tank tops and t-shirts. Come, I'll show you where. Jonas you need to find the same for yourself, that table over there has some good selections," Marcus said while pointing to a table to our left. "Lily you come with me."

I followed Marcus to the right as Jonas remained in the same spot, watching me walk away for a moment before turning to where the men's shirts were located. Once Marcus and I reached the table with the women's tops, a lady in her early 20's approached the table and looked at me for a moment before asking, "Hello. Can I help you find something in particular?"

I couldn't take my eyes off of her. She was a beautiful woman of Asian descent with very long black hair and delicate features. Marcus quickly took my hand and whispered, "Shield."

That one word seemed to snap me back to the present. Without any hesitation, I shielded myself easily and quickly. As soon as it was up, I briefly closed my eyes reveling in the warmth and silence that softly cocooned my body. As the beautiful sales girl waited for me to respond to her inquiry with a smile, I created a small opening in my shield so that I could stealthily reach into her mind. I was curious about her life. Did she have a normal life with a happy home and a lover perhaps?

I was quickly able to learn that her name was Jennifer and that she was 22 years old. Jennifer stood very still, unblinking as I held her gaze while rummaging around in her head. I focused in on her daily activities, her joys and disappointments. I learned that she was a college student at Iowa State. She was majoring in biology and hoped to be a doctor someday. Her job in the outdoor gear store was part time and that she needed the work in order to pay for the rent. She has 3 roommates and a boyfriend. She had been in that relationship for close to 2 years and didn't love him anymore but just didn't have the courage to break things off. His name was Dave and he lacked passion, vision and drive. He had been unemployed for months and had dropped out of school soon after losing his last job.

I was startled when I unexpectedly heard Jonas speak in my mind, *'Just control it darling.'*

Then Marcus took hold of my shoulder and whispered in my ear, "Okay enough. You've done well."

Jennifer blinked rapidly as I released the tether I had on her mind. With a giggle she said, "I'm sorry. I'm not sure what just happened there. I've been a little tired lately. Is there something I can help you find?"

"No, thank you," I said while looking at her with a smile. Without another word, she politely turned and walked away. Marcus looked at me and nodded, "Good. That was good," he said as he took my hand.

Our clothing-shopping excursion was relatively quick and ended not long after my interaction with the sales girl. To be completely honest, Marcus could have done the shopping for all of us. As I followed the others out of the store after making our purchases, I turned to Jennifer who had been standing not very far from the exit at a table folding shorts.

Before walking through the shop doors, I looked at her and said, "You have to be brave Jennifer. You don't love him anymore. He's just holding you back."

With a startled look in her eyes she said, "Excuse me?" But I just looked at her and smiled as realization struck her. Before she could ask me any more questions, I turned and walked out of the store to the waiting SUV.

I was the last to climb into the silent vehicle. Jonas smirked at me before asking the group, "Okay, where to next?"

"Groceries are next," Naomi replied.

We didn't have to drive very far to our next destination. The parking lot outside of the grocery store was much more crowded than the lot we had just been in. I could feel all of the external emotions and thoughts beginning to make their way into my head while still in the parking lot. Instinctively and instantaneously as my muscles began to tense I created my shield as I turned to Jonas with a smile, sensing his tension as he put up his own shield.

I extended my shield to his and asked him privately, *'You OK?'* He nodded but remained quiet as we jumped out of the car.

We walked around the store arm in arm, which made the shielding even easier. Jonas and I maintained our mental link only occasionally connecting with one of the shoppers if they seemed to have an interesting story. The more we did that, the more we realized that almost everyone we "listened" to had similar goals and worries. The humanity in the shared experiences and desires united everyone. My goals had been the same as theirs not that long ago. Worries about family, work and money were all a common threads connecting everyone.

I turned to Jonas with sad eyes and said, "Life can change in a blinding instant..."

23

We journeyed home in silence. I kept my shield up as we drove back to the compound. I could tell that I was heating up the car by doing this since Jeff and Marc had opened all of the windows and turned the air conditioning on full blast despite the 50 degree temperature that blew in from outside. I only cared but so much. I needed to feel the warm calm as I silently watched the landscape pass by outside. I had never seen such a flat terrain comprised entirely by farms the dilapidated barns and scattered farmhouses here and there. Turning onto the dirt road that led to The Homestead, I noticed that there were no indications of any sort that such an enormous compound existed here, just off the main road with a large guard house not far from the roads entrance. Could it be possible that the locals were unaware of its existence I wondered?

As we approached the gate, Jeff closed all of the windows with the exception for his. The same guard as earlier, approached the car with his clipboard. "Hello sir," he said addressing Jeff. "How many are back?" he asked.

"Six," replied Jeff.

The guard leaned into the car ever so slightly to get a look at who the passengers were but then stopped himself as his muscles tensed when Jeff stiffened and sat up straighter. Marc leaned across the arm rest that separated his seat from Jeff's and said firmly, "Mind your own business and open the fucking gate."

The guard straightened up and said, "Yes sir." He then motioned to the second guard to open the gate. The tension and pressure radiating from Marc and Jeff was intense, almost sucking the hot air out of the car.

"Alright, alright, it's over. Move on boys," Marcus encouraged.

Jeff stepped on the gas and sped past the guards, leaving them in a thick dust cloud.

'*What was that about?*' I asked Jonas as I shook my head. But his only response was a shrug in his shoulders.

"They are suspicious that you have both returned. They have memories and there are stories about the both of you that have become legendary from the repeated telling and retelling of your abilities. They all grew up here too, don't forget that," Marc explained.

I don't know why but that just pissed me off even more. I didn't realize I was heating up until the windows were opened again and the air conditioning turned back on full blast. Jonas reached his cool hand for mine and held it tightly. At least I knew I wasn't affecting him.

Turning my attention to the tunnel of trees we were driving through once again, heading back towards the Homestead Leaning, I leaned my head out of the window and deeply breathed in the air, pulling the sweetness from the shade covered earth into my body. Wishing I were out there, walking with bare feet on the moist dirt, feeling my toes in the soil. My body ached to run and fly to release some of the angst I had been feeling and to clear my head.

AFTER PULLING into the driveway in front of the house, I helped put away the groceries before running up to my room to put on clothes that I could workout in. I opened the bedroom window and just before I jumped out I reached for Jonas in the house and said, *'I'll be back soon'*. Without waiting for him to respond, I jumped up and was instantly airborne outside.

'Okay but don't shut me out while you're out there. I love you darling,' he replied.

I quickly flew to the edge of the tree line feeling immediately comforted by the sensation of openness. The wind had surprisingly turned into an ally and companion to me. Sometimes almost even taking on a personality of its own with a different mood each time I flew. I made my way deep into the trees before dropping down to the ground when I knew I was out of site from the house. Pulling the crisp air into my body with closed eyes, I drew upon the energy in my core to strengthen me as I prepared to run. Raven began to caw overhead, letting me know that he was there. Without responding to him, I broke out into a fast paced run. Jumping over rocks and roots, ducking under low branches with no idea of the direction I was headed in. All I knew and felt was the need to exert myself to release the pent-up tension and run. It felt good to push my body. To continue in this merciless fast pace until suddenly, the familiar guard station by the front gate came into view. I stopped where I was and ducked down behind some trees. I watched them pace around a bit, smoking cigarettes and laughing at something I could not hear.

While I stood there silently spying on them, I felt Jonas' energy approaching me from behind. I closed my eyes and smiled at the sense of peace he brought me. *'Hello darling. Feeling better?'* he asked.

I took in a deep breath and smiled as I turned to him.

'What are you doing?' he asked.

'Just watching is all. I was wondering if they remembered Peter. Maybe they know where he had been sent,' I responded.

'Darling, you have to let him go. He is gone. Naomi would know if he was still alive.'

'I can't bring myself to believe it Jonas. I know that Philip and the kids are gone. I saw them with my own eyes. I know my mother is gone, I saw her too. But, I can't seem to let go of Peter. Much like you can't let go of

Jack.' I thought this as I pushed the gold feather up against my skin beneath my shirt. *'I can't explain it.'*

'But what about what Naomi said?' he asked.

"I don't trust that bitch," I said loudly.

We both stopped talking with a gasp, turning to see if the guards had heard me. The soldier that had been pacing outside of the guard stand stopped and turned to look in our direction, squinting his eyes and dipping his head down to look through the tree branches. Jonas and I quickly dropped to the ground and continued to watch him over some tree roots. The guard turned and said something to his partner in the guard stand before starting to walk toward us.

'Uh oh,' I silently said to Jonas. *'What should we do? Talk to him? Fly up?'*

Jonas and I just lay there in the dirt watching as the guard got closer and closer with his very large gun. His partner stood outside of the shack watching him from a distance, weapon at the ready.

Suddenly, the guards heavy boot loudly snapped a twig not far from where we hid. Without a word, Jonas and I looked at each other and instantly flashed up over the treetops. The guards direction and speed with which he walked through the woods indicated to us that he had not seen us. He continued to make his way to the spot where we had been hiding as we silently hovered above him for a moment or two, watching him intently. Suddenly, Raven flew up beside us and cawed in a way that sounded like laughter.

It was then that the guard yelled to his partner in the distance and said, "Just a stupid crow."

I turned and smiled at Jonas before we both flashed back to the house. Once we had reached the seclusion of the house, we began to laugh uncontrollably. Raven landed beside us flapping his wings with his puffed chest feathers while moving his head back and forth, clearly enjoying himself at our expense.

I looked at Raven and smiled. "The guard thought it was you. He told his partner it was a stupid crow flying out of the woods." I began to laugh again as Raven stopped celebrating, tucked in his wings and stuck out his chest in a very masculine way, *I am no ordinary crow. I am three times larger with an IQ score that would shatter any confidence they might have about themselves.'*

"You are gorgeous, masculine and brilliant my friend. You put them all to shame," I said to Raven, bending down to kiss his head. Jonas just laughed at me. I then realized that just like that, the stress of my day had faded into oblivion.

24

The next few days were much easier on me emotionally. We trained hard during the day and at night we ate feasts and drank copious amounts of wine. We would pretend for a little while that we were living normal lives. Until one evening, there was a knock on the door as I was setting the table for dinner. Marcus stood silently in the kitchen while Marc put down the romance novel he had been reading. Jonas was still in the shower and Naomi was somewhere else in the house. Jeff slowly opened the door while I remained hidden in the dinning room within earshot.

"Good evening Sir, apologies for interrupting. I have been asked to deliver the mission paperwork for you and your team, and to also inform you that your transportation departs at 0400 hours." His voice sounded like the guard from the front gate.

"Thank you," Jeff responded formally before shutting the door hard.

I turned to look out the window and saw the guard pause when he reached the steps and turned towards the window slowly until he made eye contact with me through the glass. After a moment, he bowed his head slightly before turning to resume his descent down the steps. It wasn't until after he had driven away that I realized that he looked familiar. But not familiar from the guard gate, I knew his face from even before then.

I walked into the kitchen where everyone else had gathered. Jonas came running down the steps with his clothes stuck to his body from dressing before drying after the shower. He grabbed me by the shoulder and turned me to face him. He pushed my hair behind my ear, "What happened? Who was that?" he asked.

"Our mission paperwork just arrived," I answered him stoically.

We all turned to Jeff as he opened the envelope and removed a single piece of paper. He read it quickly before putting it down on the kitchen island. The rest of us leaned over to get a closer look. The document said:

> *Due to the Top Secret Nature of your particular*
> *circumstances, information will be provided as*
> *necessary and with little antecedence.*
> *This is for your protection.*
> *Transportation from the Homestead will retrieve you at*
> *0400 to bring you to the departure rendezvous by 0500.*
> *Get some rest and pack smartly.*

We all stood frozen in place and in silence for a few moments processing everything until Marcus finally broke the lull, "Well, dinner is getting cold and it looks like we have an early start to our day tomorrow. And I am going to drink heavily tonight. So...let's eat," he said with a smile.

"I'll grab a few more bottles," I said making my way to the wine fridge. Jonas laughed quietly knowing that we were going to be drinking with Marcus all night.

By the end of dinner, Naomi was the only sober person at the table. Even Jeff and Marc partook in the libations. Granted, they didn't drink as much as Jonas, Marcus and myself but we weren't holding that against them.

After drinking several bottles of wine and cleaning the house out of any beer, Naomi wound up having to take charge of the clean up so that the rest of us could attempt to pack our bags and get ready for our early departure. After taking a scalding hot shower, I messily threw every piece of clothing I could find into a duffel bag before drunkenly climbing into bed. Jonas was not far behind snuggling his cold body up against mine.

"Oh my God you feel like summer," he said as he snuggled in.

"Well, you're like Antarctica cold so I guess we're a good balance," I replied giggling with a small burp.

Literally 2 seconds later he was snoring beside me. I lay awake staring at the ceiling holding my gold feather while my thoughts raced a mile a minute. A tapping on the window interrupted my internal ramblings. Very ungracefully and loudly, I stumbled out of bed, falling to the floor as I tried to make my way to the window. Jonas' snoring paused briefly before resuming its rhythmic pattern not a moment later. I crawled to the sill so I could pull myself up to see Raven watching me with judging eyes.

I opened the window and whispered in a drunken slur, "Hey Raven. What are you up to? We're going on a mission tomorrow."

'Yes, I'm aware of your departure. Are you drunk?' he asked, definitely judging me now with his raspy voice.

"Here let me come out," I said while throwing one leg over the threshold.

'No! You will do no such thing. You will remain firmly grounded while you are in this condition,' he ordered as he firmly pecked at my leg.

"Ouch!" I shouted in a whisper.

After giving him a defiant look, I lifted into the sky and continued to ascend, reveling in the freeing feeling it gave me. I closed my eyes and listened to the wind whispering around me like an invisible confidant. 'I wonder what the wind will be like where I'm going.' I thought. "Are you the same everywhere?" I asked it out loud as if it could answer me.

'Lily! You are rising too far up. The air becomes thin quickly. You will lose consciousness!' Raven scolded as he followed me up.

Ignoring him I continued to rise. Nervously, he began to squawk loudly intentionally trying to bring attention to us. I could feel the air becoming colder and the oxygen level diminishing, but I continued to push on. It just felt so good to let go. I closed my eyes, attempting to block out the obnoxious sounds Raven was making and put my arms out so that I could feel this sensation in every corner of my body.

After a few moments I felt my body held firmly up against someone's body. I opened my eyes and saw Jonas smiling at me.

"Where are you going darling?" he asked.

I brushed his cheek with the back of my fingers in a tender way and said, "Hey there."

"I don't want you to go any higher than this okay?" He looked at me earnestly.

"It feels so good to let go though."

"But you might be letting go of me also and I can't live without you," he explained tenderly.

"I know. I'm sorry. I'll be more careful next time," I said after a pause.

We began flying together hand in hand at a much lower altitude with Raven beside us. It felt freeing and carefree to be surrounded by my loves, to feel cared for and protected. I smiled thinking about how lucky I was as I reached for my gold feather that dangled from my neck. It was bittersweet to see the lake in the distance as I sadly bid it farewell for now, silently preparing myself for what was to come.

25

We woke up with Naomi standing over us screaming for us to get up. We had 20 minutes before the transport would arrive. Jonas was sleeping in his usual position which was an arm draped over my body while his leg straddled both of my legs wearing absolutely nothing while I wore my pajamas. It was a new habit of his, claiming I made him too hot during the night. There were no sheets or blankets over us so Naomi got the full view of the situation in our bed.

She stormed out of the bedroom talking to herself, "In all my life. Everybody is still drunk and here we go on our first mission..." I missed the rest of what she said while she mumbled her way down the stairs. I honestly didn't care what she had to say.

"Come on," I said while shaking Jonas. "We have to take a shower. We smell like a brewery." I rolled him off of me and then unintentionally off of the bed all-together making him land with a loud thump. Marc came running in and said, "All okay?"

"Yup... Just getting ready," I slurred only to then be consumed by the need to vomit. I jumped over Jonas' naked body and ran to the bathroom barely making it to the toilet. Jonas crawled into the bathroom behind me and then sat bedside the toilet on the floor watching me hurl while rubbing my back.

"Okay. Get the poison out darling. You'll feel better soon. We'll shower and then get some breakfast." he said.

The mere thought of food made me vomit some more. When it finally seemed to be all over, Jonas lifted me and carried me into the shower, pajamas and all. The water was freezing. Just the way Jonas loved it of course. He peeled my wet clothes off of me and shampooed my hair as I brushed my teeth. *'I have to remember to pack this toothbrush,'* I said to him more of as a reminder to myself. To which he grunted in response.

After showering and dressing, we made our way down to the kitchen carrying our duffel bags while I held my toothbrush in my hand. "Put that in the bag darling," Jonas motioned to my hand. I nodded and thoughtlessly did what he told me to do.

Marcus also looked terrible. I'm sure he was still mostly drunk. Marc and Jeff had it much more together than any of us did as they sat at the kitchen island drinking coffee and eating dry toast. I joined them at the island and stole one of Jeff's toasts. He gave me the stink eye while I blew him a kiss as I slowly pulled out a pair of sunglasses I had found in one of the kitchen junk drawers and slipped them on.

The knock came at 0400 exactly. "Punctual," I slurred as I crunched on the dry toast.

The guard from last night stood at the door and looked at all of us in our several stages of disrepair. I pushed my glasses up and looked at him. I could tell he was having a hard time taking his eyes off of me. It began to feel slightly awkward. Especially since I stared back in an almost challenging way. Jonas noticed what was happening and so he made his way to stand directly in front of me to block the guards view of me.

"Is there a problem?" he asked the guard.

"No sir I apologize," the guard replied as he bent down to pick up the duffle bags. We all followed him to the SUV, I climbed in first so that I could make my way to the far back with Jonas following to sit beside me. Marcus squeezed on the other side of him. Jeff and Marc sat in front of us while Naomi sat in the front passenger seat.

The soldier drove us in the dark through the tunnel of trees. After opening my window, I lay my head in the opening, enjoying the cold wind that blew on my face, desperately trying to avoid carsickness. I reached out to find Raven to bid him goodbye to only be interrupted by Jeff as he reached over the back of his seat so that he could pull me up to sit to then press the button to close my window.

"We are pulling into the Guard Stand. I don't want any of you to be seen yet. Its best if the three of you remain unidentifiable," Jeff explained.

I turned to look at Jonas and Marcus, feeling instantaneously woozy just from turning my head. Jonas looked at me with concern lines on his forehead.

"That guy has seen us," Marcus said while pointing to the guard driving us.

"He has special security clearance and he knows the repercussions of breaking the code," Jeff answered while looking at the guard in the rearview mirror.

The guard gave a quick nod as he made eye contact with Jeff. Once we arrived at the Guard stand, the driver opened his window and told the on duty officer that seven were departing.

The on duty guard said with a salute, "Safe travels to all Sir."

The gate unceremoniously opened and off we went into the dark Iowa countryside. As we continued down the main road in the opposite direction from the city we had visited, I had to open the window again. I was starting to feel so sick the heat was rising in the car, to the point that Naomi herself turned the A/C on full blast.

"I'm sorry." Was all I could say as I stuck my head out of the window.

It had started to drizzle softly and the cool water droplets felt so good on my face. I breathed in a sigh of relief as I heard Raven caw loudly in the distance.

'I'll see you soon my friend,' I said to him hoping he could hear me.

WE ARRIVED at an airport just as the edge of the sky had begun to lighten. The entrance was heavily guarded, with at least five soldiers pacing around the gate and guardhouse, fully armed of course. Barbed wire lined the chain linked fences clearly marked with warning signs about electricity posted every few feet, running along the edge of the property. We arrived in an unmarked hanger and as the SUV pulled into the building the doors shut behind us and locked loudly. Perhaps my hangover made the sound much louder in my head than it actually really was, I thought doubting my hearing.

Marcus said, obviously having heard my thoughts, "Nope, that was loud for real." I turned to him and smiled as he rubbed my leg.

"You Okay?" Jonas asked. "You look a bit green."

"I feel a bit green. I hope they serve breakfast on this thing," I said gesturing to the large military plane located in the hanger with us.

"They'll have chips and soda on there," Naomi answered as she closed the visor in front of her, using its mirror to reapply her red lipstick.

Our driver jumped out of the car and walked towards two men standing at the base of the steps that led up to the plane. When he reached them they all saluted before he said, "I have the cargo. Are you ready for them to board?"

Alcohol must have heightened my hearing because they spoke softly, feet away from where we were and I was able to clearly hear them.

"Did he just call us cargo?" I asked sluggishly to no one in particular.

Marc laughed out loud at that, Jeff gave him a smile and shook his head at him.

"We are all military. Just tools in an arsenal...weapons. It makes this more difficult if they acknowledge our humanity," Jeff explained as I looked at him in shock.

"Just The Homestead guards treat us that way. They have been given some information about us. They saw us change from an early age. They know we are modified. Other members of the military will not treat us differently, they don't know who we are and all they know is that we are vital members of the team. They know not to ask questions. Their job is to follow orders," Marc explained.

Jonas was in shock and didn't know how to respond.

I began to sit up straighter and whispered with a worried grunt as I opened my window, "Oh mother fucker!" Turning my head just in the knick of time, I quickly throw half my body out the car window before the vomit exploded out of me and splashed all over the concrete hangar floor.

I heard Marcus ask Jonas behind me, "Can I video this?"

Jonas said firmly, "NO!" as he rubbed my back, "It's okay darling. You're safe, let it all out."

I pulled my head back into the vehicle and said as I pushed my sunglasses back on my face, "Much better thank you."

Jeff handed me a cold bottle of water just as I began to think how completely embarrassing this situation was. It was certainly a nice way to start my first mission, I thought sarcastically. Good impressions all around, lovely.

I sat back and took a sip of the water to clear some of the vomit out of my mouth until suddenly and in unison, everyone in the car, including Naomi, broke into a loud guffaw. I slid down in my seat while pushing my sunglasses even further up my nose as Jonas pulled me to him so I could lean on his chest.

"We love you Lily. This was the perfect ice breaker," Marc said while he rubbed my knee and smiled.

And with that, I smiled and began to laugh as well. "Assholes," I slurred.

WE CLIMBED into the small plane with its flanking double seat rows. I chose a seat close to the front of the plane before plopping myself down roughly. Jonas sat across the isle from me. Marcus took the seats behind me, Jeff and Marc sat behind Jonas. The sun was beginning to rise outside which caused an intense glare that reached through the now open hanger doors all of the way to my window. I was thankful that I had kept the sunglasses on the entire time. It was obvious that despite my recently discovered abilities, the quick metabolism of alcohol and hangover reduction were not one of my abilities.

Before closing the window shutter beside me, I noticed a figure standing outside of the plane watching me. It took me a moment to register that it was the guard that had been charged with getting us to this destination. I stared back at him so that he knew I had seen him. He bowed his head at me slightly before turning around and walking back to the SUV. As he sped away I turned to Marcus and said, "What the hell was that about? Did you see that guard staring at me?"

Jonas jumped across the isle and was practically sitting on top of me to be able to look out the window, "Did he just leave?" he asked.

"Yeah he just drove off. He was just standing there watching me. He looks really familiar to me," I said with a shiver.

Jonas turned to the rest of the group and asked, "Who is he?"

"Well, he grew up with us of course, like all other personnel living in the compound. He remembers you. You and Jonas coming back is a big deal. It signifies the culmination of all of the work everyone has been involved in. I'm certain he wants to know what your abilities are and the level of your strength. Why didn't you read his mind?" Jeff asked me.

I hesitated a bit and then finally said, "Well...I think I may still be a little bit drunk and so I didn't think about doing that."

"You need to reach out your mind at all times and in all ways Lily. You must get used to doing that," Naomi said authoritatively.

I rolled my eyes behind my sunglasses as I mocked her voice softly while speaking gibberish. Jonas looked at me, smiled and then kissed the top of my head before returning to his seats.

There were few pleasantries from the flight crew before we took off. Surprisingly there was a flight attendant. She came around about an hour after our departure and handed us a bottle of water along with a bag of chips each.

"Well, this is going to be a long flight," Marcus said as he opened his snack. "How long is this flight anyway? Are we allowed to know where we are going yet?" he asked.

"Only the pilots know at this point," Naomi responded.

I looked at Jonas, giving him a fake toothy smile and then leaned my head back while pushing my seat back to reclining, which is a joke because it's essentially a 2-inch difference from upright. I closed my eyes fearing that my hangover would worsen and that airsickness would kick in. I had already scoped out where the bathrooms were just in case. Gladly however, the opposite happened. I fell asleep.

I WOKE myself up about five hours later with the sound of my own loud snoring as drool ran down my face. I looked around the plane, nervous that everyone had just witnessed me at my most unsexy, but was relieved to discover that it seemed everyone else had been in the same disposition, with the one exception of Naomi who remained awake, typing feverishly on her laptop. I got up and walked past her to the bathroom. After brushing my teeth and relieving myself, I walked back towards my seat but decided to sit down across from her. She did not acknowledge me at all, but kept on typing. I closed my eyes and reached out to her mind, hoping to find some information or at the very least get her attention. I have so many questions that I need answered. Where are we going? What is the plan for us? And most importantly, where had Peter been laid to rest? I had to know where I could visit his grave. I had to try to feel his energy, if there was anything of it remaining.

The moment I reached her mind, I could feel myself hitting a barrier. It was so unexpected it made me gasp. Naomi stopped typing and turned to me with venomous eyes and said, "Don't even try Lily. I have no tolerance for privacy invasion, aside from the fact that I have no answers for you."

I straightened my back in my seat and began to explain. "I apologize. I'm just hurting Naomi. I've had a lot happen to me in the past few years... I just have so many unanswered questions. I find it hard sometimes to keep myself from sinking into the darkness with this entire world of unknown I seem to have found myself in. I know we have all been through a lot. I know you've been through a lot as well..." I could feel her anger and contempt as she glared at me. Realizing that she was not going to give me an inch, I nodded in understanding as I stood and returned to my seat.

After sitting down, I turned and looked at Jonas as he sat awkwardly in his seat watching me while giving me a small smile. *'I'm sorry. I know you're sad. I know that I'm not enough for you. Just know that I love you more than my life and I know how you feel. We will find answers. I don't know how but we won't give up. Okay?'*

I stood and walked to the seat beside him pushing his leg down to the floor so I could sit down. I reached for his hand and squeezed it tightly. Leaning my head back in the seat I closed my eyes and responded. *'I love you so much Jonas. You are my anchor and my only reason to continue. I'm sorry if it seems that I don't appreciate you. Please believe me when I say that you are enough for me, you're my touchstone. You are all that I have and I couldn't be happier about it. I love you. You are everything to me. Please trust that.'*

He leaned his head on mine and responded, *'We'll get through this together. And when we are done with this mission we will move to a Caribbean Island somewhere and live in peace.'*

We looked at each other for a while and smiled. He hurts just as much as I do. We would find answers as we journeyed together I thought to myself just before we both fell asleep beside each other.

WE TRAVELLED for 9 hours before reaching our destination. My body hurt from trying to sleep in those ridiculously small seats. Jonas had assumed his regular sleeping position, which is to have as many body parts on me as possible. I had really grown to love the feeling of safety and reassurance that I got from him sleeping like that. It had gotten to a point where I actually needed it to sleep. But having him sleep like that in my hung-over condition in the small airplane seats did not make for a comfortable trip for me. The only reason why I was able to sleep was because it was more of a loss of consciousness as opposed to actual slumber. There was still a copious amount of alcohol flowing through my veins for a majority of the flight.

We landed without a word from the crew. The flight attendant collected our empty bag of chips and gave us a second bottle of water during the flight, but then that was the last time we saw her until the plane was on the tarmac. Marcus opened his shade to investigate where we were but we arrived during the night so there was little visibility past the borders of the runway. Marcus turned to Jeff and Marc, mentally asking them where we were, but they both just shrugged in response.

"Where are we Naomi?" Marcus asked irritably.

Naomi stopped typing and looked up at Marcus before saying, "Tunisia."

SOMEWHERE IN TUNISIA

26

'*T*hat bitch knew the entire time where we were going?' I thought through gritted teeth to all of the boys. I took in a deep breath and shook my head trying my best to stay calm and in control. Jonas just looked at me and shook his head in disgust.

"You're not a good team player Naomi," I said with disgust.

She looked at me and said, "I am meant to lead all of you, not be part of you."

I caught Jeff and Marc looking at one another quickly and shaking their heads subtly with disapproval.

I try really hard to open up and be friendly to her, try to be inclusive but all I want to do is punch her in her stupid Barbie doll fucking face.

Jonas snickered, '*She's just doing her job darling.*'

Marcus pulled his duffel bag out of the overhead storage compartment and walked toward the front of the plane waiting for the door to open. The flight attendant, who had essentially hidden from us in the galley during the entire flight, saw Marcus walk toward her. In a panic she abruptly rushed to the cockpit door, knocked her secret knock before she was pulled in presumably by one of the pilots. Who then slammed the door behind her with a loud click of the lock.

Marcus turned to all of us with a confused look lifting his hands as if to say, what the hell was that about. Jonas and I shook our heads in unison as a response.

"I need to say something before we disembark please. It is imperative that you follow these orders. You are absolutely under no circumstance allowed to outwardly demonstrate your abilities. We will be surrounded by the unmodified and they cannot know what you are capable of. Please. I know you all dislike me. Don't forget I can hear you. Just please do what you are told right now. It will all make sense as we move forward. This location is just a stopover for acclimation purposes. We are here for approximately 48 hours and that is all," Naomi explained in an almost imploring tone.

'This feels intense and urgent,' I said to Jonas privately.

'Yeah, this is serious. I can't get a handle on what the hell it is we are doing here. She has a tight seal on her barrier. She worked at that ability that's for sure. I've been trying to break into it the entire flight. Why Tunisia?' Jonas responded to me.

Naomi then nodded, mainly to herself, walked to the cockpit door and knocked. "We are ready to disembark please," she said speaking to the pilots through the door. Within a few moments we could hear gears and latches turning before the door opened abruptly from the outside. Standing at the top of the moveable steps stood a very large man dressed in military garb waiting for us to come through the door. As we each walked past him he kept his gaze down so that all he saw were our feet walking past him.

As soon as I walked off of the airplane the dry heat impressively struck me. It felt positively delicious on my skin and in my lungs. Once I was off of the steps and onto the ground I secretly brought the breeze to me and made it swirl around my body. I closed my eyes and turned my face to the sky as I subtly lifted my arms. *'Hello my friend,'* I thought as I pulled my invisible colleague over to me and had it wrap itself around my body in a tight hug. I wanted to allow myself to soar, to feel it lift and hold me high above the earth. Suddenly, Jonas reached for my hand and pulled me back to reality, gently reminding me of our restrictions while we were here.

I gasped at the sudden interruption. "Sorry," I said in a barely audible whisper to my teammates. Naomi glared at me with fury with fury burning in her eyes. I felt sorry for having done, I honestly didn't mean to have that response to the wind, it just happened.

"Can you just get in the vehicle please?" she demanded of me with an annoyed tone.

As per our usual travel accommodations, there was a large black SUV awaiting our arrival. The government must buy these in bulk at cost, I thought jokingly. Jonas and I took our usual seats in the far back with Marcus beside Jonas. Jeff and Marc in front of us, while Naomi rode in the front passenger seat. The same large soldier who met us at the top of the steps of the plane drove us off the tarmac. His hands were gigantic as they tightly grasped the steering wheel making it look like the wheel of a toy car in his hands. His head was shaved down which was a good thing since it was about a centimeter away from touching the roof of the car.

Silently, we made our way out of the airport, through a highly guarded gate and then onto a dusty, sandy road. There was no stopping to check for documents at the gate or confirming against a lists for permission, we just sped right through the guards. The sandy earth seemed to wash up against the side of the car as we sped through the desiccated terrain. As I had done in the past, I opened my window once we had passed the guard station. I needed to become acquainted with air in this part of the world, loving the grit it left on my skin from the flying sand.

Every road we took on our journey was unpaved and for some reason that made my anxiety level escalate despite my attempts to tamper it down. With my sunglasses and the heat level in the vehicle rising, everyone began to feel uncomfortable as sweat rolled down their skin. Everyone in the vehicle, with the exception of the driver knew that heat we were feeling was not just coming from my open window. Without conferring with me first, the driver shut my window just as he turned on the air conditioner. I couldn't help but feel sorry for him because little did he know that we were all doomed to an uncomfortable and sweaty trip despite the cool blast coming from the vents.

'I'm sorry everybody. I'm trying to turn down the heat but I'm so anxious,' I explained silently to everyone.

'It's okay darling. We're all a little anxious. Let me see if I can help a bit here,' Jonas responded. With that, a cool breeze began to radiate from his body, helping drive the temperature in the car down. I could see muscles begin to relax as sighs of relief echoed in the car. Naomi turned to look at Jonas with the intention to reprimand, but since there was no visible evidence that the two of us had anything to do with the temperature variances in the car, she grimaced before turning back around to face the road. Annoyed by her disdain, I flicked her the bird to the back of her head. All of my boys smiled coyly at my rebelliousness.

WE DROVE through the night at an unrelenting fast pace, through the strong sand carrying winds, without ever seeing any structures or evidence of humanity at all. As the sun began to rise in the horizon, its light reflected on the sand and dunes that strung together like beads in a necklace for as far as the eye could see. I watched the peaks and valleys go by while everyone by myself and the drive slept. His stamina was amazing. We did not pull over once for anything, not that there was anything to stop for. My stomach rumbled from hunger, my tongue felt rough from thirst and I had to pee like a race-horse but was too nervous to ask him to pull over. He caught me a few times watching him in the rearview mirror, never speaking a word. He just made sure to avert his eyes when he noticed mine staring at him through my dark sunglasses.

Out of boredom and the need to take my mind off of my bodily discomforts, I reached into his mind and was able to learn quite a bit about his personal life. His name was Manny and he was 32 years old. He had been married for 12 years to Norma and they own a home in

Idaho. They have a son, David and a daughter, Elena. He loves his life as a soldier and couldn't imagine doing anything else with his life. He loves his family but prefers his life here with his military brothers. He married Norma just a few short years after entering the military at the age of 18, but despite his many years of wedded bliss, he had no idea about how to be a family man. His trips home were often awkward and he would often find himself counting the days before he could return to his real life. Despite all of this, I could feel that he was a kind man.

By the time we arrived at our destination, the sun was well above our heads and Jonas had to increase his output of cold to keep everyone comfortable in the car. We pulled up to a small military out posting, composed entirely of beige tents that easily blended into the sandy surroundings. As soon as the vehicle came to a stop, four soldiers came out of their tent, all dressed in beige military camouflage gear just like our driver.

After coming to a full stop, Manny jumped out of the car first. Just as his door slammed shut, Naomi turned to us and said, "Wait in the car until I come for you please."

I looked at her and said, "If you don't get me out of this car immediately I am going to pee in this seat."

"Dido," Jonas agreed.

The rest of the boys all nodded in agreement. Naomi rolled her eyes and let out an exasperated breath before opening her door and jumping out, landing roughly on the sandy ground with her black military boots and her petite frame. It surprised me that she could even get into this SUV without a step-stool. She must be missing her high heels, that's for sure, I thought.

Marcus watched her intently communicating with the soldiers since they were on his side of the car. Just as soon as Naomi had finished speaking, she motioned to Manny to let us out of the car.

'What did they say to each other?' Jonas asked Marcus.

'I couldn't hear anything because she did all of the talking. They just nodded their responses. I must admit her barrier is strong and she's no dummy. She knows we're listening,' he explained.

One of the other soldiers opened the door and stepped aside while averting his eyes to the ground. I turned to Jonas and Marcus and mouthed "What the fuck?"

In an almost defensive way I reached for his mind and quickly discovered that his name was Drake. At 24 years old, he was the rookie in the group. When he's not out in the desert with his military brothers, he lives in California, where surfing is his passion along with his girlfriend, who desperately awaits his return. His desire to be back in the ocean was palpable, but because he had some petty crime on his record, he was committed to his time in the army. Other than that, he was innocent and the men treated him as if he were their jokester little brother.

I shared all of the information I garnered as I filtered through his mind while each of my boys smiled subtly as they passed him through the open door. I was the last to get out of the car and just before my foot touched the sand I made sure my sunglasses were firmly up on my face. Glancing up at Drake as I passed him, he did not waver his downcast gaze, strictly following the orders he had received from Naomi.

A third soldier approached us, again not looking at us but at our feet as he spoke. "Follow me," he ordered.

'This guy is a giant,' I thought to the team, who all silently nodded their heads in agreement.

I reached into his mind and discovered that his name was Gunther. But his military brothers call him Grunter because when he speaks it sounds as if he has a mouth full of marbles. He is single, rarely takes his available leave and has actually given his time off away to other soldiers in need. He has a small family home in Mississippi but no actual living relatives. He is the oldest in the group, at 59 years old. He is a simple and good man, who avoids complications at all costs.

'You are getting very good at this darling,' Jonas said as he held my hand.

'Yes, you are and I'm really enjoying these little tidbits we are learning,' Marcus said.

We followed Gunther into a tent that contained a metal table in the center with several bottles of water and granola bars. I was parched but couldn't even think about drinking anything until I emptied my bladder.

Almost as if on cue, in strode Naomi. "The bathroom is straight through there," she said as she pointed out of the tent in the opposite direction we had just walked in.

In a brisk pace, I crossed the tent and walked back outside, instantly glad that I had left my sunglasses as the bright sun burned overhead. The outhouse was simple, made up of wooden panels that left a large gap between the bottom of the wood and the sandy ground along with another gap between the paneling and the beige variegated plastic roof. I swung one of the hinged panels open discovering a metal drum that had been cut open on both ends was buried half way up, so that all bodily evacuations would fall straight down the deeply dug sandy hole at the bottom of the drum. The top of the drum actually had a toilet seat, which I found to be a relief and I was even more relieved to find that there was actual toilet paper. But despite all of this, I couldn't help but feel absolutely horrified when the stench hit my nostrils and a black cloud of flies and mosquitos lifted into flight from the pile of human waste that sat at the bottom of the drum. The unintentional breeze I had created by opening the door disturbed them from their meals, sending most of them swarming around my face while others flew higher to land on the beige ceiling, turning it black with their shiny bodies. All I could think about was how I had to contain my screaming if they flew onto my naked delicate parts as I peed. After a few seconds of debate while I did the pee-pee dance, I called on the wind to cause a bit of a breeze in this disgusting place to help address the odor and the mosquitos. I pushed the gigantic flying beasts out of the outhouse, congratulating myself at my own brilliance before sitting to pee for what felt like 5 minutes straight, actually feeling my bladder deflating in my body. The relief of the release felt euphoric.

I strode back into the tent, gave Jonas a wink and thought, *'Good luck darling.'* He looked at me and furrowed the space between his eyes before walking out to the outhouse. I could feel his disgust as he entered the odiferous space. With a quiet chuckle I lifted a bottle of water to my mouth, guzzling the entire thing in one go. I hadn't realized how thirsty I had been until after I had emptied a third bottle.

As I reached for a granola bar I softly said to myself, "I would kill for an apple." Gunther, who had been standing not far from me, quickly exited the tent and when he returned he handed me a large green apple. Surprised by this act of kindness, I took the apple from his hand and smiled at him. He looked at me slightly from the corners of his eyes, attempting to keep his gaze turned to the ground.

"Thank you," I whispered. After giving me a slight bow of his head, he turned and strode out of our tent.

27

The next 30 hours went by very quickly. We were asked to remain in our tent at all times with the exception of outhouse breaks. We were to remain out of the soldier's tents and they were to not come into ours, which suited them well since they all seemed to avoid us at all costs. Curious, I reached into Drakes' mind and discovered that they really were not told anything about who we were. Their orders were simply to keep us safe and that our presence here was top secret. But most importantly they were ordered to avoid contact as much as possible. They were told that we needed to maintain our anonymity, which is why they were not permitted to look at us. The no contact order included not only physical but verbal contact as well which was a bit disconcerting for me in the initial hours but then I decided to respect that they were simply following orders and that their role was brief in our route to our ultimate destination. Wherever that might be.

Breaking the rules ever so slightly, the five of us went for short walks around the tents in the bright hot sun to stretch our legs and avoid boredom. I welcomed the heat as it kissed my sweat-streaked skin, pulling the wind around my body. It was in this random sandy land that in our semi-captivity that I began to refer to the wind as my brother. My brother wind, with its unintelligible whispering that I sometimes heard, also occurred out in the desert, making me yearn for solitude and privacy so that I could work on developing this ability that seemed to want to shine through.

The wind in the desert had an element of harshness and aggressiveness to it, as it moved unobstructed over the land without the burden of trees or mountains to dampen its strength. But despite this perceptible hostility, I still called to it. Pulling its invisible arms around me to lift me ever so slightly before returning me to the ground. Naomi of course had forbidden that I rise up into the sky out of fear that someone would see.

Our time in the tent was comfortable thanks to Jonas, who would cool things down to 65 degrees, unleashing an unanimous sigh of relief from everyone, knowing that they would rest a bit more comfortably. Gunther had been assigned to bring us all of our meals. He was very pleasantly surprised to feel the cool air the first time he came into our tent. Nonchalantly, he searched for the cooling system every time he walked into the tent, but of course was unable to locate it. After his initial visit it seemed he would find reasons to come into the tent, always being very careful to keep his eyes fixed on the ground and without speaking to any of us.

"Are we able to shower Gunther?" I asked him during one of his visits. He was startled a bit at my speaking to him directly but then I heard him think, *'How does she know my name?'*

'Jesus Lil!' Marc reprimanded me.

'I'm sorry. Honest mistake you guys. I apologize,' I responded to all of the boys.

Gunther just subtlety shook his head before walking very quickly out of the tent.

"Well, I'm glad you asked because I could really use one. I'm beginning to smell," Jonas said.

"What do you mean beginning to smell?" I said jokingly.

"Yeah you stink man," Marcus responded as well.

I know that Jonas could technically use his ability to create a lovely spa oasis in our tent so we could all freshen up, but I was certain that Naomi would shit her pants if she found out. Needless to say, we were all doomed to fester in our stenches for the unforeseeable future.

The guards slept in shifts, ensuring that there was always someone watching over the campsite and us. What were they afraid would happen? Perhaps that we would run away or that some unknown enemy would sneak into the camp and kidnap us? Whatever the reason was, I felt sorry for the unlucky fellow who drew the short straw and had to babysit us from outside of our tent.

"I mean really, what do they think we're going to do?" I asked at some point.

"We are a valuable secret that must be guarded at all times," Marcus said in jest.

"I realize you think you're joking but that is precisely the case Marcus. All of us at The Agency have gone through immeasurable lengths to ensure that you and your abilities remained undiscovered." Naomi paused for a breath, "All of your missions will be undocumented so that the secrecy can be maintained. Your identities outside of the agency have been completely expunged to keep you from being linked to the missions and ultimately The Agency. The soldiers that guard you now have top-secret clearance. Having said that, they have no knowledge of why you are to be under guard at all times or even who you are for that matter. You are never to discuss who you are and what your abilities are with anyone outside of The Agency," Naomi ordered. "Now try to get some sleep, we are leaving at 0400 for our final destination."

Nobody spoke another word as a somber feeling swept through the tent. Jonas and I slept on an air mattress on the sandy floor. Well, Jonas slept while I stared at the tents roof, unable to slow my mind down enough to allow me to sleep. My mind raced with questions and fears about what Naomi had said. I hated hearing that I was dead to everyone outside of The Agency. My life had become so unusual with so many changes and discoveries that I had neglected to process what it all really meant for when we get out. If we ever did get out. Where would I live once this was all done? Naomi had said one mission and then we could go on our merry way until they called us back. Well, where would I live? Could I go back to working as a nurse somewhere? Jonas and I hadn't even talked about any of this. Obviously I would go wherever he was going, that went without saying. But where would he want to go? Would the others come with us? I had become so attached to Marc and Jeff, not to mention Marcus. Would they come with us? I didn't want to be away from them.

'Stop it darling. You're keeping all of us awake. We will all have to sit down and discuss all of this when this fucking mission is over and done with,' Jonas said as he draped his body across me in his usual sleeping position, squeezing me as he did so.

'We love you too Lily,' Marc and Jeff said simultaneously.

'Get some sleep Lil. We'll figure all of this out, don't worry. I don't want to be apart from any of you either,' Marcus explained.

'Sorry boys, I love you. Sleep tight,' I said.

I snuggled into Jonas and closed my eyes, but it was useless. My mind was like a runaway train, percolating with angst about our future. Taking deep breaths, I tried to focus on the present to slow my mind and lower my anxiety down a bit but then I realized where I was physically laying down and then all I could think about were scorpions. I started to imagine them crawling under the covers and up my legs making their way up to my face.

'Holy fuck! We are all going to be killed by scorpions while we sleep!' I screamed in my head.

Once my focus shifted to our impending slaughter at the hands of wild scorpions there was no turning back. Jonas must have heard my internal monologue because he tightened his arm around me while draping his leg across me further before getting really close to my ear so that he could shush me softly. I tried to take control of my mind, trying to keep myself from thinking about the scorpions but it was pointless, it was like getting a song stuck in your head. It just kept playing over and over again ad nauseam. I started to imagine one of them walking on my eye while another crawled in my ear, making me itchy all over ensuring my night of insomnia.

That night lasted an eternity as I listened jealously to the boys snoring around me. After several hours Gunther came in and shook Naomi awake. She was startled initially but then sat up and thanked him. As he walked out of our tent he snuck a peak at me lying beneath a naked Jonas as he draped himself across my body. I smiled and gave him a small wave, making him flinch slightly in response before quickly looking back to the ground as he raced out of the tent ashamed of his own weakness.

Naomi woke the boys up in her usual authoritarian and unpleasant way. We all gathered our belongings and stumbled into the waiting black SUV. We sat in our usual seats as we sped to our next destination with Gunther behind the wheel this time, barreling us through the dusty sandy road. Our drive through the empty desert was not long. Ultimately turning off onto a barely defined road that led onto yet another tarmac. With a grunt I looked around and noticed that this particular landing strip was very different from the one we had landed on just a few short hours ago. There were beige structures flanking the tarmac perfectly camouflaged into the surrounding tones, surprisingly hiding the giant monstrosity that awaited us. Instead of the usual passenger plane, we were now met by a behemoth of a cargo military plane, large enough to move a tank or two.

Gunther opened the door for us while keeping his gaze fixed on the ground. Again, I was last to jump out of the SUV and as I walked by he whispered, "Take care miss."

Barely turning to him, I whispered back, "You be careful out here Gunther. And thanks for everything my friend."

The boys had already boarded the plane, climbing up through its open mouth located at the tail end of the aircraft by the time I myself started making my way up the ramp. Once I reached the top I noticed another soldier standing silently to the side of the entrance as he watched each of us boarding the plane. He was unabashedly examining each and every one of us. I looked at him in return almost challenging him as I slid my sunglasses up my nose. I could feel that he was similar to the military folks we had encountered at The Homestead.

"Hello. I'm O'Connell. We need to depart now. Please go on in and buckle up. I'll be riding in the back with you all in case you need anything," he said in a friendly tone.

I made my way to a seat between Jonas and Marcus, while privately saying to the group, '*Wow. Eye contact. And this one can speak.*'

As the hanger doors began to close, I leaned down to search for Gunther, who had remained at the bottom of the ramp watching me with a broad smile. When he noticed my gaze finding him, he brightly waved me goodbye. I smiled and waved back hoping that our paths would cross again, before the doors slammed closed with a loud bang.

THE FLIGHT WAS PHYSICALLY PAINFUL. The seats had zero cushioning and the backs almost forced you to lean forward slightly because they were so erect. The seating configuration had us all facing the center of the plane, which meant that there were no seat back trays, no meals, nothing. The turbulence was almost constant and at one point it became so intense that it lifted me from my seat repeatedly resulting in a hard landing each time. After a few episodes of this, Jonas and Marcus both reached across my lap to help keep me in my seat.

With the merciless repeated back injury, I was again unable to sleep on the plane, elevating my level of exhaustion to an all time high. I began to lose track of when my last good night of sleep was. Could it be 4 or 5 days ago? O'Connell kept his word, he stayed in the back with us for the duration of the flight. His body seemed to know how to land during the most intense turbulence. Jeff and Marc sat beside each other across the aisle from us with arms touching, never breaking contact, surprisingly sleeping through all of it.

I turned to Jonas and said while gesturing towards J&M with my head, "I think they're narcoleptics."

Jonas smiled and Marcus laughed out loud. Naomi, as per her usual just typed away on her computer through all of it as well. "What the hell is she typing? She's constantly typing. She's seriously making me paranoid," I said to them out loud not caring if she heard me.

It was then that we hit an especially angry pocket of turbulence and the plane began to lose altitude. The pilots obviously were trying to take control but were having some difficulty as the caution alarms began sounding loudly in the cockpit. As my back began to scream and the airsickness started to rear its ugly head, my extreme exhaustion and frustration seemed to get the better of me and much against my better judgment, I unbuckled my seat belt before calling upon the air outside of the plane to lift me off of my seat. Quickly floating my way to the center of the plane, I lifted my arms on either side of my body as if I were a bird stretching its wings.

"You have to remain..." O'Connell had started shouting, stopping short as he saw me lift into the air.

The engine roared loudly, the warning lights flashed and the alarms rang loudly around us. Jonas and Marcus just watched me with grins on their faces knowing exactly what I was going to do.

Reaching far outside of the plane with my abilities, I forcefully grabbed the turbulent air and pulled it tightly around my body as I continued floating inside of the plane. Relishing in the power and euphoria I felt, I began to move the air, pulling and pushing it around the plane until I gained control of its metallic body, forcing it to move with the air and not fight it, caressing it into tranquility. The alarms silenced and my muscles relaxed as the plane steadied.

As soon as I felt the pilots regain control of their charge, I released my hold on the wind and gently placed my feet back on the floor before returning to my seat. After buckling myself back in, I closed my eyes as the sensation of Naomi's burning glare beat upon the side of my face. With adrenaline still coursing through my veins, I glared back at her, fearlessly challenging her authority over me. Her anger, contempt and lack of gratitude were palpable beneath my own skin.

Jonas pulled my mind away from her discontent with a squeeze of my hand. And as I turned to give him a smile, I caught O'Connell watching me with a small grin on his face, instantly giving away that he knew exactly who we were.

SOMEWHERE IN AFGHANISTAN

28

The flight continued on for several more hours after my inflight flight. After returning to my seat, I slipped my sunglasses back on my face and I kept them on for the remainder of the trip in the hopes that I could at least get a little catnap. As we approached our destination, O'Connell astutely recognized my level of exhaustion and kindly made me a very large cup of strong coffee to help me be more alert by the time we landed. The others seemed bafflingly relaxed as they snored away. Marc and Jeff had been asleep for pretty much the entire flight, including during my "little moment" where I helped the pilots out a bit. Marcus snored beside me and Jonas drooled on my shoulder while the relentless uninterrupted sounds of tapping on a keyboard echoed in the large space.

I wondered what the hell she could be doing on that thing. Is she surfing porn or perhaps online dating? I thought to myself jokingly. She can't possibly be writing about us for 72 hours straight. What could there possibly be for her to say?

After taking a few sips of coffee, the pilot came on the speakers and told us to prepare to land in the next 5 minutes. With a big yawn I stroked Jonas' face and squeezed Marcus' leg. Jonas sat up with startled as he wiped the drool off his face. "We're landing soon," I explained as Marcus grunted at me.

Marc and Jeff surprisingly woke up when the pilot spoke. I looked at them with confusion while shaking my head. Jeff gave me a small wink before turning his attention to Marc. I held on to my coffee and took small sips of the scalding hot liquid as I braced myself for the landing. We are a strange group, I snickered to myself.

THE PLANE LANDED SMOOTHLY ENOUGH with the cargo door lowering to the ground soon after we came to a stop. The bright sunshine hit me quickly along with the dry smell of desert air. Naomi went down the ramp first followed by the boys. I could feel their excitement and curiosity at lay ahead as I remained in my seat for a few additional minutes, enjoying the stillness of my muscles. Before rising to disembark, I closed my eyes and reached out to all of the hearts beating that I could sense standing at the base of the cargo doors. With the sensation of each individuals particular beats, also came the emotions that they carried within their chest. I could tell that everyone outside was male with the one exception of Naomi. They were all Solos, military and all were heavily armed. Confirming that there was no eminent threat I pushed myself off of my seat while reaching down to grab my duffel bag. With a deep breath and a large gulp of my coffee, I propelled my exhausted body down the ramp and off of the plane.

My boys stood behind Naomi while she greeted a very serious but distinguished looking man wearing a beige camo uniform. He had deep black hair with silver at his temples. He was clean-shaven and had a strong build. And he was obviously the man in charge based on his demeanor and the way his men respectfully stood behind him. All of his soldiers wore white T-shirts in various stages of cleanliness along with their tan camo pants. As my feet stepped off of the plane, my attention was quickly stolen by the wind that encircled my body. I took in a deep breath, relishing in the delicious heat that filled my lungs as the suns rays touched my skin. The combination elicited an instinctive response from me where I opened my arms slightly to welcome the breeze as it barely perceptively lifted me.

My elation was short lived as Jonas pulled me back to reality by grasping my hand and whispering, "Come on darling. We'll find time later."

Bringing myself back down to the moment I was struck by the intense gazes of the men as they watched from behind their commander. Breathing slightly fast from the euphoria I had to so suddenly relinquish, I held onto Jonas' hand firmly and followed him so that we could join our small gang. Hiding my eyes behind my dark sunglasses, I intently examined the military men wondering if these were the men we grew up with back in Iowa. Did they know Peter and how he met his end? I asked myself.

Once Naomi had finished speaking with the head of the men, he turned his attention to us and said, "Hello. I'm Major Roberts and I am in command of this base. We have been looking forward to working with you all. The squad standing behind me is called Corvus or The Black Bird squad. Officer James here will show you to your bunker where you can drop off your bags," Major Roberts said with the confidence that came with authority.

I scanned the men's faces as he spoke. I heard a few of them call me the weak link noticing my inability to let go of my boyfriends hand. Jonas and I smirked simultaneously as we heard that.

'Well this is going to be interesting,' I said.

'There is some serious testosterone in this camp,' Jonas responded to me.

'Yeah, along with the smell of sweaty ass,' Marcus chimed in.

Jonas and I both turned to Marcus and gave him a small chuckle. Naomi cleared her throat in an attempt to get our attention while also silently reprimanding us.

'I'm so over that bitch,' I said to Marcus and Jonas as I resumed my glaring of the men standing in front of us.

Major Roberts turned his gaze back to our group while gesturing for us to follow Officer James. There was something about him that triggered a curiosity within me, sensing an energy of concealment. I watched him for an extra beat before our guide led us away.

Officer James oozed the feeling of hesitation and nervousness to be near us. I could tell that we petrified him. His hands clearly shook as he pointed in the direction we were heading in. His hidden emotions conveyed that if any of us were to make any sudden movements, he would unashamedly run away screaming. As tempted as we had been to see him run away from us, we followed him respectfully, knowing that we needed to treat him with kid gloves. Naomi did not join our group, remaining behind to speak with Roberts as they walked to one of the other buildings. His men, on the other hand remained silently behind tracking us as we moved away from them.

Our barracks looked as I imagined it would with thin mattresses on metal cots each with its own footlocker and a bedside lamp on a simple nightstand. The wood floor was covered with sand and the walls were a fake wood paneling. It was a dark and uninteresting room with only one small window allowing for little natural light to filter in. There was a soft constant whirring from an old air-conditioning unit built into the wall below the window. We each randomly claimed a bed by placing our duffle bags on the respectful footlockers. Jonas and I were beside one another of course, with Marcus on the other side of me. Jeff and Marc chose the cots across the small isle in front of our beds. There were no extra beds which lead us assume Naomi had her own private room somewhere else on the base. After inspecting the room, we all looked to James simultaneously waiting to hear what our next instructions would be.

"I will be back in an hour to get you. Bathroom is out to the right of the door. Please keep showers short, we have limited water supply," James instructed before turning on his heels and quickly exiting the room. As soon as the door had slammed shut loudly behind him I said, "Poor guy." With legitimate pity for how we made him so afraid.

Marc turned to Jonas and said, "Cool it down in here would you?"

"Certainly," Jonas replied then closed his eyes as a rush of cold air poured into our small room. The temperature dropped so low and so quickly, I actually began to shiver while wishing for a sweater as the others sighed in relief. I curled up on the firm cot, careful to not get my shoes on the bed as I held onto my gold feather that had remained safely hidden beneath my shirt.

"Funny that the squad is called Corvus, huh?" I asked no one in particular as I shut my eyes.

"They were ours," Jeff replied emotionless.

I nodded since I had sensed that already. "They knew Peter. They know what happened to him," I stated matter-of-factly.

Jonas leaned down and rubbed my shoulder before sliding his cot across the wood floor until it was touching mine. With heavy eyes I wished for a 10-minute nap feeling my muscles loosen in my repose. After a few minutes had passed, I forced myself to fight the exhaustion and push myself up on my elbow to reach for my cup of coffee that I had placed on the nightstand. Taking a large sip, I grimaced before swallowing the cold and bitter black caffeinated syrup. Jonas took the cup from my hand before unceremoniously dumping it into the trash bin. As he walked back towards me I quickly stood, grabbed my duffel bag and began to make my way out of our room.

"I'm going to take a hot shower. It's freaking freezing in here," I said.

Jonas grabbed his bag and followed me out. The bathroom building was easy to find. The structure itself was right beside ours down an uncovered sandy path open to the suns bright rays and it's welcoming heat. Pulling the heat forcefully into my lungs, I slowed my stride to prolong my time in the warmth.

The bathroom building had no fanfare as expected. There were four shower stalls separated by half metal walls and a shower curtain entry. The toilets were located on the opposite side of the showers with an island in the room's center containing three sinks. The entire room was white and surprisingly clean. Jonas and I undressed quickly and stepped into one of the stalls together. The hot water felt delicious making my muscles relax euphorically.

"Give me the shampoo, I'm going to wash your hair. You haven't been able to sleep because you're so tense. Relax darling, relax," Jonas said as he began scrubbing my scalp.

A few moments later Marcus came into the bathroom and began showering in the stall next to us. The three of us stood silently beneath the waters stream rinsing away 3 days worth of stink along with all of the sand and grime we had managed to collect in our pores.

"These men were wiped obviously. But Major Roberts knows exactly who we are," Marcus said suddenly shattering our silent oasis, making me flinch slightly.

"I agree with you," Jonas responded. "I wonder if they had similar experiences as ours you know? Were they raised by handlers and then just happened to sign up for boot camp when they turned 18?" Jonas stated cynically.

I quietly listened while holding onto my necklace as the stream rinsed the shampoo out of my hair. Jonas then very meticulously applied conditioner while massaging my scalp. Once my body was washed I stepped out of the shower and dressed in the cargo pants and T-shirt I had bought at that outdoor store back in Iowa. It felt wonderful to put on clean underwear.

Jonas and Marcus stayed in the shower as I made my way back to our barrack, passing by Jeff and Marc as they walked to the showers. The air in our quarters was freezing making me shiver, but the silence and solitude encouraged my mind to relax despite the cold. After removing my sneakers, I slithered my way beneath my covers allowing my muscles to soften as I closed my eyes, hoping for just 15 minutes of sleep.

I WOKE-UP to the sound of Officer James speaking in a very monotone but hurried voice. "We are to meet in the conference room. Please follow me," he said.

After stretching for a moment, I stood up and put my sneakers on grateful for the few minutes of shut-eye I was able to squeeze into my day. Jonas stood at the door waiting for me with his outstretched hand as I slipped my sunglasses back on. As we stepped over the threshold, I quickly placed a protective shield around our barracks. I wasn't sure why I felt the need to, I just needed to feel protected.

Turning left this time, we walked out of our building toward a small courtyard created by the strategic placement of small sand colored buildings. Officer James led us toward a larger structure located at the far end of one of the rows. The front door of the single story building led to a very nondescript beige colored hall flanked by four closed doors, two on each side of the hall. The fluorescent lights flickered and hummed as we made our way to the first door on the left. We walked into a windowless conference room with walls that were covered by topography maps and a dry erase board. There were two large tables on the far corners of the room, each with its own computer and at the center of the room stood a large conference table with piles of papers scattered everywhere. Major Roberts stood beside Naomi facing the center table with his 13 soldiers standing on the opposite side of the table facing us.

When the Five approached the table, the room became deafeningly silent. With the lift of a hand, Officer James instructed us to join the others around the center table. As soon as my thigh came in contact with the table, I nonchalantly began to examine the papers on the table in front of me as well as the maps on the walls, trying to figure out where we were and what the heck we were supposed to do here in order to earn our delusional freedom.

"Major Roberts, thank you for hosting the team. Allow me to introduce Jeff, Marc, Marcus, Jonas and Lily. They are the Five," Naomi said shattering the silence in the room.

Keeping our focus on Roberts as his gaze shifted down our row as our names were spoken, his men remained immobile as they flanked him, watching us skeptically with their firm straight backs and puffed out chests. The room smelled like stale cigar with a hint of man stench as the air conditioning unit whirled and struggled to keep up with the demand to cool a room full of sweating man bodies.

"Welcome Five. We are happy to have you. You are in an undisclosed location in the country of Afghanistan. Just a few miles away from us, there are enemy groups that we have been charged with eliminating. We were just debriefed by Naomi here. We are aware that each of you possess special skills that may help us succeed in our mission." He paused briefly scanning our faces before continuing. "Our particular mission and location is vital based on its remote location within the country but most importantly because in this small targeted village, there currently resides several militant group leaders. These enemy combatants have been identified as the leaders of several satellite terrorist cells both here in Afghanistan and in other parts of the globe," Roberts explained with intensity in his voice. "The only way to weaken these satellite cells is to throw them into chaos and the best way to do that is by eliminating their leaders."

The Five of us stood motionless, intently staring at him. I quickly glanced at Naomi and caught her glaring at me, which I reciprocated with my own glare in return. After a few moments, I turned my attention back to Major Roberts as he commanded firmly, "You are not to leave the premises without an armed guard..."

'This guy has no idea what we can do,' I thought to my boys.

'Lily... Never disclose everything to these people, understand? Stand still and silent. Do not avert your gaze from him,' Jeff warned us.

"...You are within an easy range for a well trained sniper to just take you out. Do not underestimate these people because of what their environment looks like. They are lethal, they are armed and they are not afraid to die for their cause," Roberts continued.

I stood beside Jonas holding his hand trying to not let my dismay show. The reality that we were told that we would be killing people or at least helping these men kill people was alarming to hear. But this is what we were created for. This was our purpose within The Agency. We needed to get out as soon as possible I kept repeating to myself. All we needed to do was get this job done so that we could figure out the rest of our lives. Jonas squeezed my hand while holding it behind my back, sensing my inner struggles. The desire to walk out of the room and run into the warm desert air, to feel the blood pump through my body was all I could focus on as Roberts continued to talk at us.

"...It is now approaching 1700 hours, Officer James will lead you to the mess tent for some supper. I strongly encourage you to get a good meal and then promptly return to your barracks for some needed rest. You all look like you could use it. James will retrieve you in the am at 0600 hours. Sleep well." Roberts finished, turned around and left us standing there. His men continued ogling us as Officer James motioned for us to exit.

Before leaving I was able to quickly garner some information from the men. All were good and genuine men juggling their military lives with wives, partners, homes and children. They had seen some horrible things out in the desert and secretly carried profound fears within themselves. Along with this inner turmoil there also was a deeper fissure within themselves that I could not penetrate in this brief encounter. This was not only confounding me but it was something that they themselves did not realize resided within their psyches. I needed to figure out how to crack those fissures wide open to let all of their buried minds be exposed into the light of day. Hoping to learn about their time at The Homestead and to determine if they had any information about Peter.

29

I woke up shivering in our subarctic room. Sleeping in the small uncomfortable military cot alone was quite a change from my sleeping arrangements compared to the past few weeks. Jonas was in his bed beside me, which meant he couldn't hold me like he normally did. Carefully lifting my arm so that my wrist was accessible just beneath the blanket I glanced at my watch and saw that it was only 4:30 in the morning. I lay in the dark holding my gold feather as I stared at the ceiling while listening to the boys snoring away.

After a few moments of contemplating my latest dream about Peter, I decided to quietly dress in my running clothes and go for a quick run before Officer James came to fetch us at 0600. I managed to silently leave our room and make my way to the tarmac where our plane had landed the previous day. The desert silence around me was glorious. The heat worked quickly to thaw my cold limbs as the breeze wrapped around me in a small whirlwind. In the far distance I could make out the faint glow from city lights. Presumably that was the location of our targets. Breathing in deeply I pulled the warm air into my lungs and bathed in the bright glow of the full moon. The stars shone brighter than I can ever recall seeing. The desert was full of unexpected beauty and mystery, I thought to myself, such a shame that there was so much turmoil.

I began to jog slowly at first in the opposite direction of the city lights, just to get my limbs warmed up until they felt ready to pick up speed. The feel of my muscles pushing and propelling me on the sand covered pavement felt delicious. After picking up speed and finding my paces sweet spot, my thoughts wandered to Jonas and keeping him safe, completing this mission successfully to then hopefully and ultimately have the ability to start my life outside of the Agency and the Homestead.

I ran until unnoticeably, the sun began to rise, brightening the sky with its pinks, oranges and yellow lights streaming from the horizon. My legs moved me away from the base into a completely desolate sandy planet surrounded by nothing except for the dunes that now glowed pink as they reflected the morning sky. After a while I began losing track of how far I had gone. Without slowing down, I turned to discover that the base could barely be seen behind me, fading so easily away into the sand. Could I just run away? Just leave it all and take my chances with whatever the consequences might be out here, I wondered. It would be so easy to just leave. But I could never abandon Jonas. I could be away from him.

I continued to run away as my thoughts brought me to far off lands where new lives could be lived with no history to hold us back. My daydream was abruptly interrupted by the sound of feet running behind me. Slowing my pace slightly, I turned my head to discover a frantic looking Jonas running towards me as tears glimmered on his cheeks, reflecting the rising suns light. Sensing rage coming from his skin I stopped running and waited for him to reach me.

"What the fuck are you doing Lily? Where are you going?" Jonas yelled at me.

"No, no, no please," I pleaded. "I was just going for a run. I'm not leaving you. Never," I said in a panic as he panted for breath in front of me. I reached up and pulled him down into a tight hug.

"I heard you. I could hear you debating to just leave Lily and to just keep running away from all of this. You know running away will also take you away from me," he said angrily.

"Yes, I thought it...daydreamed about it really. I would never leave you. I would leave all of this, yes. But not you please believe me. We are getting out of this. All Five of us and we are going to live lives away from all of this," I implored.

He squeezed me back before pulling away to say, "We have to go back. They'll be waiting for us." I could feel that he was still angry with me. I looked at him and smiled while nodding readiness to return to the base. We ran back in tandem, side by side, keeping perfect pace with each other. When the base came into view, I picked up speed and he did the same. We raced back laughing and huffing as we pushed ourselves to run as fast as we could. He beat me by a millisecond and as he entered the base he turned and gave me a high five.

"I will never leave you Jonas. I swear," I said seriously.

He nodded and said, "I believe you darling."

Headed back to our quarters, we walked through the center courtyard passing by the outdoor mess hall with its large picnic style tables that were covered by beige colored plastic tablecloths that blew in the breeze. Two men sat at one of the tables drinking coffee with a big plate of eggs, hash and toast watching us as we passed them, surprised to see us. Leaning down into a big black barrel I grabbed 2 water bottles and sat across from them as Jonas sat beside me.

"Good morning," I said to them with a big smile.

They watched Jonas and I take our uninvited seats. The man sitting in front of me said, "Nice run? You could have been killed you know."

I turned to Jonas and smiled, neither of us responding to him.

"You do realize that if anything happens to you then all of our efforts out here would have been for nothing," he said with a harsher tone.

I reached into his mind and learned that his name was Emilio. He had been raised at the Homestead even though he had no memory of it. His memories had been cleared when he was 17 years old. That was when he was sent to live with a Mexican-American family, agency personnel of course. But he believed that they adopted him when he was an infant. He spent a year in Southern California until he enlisted in the army at 18 along with his adoptive brother Gustavo who was 18 at the time as well. Gustavo sat on the other side of Emilio silently eating his omelet. Since enlisting in the army, they have only returned home twice because they have no remaining living relatives. They are both single and never leave each other's side. Sensing their need for proximity to one another, I began to wonder if they were perhaps failed Duals? Jonas listened intently as I made these discoveries.

"Nothing will happen to us Emilio, I promise. And we will make sure no harm comes to you or Gus," I said while Jonas smiled at them.

"How did you know our names?" Gustavo asked as he looked at Emilio.

"We have more things in common with the both of you than you realize Gustavo," Jonas replied. "We are here to help you. The team will succeed in its mission. Whatever that mission may be. Trust us."

With a smile Jonas and I stood while the brothers watched us with confused looks. Leaving them pondering the little we had just revealed, we headed to our room to gather shower supplies.

"That was fun," I said as we walked hand in hand. Jonas grunted in agreement.

Naomi was waiting for us in our room. She glared at us as we came in. *'She hates my guts,'* I thought out loud.

Jonas pulled my hand slightly and led us to our beds.

"I'm here to let you all know that I am being sent to another location. This means that you will remain here under Major Roberts' command. I am uncertain of when I will be returning," Naomi explained.

"Congratulations... Hey before you go I do have some questions. What the fuck are we doing here? What is this mission everyone keeps referring to and how long will it take? And, when it's all said and done we are done right? As in I can live a life away from all of this right?" I said in a tone that conveyed slight aggression and annoyance.

"You will be debriefed on your mission later this morning. The length of time you spend here will depend entirely on how long it takes you to complete your tasks. You can begin a life outside of the Agency once you are finished. But let me say what you already know. We can track you down. We know how to find you. And you will certainly be pulled into future missions as needed. You may begin your lives, but you will forever be an Agency Dual," she replied smugly.

"Great, I need a shower," I said while looking at Jonas. I walked passed Naomi on my way to the door pausing only to give her a quick glare.

JONAS and I took showers in separate stalls. He could tell I needed some space. I felt trapped in my life. Jonas and I along with the others could be very content living together, supporting one another through all of this, but I knew that Jonas and I, and even Marcus for that matter would always feel like something was missing.

I dragged out my shower for as long as I could before Marcus reached out to us, telling us to hurry because Officer James was about to short circuit from anxiety of being five minutes late to our morning meeting.

After quickly dressing in a clean white tank top and black cargo pants, I threw my long brown hair into a bun at the top of my head and put my sunglasses on. Jonas and I made our way back to our barrack and were instantaneously able to witness first hand what Marcus had been talking about.

"We must go now. Two of our team members have just returned from a nearby base with information that could help us succeed in our mission. Major Roberts prefers that everyone is debriefed at the same time," Officer James said in a panic.

"You were missing two?" Jeff asked.

"Yes, we are fifteen strong, had you not noticed that there have only been thirteen of us at all of the meetings?" James asked in a huff.

"We were never told that your team had fifteen members," Jeff said with an annoyed tone.

"My apologies, I assumed that your guide, Naomi, would have debriefed you before your arrival here," James explained. "It doesn't matter. We need to go now."

"What the hell else did she not debrief us on?" Marc asked sarcastically.

Officer James walked out of our sleeping quarters with us in tow. Jeff and Marc were obviously perturbed by this news while Marcus, Jonas and I didn't really care either way. I honestly wasn't surprised to find out that Naomi had withheld information from us.

We followed behind James to one of the airplane hangars on the outer perimeter of the base. Standing there waiting for us was the entire team of soldiers. All fifteen soldiers were present with their back facing, James broke off from us and took his position at the end of the line of men. They all stood at attention facing the inside of the hangar behind three long tables that were lined up in a row by the entrance of the building. Major Roberts silently watched us approach as he stood on the other side of the tables facing his men. There was complete silence with the exception of the wind softly blowing, whistling on the edge of the building. Only Roberts gaze landed on us as we made our way inside to stand together as a group at one end of the tables. He glared at us as we settled into our spots.

"I realize that you all are not military trained and so lack the knowledge of protocol. Let this be my first and last warning to you all," Major Roberts said while looking in our direction. "Don't ever be late to a debriefing again. Do you understand?" Roberts shouted at us. "You are wasting mine and my men's time."

I became so annoyed and frustrated that before I realized what I was doing I squeezed his throat shut with my mind subtly and slightly, making him repeatedly try to clear his throat as he tugged at his tight collar. Once I realized what I was doing I released him and watched him cough frantically.

'Oh jeez, That was totally an accident!' I thought to the Five with mock self-deprecation. After a short pause I thought, *'I must admit though it was shamefully gratifying.'*

'He is going to be so pissed if he discovers how that just happened,' Marc said.

"Can I get you some water sir?" Officer James asked Major Roberts.

"No!" Roberts replied curtly as he continued to cough.

We all stood straight-faced watching him recover until he was able to speak easily. Once he had composed himself he continued to berate us.

"I was reassured by Naomi that you are all ready to begin immediately," he said with annoyance. "Therefore, we will begin by taking you all into the field today. We have received reports of enemy activity in the center of the city located not far from our present location. Specific targets have been identified and are currently seeking protection there. You are to eliminate them with as few casualties as possible, silently and with as little commotion as possible. Four of you will accompany two small groups of my men to where we believe they are being sheltered," Roberts explained. "We do not want attention, understand?"

Processing the repercussions to what we were being tasked with, my attention was suddenly pulled away from Roberts' words to my gold feather, which had begun to heat up and vibrate against my skin. Grasping the pendant through my shirt, I turned to my left to look at Jonas to show him what was happening. But my attention was quickly deviated from the burning I felt on my chest to Jonas, as he stood motionless and barely perceptibly breathing as he stared intently over my head and to my right at one of the military men. Feeling a sense of urgency and warning, my body immediately tensed as my defense mechanisms were engaged. I turned my head, following his gaze almost afraid to see what it was that had caught him so off guard as I asked, *'Hey. What's going on?'*

He gave me no response and had intentionally closed me out of his mind.

Sensing the temperature increasing as my body slightly shook, I started breathing deeply and slowly when I began to taste blood in my mouth. After realizing I had accidentally bit down on my cheek in an effort to control my ability, I balled my free hand into a fist when Jonas moved his body to stand to my right as he wrapped his cold arm around my torso, pulling me to his chest as he began sending a cold blast into my body. Roberts' yelling became barely audible in my ears as my brain became fuzzy and unable to process his words.

Staring at Jonas with a burning questioning look, he avoided my gaze and continued to shut me out of his mind while I continued to probe him and the rest of the boys desperately trying to discover why they had suddenly become so alarmed. All of them were blocking me out.

Roberts saying, "Lily and Jonas you will be accompanied by Captain Jagger," suddenly brought me out of my stupor. "Jeff and Marc you will be with Paulson, while Marcus remains on the base to help with navigation."

Standing immobile as my heart beat hard and fast in my chest, loud enough for me to hear the blood flowing in the arteries in my neck, my pendant continued to heat up as I pushed it up against my skin. Jonas tightened his hold around me flooding my body with cold. *What the hell is happening right now?* I thought out loud.

'It's Okay. I've got her boys. No attention or commotion please, it will just amplify things. Just continue as planned,' Jonas said to our group.

All consented silently as they briefly glanced at me before making their way to their assigned groups. Confused at what was happening to my body and what Jonas meant by his words, I didn't question any of it, afraid that the distraction would make me lose control of myself.

After releasing his men, Roberts escorted Marcus out of the hangar towards the command station. I could hear Jeff speaking with someone named Officer Paulson about the logistics of the mission.

Focusing my eyes in front of me, I saw the man called Captain Jagger make his way towards Jonas and I. As he approached, my breath hitched in my throat making me gasp for breath as the shaking in my body worsened almost as if I were having a panic attack. Captain Jagger stood in front of me watching me with a concerned look.

Before I could stop myself I grasped his face with both of my hands and began stroking his cheeks as I looked into his familiar green eyes. The tears began to silently slide down my cheeks without my awareness before the name I said nightly found its way out of my mouth in a shaky whisper.

"Peter..."

30

With a confused look, Captain Jagger stepped away from my outstretched hands and said, "Hello Lily and Jonas. I'm Captain Peter Jagger. I will be leading us on this mission," he said politely but authoritatively while looking at Jonas.

Peter was taller than I remembered with much bigger shoulders. His blond hair had been cut short. His face was slightly obscured by his facial hair. But I would know those eyes anywhere. They were unmarred by the passing of time. The beautiful boy I knew long ago, who continued to appear to me nightly was now the grown man that stood before me.

"Hello Peter," Jonas said hoarsely while clearing his throat. I turned to Jonas blinking quickly in an effort to keep any more tears from escaping. Jonas looked at me sadly and whispered in my head, *'He doesn't remember darling. Keep control and don't say anything.'* I shook my head in acknowledgement as Jeff and Marc watched us from a distance.

'Be strong Lil. They were all made to forget. It's not his fault,' Jeff said.

'This mission is important Lily. Stay focused. We'll figure all of this out,' Marc finished.

Jonas and I stood firmly as I wiped my eyes discreetly while turning away from Captain Jagger.

"These are the men...O'Connell, Martins, Charvis, Brody and the Gonzalez brothers, Emilio and Gustavo," Captain Jagger explained while pointing to each member of his team.

Jonas gave them each a nod as I stood silently in shock. The gravity of it all was making my head spin with questions and emotions. My hold on Jonas' arm continued to tighten out of fear of collapse sensing my skin turning pale as beads of cold sweat formed. Peter was alive and standing right in front of me. I began feeling a bit faint remembering the pain I had felt thinking that I had lost him forever. Why was I lied to? For what purpose? Unless Naomi did believe he was dead as well.

I silently watched Captain Jagger as the rest of the men prepared their gear for departure. The man that stood before me as I hid slightly behind Jonas was certainly Peter but not the Peter from my youth. He was different. His warmth seemed dampened.

"Are you all right?" Captain Jagger asked while trying to get a good look at my face.

I nodded in response unable to make my voice work.

Accepting my response, Captain Jagger laid a map down on the table and showed us the layout of the city that we would soon be traveling to. Our main target was presumably being sheltered in a building almost in the center of the city. I watched his hands float over the map indicating what our approach would be. I listened to his voice intently hoping to hear a familiar inflection or pronunciation to remind me of my old love. His body was larger and more muscular, his hands looked rougher and much stronger. My breath kept catching in my throat as I continued to press the hot gold feather pendant up against my skin, feeling the pain it was causing me as I kept repeating to myself, how the fuck is this happening?

"This mission must be handled very delicately because we only have one chance to get it right. Failure of our part means failure for the entire unit." After a short pause he asked, "Ms. Lily are you feeling well? You seem a bit pale," Captain Jagger asked with some concern in his tone.

My brain was unable to process his words nor formulate a response despite having clearly heard his words. "She's just fine. Just a little jet lagged," Jonas responded for me politely.

"Very well," he said as he looked at Jonas. "Now, we were told that you and Ms. Lily have, I'm not sure what to call them... abilities? And that these abilities can be used to help us succeed today." Pointing again to the map he said, "Between them and us, there are hundreds of mines buried out there in the sand. It's impossible for us to know where they all are and this will be our first time to take this particular approach into the city. It was explained to us that you could help us navigate through those mines and perhaps even disguise our approach. Is this correct?" he asked while keeping his focus on Jonas.

Without saying a word, Jonas and I just stood stock still with wide eyes staring at him in disbelief. Shocked to hear someone besides our small group talk about our abilities. It felt violating but at the same time validating that this was all legitimate.

"Should I take that as a yes?" Jagger asked. Nodding our assent, he continued to explain the plans for the mission. "One of our contacts has informed us that the targets will be leaving in a few hours. Attacking them in the daytime is definitely riskier and not our preferred plan but we have no other options at this point. We have to limit our exposure and civilian involvement. The risks are great but we are counting on you both to help us minimize them," Captain Jagger explained.

He stood there for a moment silently waiting for us to ask him questions, when none came he nodded and turned to his men silently giving the signal to begin mobilizing. They were quick and efficient grabbing their gear, weapons and helmets before jumping into the large military truck. Jonas and I stood back watching from a slight distance while he continued to cool me down as I tightly held his arm.

"Come on love birds, let's get in Melissa," Gus said gesturing to the large military vehicle while Emilio stood beside him.

"Melissa?" Jonas asked as we slowly made our way to them.

"It's the passenger HUMV we'll be traveling in," Emilio answered with a wink.

It turned out that Melissa was a tough vehicle made of thick metal painted a color that made it a bit easier to blend into our sandy surroundings. Everyone climbed inside and sat snuggly together with little wiggle room. Captain Jagger sat shotgun with O'Connell behind the wheel. When the key was turned the engine roared to life as the loud protesting sounds of Rage Against the Machine blasted from the speakers in surround sound. Jagger quickly reached over and turned the music off as he glanced at me as I sat behind O'Connell. My seat location facilitated my continued examination of Captain Jagger. My eyes were glued to him, my attention completely captivated by him and nothing else. Jonas sat beside me with Brody on the other side of him. Charvis, Martins and the Gonzalez brothers sat in the far back.

In an attempt to bring myself back to reality, I looked at Jonas and asked quietly, "Marc and Jeff?"

"Where will Marc and Jeff be going?" Jonas asked Jagger.

"They will be approaching from the opposite side of the city," Brody explained as he held his very large gun on his lap.

Our vehicle along with the vehicle that Jeff and Marc rode in, departed the hangar simultaneously. I watched them through my window full of worry as we broke off in opposite directions. *'Be safe out there,'* I said quickly as they subtly nodded to us. We watched each other continue on our separate paths until we were no longer in each others line of site.

THE TRIP WAS LONG, hot, bumpy and sandy. I had put my sunglasses, trying to prepare myself for whatever it was Jonas and I would need to do out there in the desert. My body felt tense and exhausted to the point where my joints hurt. The heat from my pendant had diminished significantly but had not cooled down by any means. My skin beneath it definitely smarted when I touched it.

"How long have you guys been a couple?" Brody asked from the other side of Jonas.

"We are not a couple Ken. We are called Duals. We are very much like brother and sister," Jonas answered drily without looking at him.

"How did you know his name?" Gus asked surprised.

"We know all of your names Gus and what your stories are," Jonas responded while examining my hand as he held it on his lap.

"Is there like a file about us or something?" Emilio asked annoyed.

Jagger turned his head slightly as if trying to get a better listen of the conversation. Holy shit how could this be happening? I blurted to myself in my mind. Eliciting a response from Jonas immediately alerting me that I had just blurted that out to all of the boys. I closed my eyes and tried to focus on breathing as my body was gently tossed in the moving vehicle. Did Naomi intentionally lie to us? Was it coincidence that she left just as he returned? I don't understand what the point of lying was, if in fact she had been lying.

"There is no chart Emilio. We have abilities. That's why we are here. Remember?" Jonas said while turning to Emilio.

Stop it! I said reprimanding myself. I have to keep my head straight despite the need to fly up into the sky screaming with rage and relief. My emotions felt as though they were going to burst out of me. Let's get this shit done and then figure all of this out, I said to myself as I intently watched Peter while he remained focused on the terrain outside. He was still so beautiful and my attraction to him felt like a magnet pulling at my core. Just looking at him brought me back to the memories I had been forced to forget. How could I possibly be expected to work with him and pretend that he hadn't been mine and I his a lifetime ago. How do I push it all aside when all I wanted to do was jump on his lap and look into his eyes? I watched his lips move as he spoke with O'Connell. All I wanted to do was caress them with my own lips. I wanted to grab him by the shoulders so that I could shake him as I screamed remember me! Will he remember me? Please remember me.

Jonas squeezed my hand and turned his eyes to me. I could feel his stare on my blushing cheeks. *'Stop it darling. I can feel all of this and it feels horrible. I promise you we will figure this all out. I promise. Please keep your head in the game until we get through this. Please.'*

I turned and looked at him aching to release all of this tension as I shook my head in acknowledgement. Turning my focus out the window, I watched the desert world surround us with its nothingness. After taking several deep breaths I turned my attention to the task at hand and began to plan for what was potentially to come as we approached impending hostility.

'Jeff and Marc, can you hear me? Can you send an electric pulse over the entire city to disable their electronic devices? There can't be pictures, videos and phone calls while we are there,' I explained.

'We hear you Lil, good thinking. Jeff and I can handle that,' Marc responded.

I turned to Jonas and he shook his head in agreement.

"Can you guys talk to each other like in your minds?" Ken Martins asked from behind us.

I took in a deep breath, held it for ten seconds and then released it as I began to feel my body shake with bitterness and exasperation. I was in no mood for chitchat. I would have rather walked honestly. I sent my mind to the stereo and turned Rage against the Machine back on full blast just to stop the chitchat. O'Connell and Jagger jumped in surprise and then both fiddled with the buttons in an effort to turn it off but the stereo would not respond to them. Shaking my head to the beat, Jonas gave me a stern look as the sensation of eyes burning the back of my head sunk in deep. I rolled my eyes at Jonas before turning the music off.

With a deep sigh I said, "Sorry."

Gazing back out the window I noticed that there were sand mounds in several areas. O'Connell was doing a good job at avoiding them. With a little focus I discovered that the small mounds radiated a faint heat from them.

"We're surrounded by explosives you do realize that right Brian?" I asked Brian O'Connell.

"Yes, I know. I can see them," Brian responded.

"Wouldn't it be easier if they were just detonated or moved?" I asked.

"Sure, how do you suggest we do that Lily?" Brian asked in a condescending tone.

"Stop the vehicle. Do you have a preference over whether they are detonated or moved?" I asked.

"Blow it all up," Ken Martins shouted excitedly.

As Brian slowed the vehicle down and I jumped out before coming to a full stop. Jonas watched me intently through the window with a grin on his face. I could feel his excitement and readiness at letting our proverbial cat out of the bag.

'Just control it darling,' Jonas thought.

'Jeff and Marc, the explosions you are about to hear are me detonating these buried baby bombs. Don't worry. And be careful they're everywhere,' I warned into the distance.

'I'm sad we're missing that. We're ok so far. Good luck and have fun Lil,' Jeff replied.

"Stay in the car!" I yelled while making my way away from the vehicle.

Closing my eyes, I focused at pulling the fire within me to the surface of my body instantaneously feeling the surge of power in my hands as I did so. Calling on my brother wind, I was lifted into the air while reaching for the heat sources that called out to me from below their sandy shelters. With slight movements of my hands, I touched the little sources of energy and began lifting them easily through the sand and up into the air until they were at my height in the sky. There was must have been one hundred or so bombs floating in the sky. They had a noticeable weight to them forcing me to fight gravity as it tried to pull them back down.

'Hey Lil, probably shouldn't detonate them, that would announce our presence,' Jeff said suddenly.

'He's right darling,' Jonas agreed.

Silently agreeing with their recommendation, I disappointedly moved the hundred or so bombs onto a single mound while hearing the sounds of their mechanics and electronic connections being modified from afar. Smiling at what we were achieving together, I silently thanked Jeff and Marc for deactivating the bombs. With the task at hand complete, I landed back on the sandy earth, feeling better with this small release of energy as I looked at Jonas and smiled.

I climbed back into a very silent vehicle as the men watched me with open mouths.

Jonas gave me a quick nod and said, "Detonating would announce our presence. Jeff and Marc deactivated them for Lily," Jonas explained as they sat mesmerized.

It was Captain Jagger who finally broke the deafening silence by looking to O'Connell and saying quickly, "Okay shows over, let's go." And with that command, we were on our way again.

We drove in silence to the city limits. "Since we are just learning about your abilities, you wouldn't be able to camouflage our arrival would you?" Jagger asked as he looked at me.

I turned to Jonas with a nod before he closed his eyes and began to emit his energy into our intertwined hands, strengthening and broadening his power until thick dark gray clouds filled the clear blue sky bringing with them booming thunder along with streaks of lightening that slashed deeply in the blackened sky bringing with it thick torrential rain. The cold rainwater quickly turned to vapor as it hit the hot sand, creating mist and fog that engulfed and disguised us.

After his initial shock subsided, O'Connell jumped at the opportunity that had just been presented and sped the HUMV down the main road for several minutes until we made it into the city limits. Driving quickly past the small concrete and mud homes that bordered the city limits, we swerved by pedestrians running to seek shelter from the sudden storm. Jeff and Marc sent their energy from the opposite side of the city, debilitating all electronics until their ability reached all the way across to our location. Feeling relieved at their success, I reached out to some of the city inhabitants in their homes and discovered that despite our efforts, our presence had nonetheless been announced from neighbor to neighbor as they ran passed us on their way into their homes. We had also been hopeful that the sudden and unexpected environmental changes would have forced all of the residents indoors, however a few men and women braved the storm to make their way up to their rooftops with malice in their minds and weapons in their hands as they watched us lurch through their city.

"I'm putting up a shield. We've been spotted," I said out loud as I watched the rooftop of the taller structures.

Summoning the fire within me, I pushed the energy out and around us like a bubble that blocked the rain and fog. Reaching far across the city, I was easily able to locate Jeff and Marc with their military team. With a little concentration, I successfully shielded their vehicle as well from potential attackers. With a new sense of safety, O'Connell stepped on the gas and began speeding around the twists and turns of the small city streets. Jonas' senses and mine were on high alert as we drove. We felt mentally sharp and clear headed as we prepared ourselves for the worst.

As we made our way deeper into the city, I kept waiting for the distinct pop of a gun, surprised that we had not heard one yet since our presence was definitely known to many of the dwellers. We were able to reach our targeted building much sooner than we had initially anticipated. This was incredibly serendipitous because the news of our presence had not yet travelled this deeply to the locals. Wanting to take advantage that the element of surprise was still on our side, I sent my ability out into the building, scouting for heat sources generated by the beating hearts within the structure, tracking them like a hunter tracks its prey.

The targets paced nervously as they argued while plotting their nefarious schemes for multi-country attacks, seemingly oblivious to the weather happening outside. Voicing anger and contempt at the non-believers both in and outside of their homeland, spewing fury from every pore in their bodies creating a palpably thickened air in their simple abode. Listening in, Jonas and I silently conspired our own plan of attack. My initial goal was to just have the two of us take care of this business ourselves while leaving the soldiers locked and contained in the vehicle, safely away from any possible danger. Jonas of course vehemently disagreed knowing that this would anger and potentially turn the team against us. But most importantly, he knew that my primary goal in locking the men up was to keep Peter out of harms way.

As we argued silently, I could hear the soldiers whispering beside us. Discussing what their own plan of attack should be as they also debated whether Jonas and I were having a telepathic discussion. I couldn't help but laugh as they debated with each other. Turning my attention back into the HUMV, I caught Jagger's bright green eyes watching me intently.

"You ready?" he asked me directly.

I nodded before unceremoniously opening the vehicle door and jumping out onto the muddy road. With a silent order from Jagger, the rest of the team immediately followed my lead and then proceeded to take their positions up against the buildings wall holding their large guns at the ready, preparing for the inevitable onslaught from our still hidden adversaries. Reaching my senses to the targets above us, I marked their positions within the structure and silently conveyed that information to Jonas.

Before Jonas and the team began to climb the dark and narrow steps to the third floor, I created another shield around them just as I myself took flight. As I hovered unnoticed outside of the window to the third floor apartment, I watched the men and women continuing to argue as they paced around a map-laden table. They were speaking to one another with an agitated tone as their tempers flared at one another. As I was about to make my way in through the window, my attention was drawn to a teenage boy who ran into the building behind my team.

'Jonas! There's a boy coming in behind you. He didn't seem armed but he is here to warn our targets inside. I'm going in through the window,' I said to Jonas hurriedly.

I felt him acknowledge me and then turn to tell the Gonzalez brothers who were climbing the stairs behind him. When the boy caught site of the team, he made a very small startled sound before Gus covered his mouth with his hand, shocking the boy into a petrified submission. But despite the quickness of Gus' response, the boys' warning was enough to trigger those in the dwelling into motion where each occupant reached for their weapon and then simultaneously aimed at the door.

As Jagger and O'Connell came bursting into the apartment, the targets opened fire reflexively without even seeing who had come for them. Frantically holding down the trigger on their weapons, the heat from their firing weapons along with the smell of igniting gunpowder filled the small apartment until their guns were completely emptied. Despite this onslaught the men stood unharmed as each bullet disintegrated on contact with my protective shield. Not a single bullet had reached its mark. Both groups stared in shock for a brief moment trying to make sense of what they had just witnessed. In the silent pause, I sent a heated pulse at the apartment windows blasting the glass in a loud boom, sending a million shards into the room while directing the sharper edged pieces into the legs of the targets. Screaming from shock and pain, they all watched me in horror as I silently hovered into the apartment, never setting foot on the glass covered floor. The enemy moaned quietly with their bleeding extremities as they tried to move away from me in shock and fear searching for additional ammunition. I remained airborne until I reached a clearing on the floor beside the map covered table.

My team, still protected by my shield, watched in amazement, amusement and delight at what had just transpired. All of them smiled but Jagger who remained stoic. Jonas' chest puffed with pride as he watched from the front of the group, at the ready to jump in and engage if needed. Sending silent encouragement, he urged me to just let the power within me unleash and not hold back.

After a moment of contemplation, I lifted my arms up beside my body and with my palms up I pushed my energy to my finger tips until my hands felt like they would explode from the power surge flowing from my core. With a gasp, I released the heat out into our opponent's chests where it gripped and twisted their beating hearts. After a brief second, each target dropped in unison to the floor with a heavy thud as their hearts exploded in their closed chests.

Pulling the energy back into myself in a rush, I looked at Jonas full of nerves searching for confirmation that what I had just done was acceptable as my mind raced with both fear, shame and amazement at what I had just achieved. I felt immediate relief when only pride reflected in his eyes. I smiled and said, "You can stop the rain now."

The silence was sudden and deafening in the apartment when the rain stopped falling outside. The heavy astonished panting from the men was the only sound in the apartment. My eyes met Captain Jagger's stare as he left the safety of the shield and with long strides made his way towards me almost as if he was in a trance. His face remained stoic as he took my hands in his, never deviating his eyes from mine. My breath caught in my throat with surprise from this unexpected touch. Turning his attention to my hands, he examined them for evidence pointing to the source of what could have inflicted such an immediate end to our mission. Not finding anything, he looked back into my eyes with wonder. As we stood there holding each other's hands, I silently begged for his memory to return even for just a moment, just a glimpse at who we were all of those years ago. As my eyes began to fill with tears, he reached up and stroked my cheek gently. Instinctively, I leaned my face into his hand and closed my eyes allowing the feeling of joy he triggered to flow through my body. Until one of the men cleared his throat, bringing us back to our reality. Captain Jagger quickly removed his hand from my face as if the hypnosis had been abruptly terminated.

"What should we do with the boy sir?" Steven Charvis asked Jagger.

Turning his attention back to his men, I closed my eyes as the sensation of him disconnecting from me again returned. I took in several breaths as I wiped the tears from my face. Bringing myself back to reality, I noticed the glare of a young boy of maybe thirteen years. He had beautiful round deeply set brown eyes that looked at me with awe. Reaching into the boys mind, I discovered that he was the son of our primary target. He was not here to warn them but to see his father, whom he admired greatly. He would have done anything his father would have asked of him. This caused his mother great fear and heartache as she anxiously awaited for his return home. The boy continued to watch me intently while formulating a theory about the day's events. He believed that the rains had been a bad omen and that I was a witch. Jonas and I contained our simultaneous chuckle at this discovery out of respect for the boy's loss.

"He is an innocent. His father was the main target and he just witnessed his demise. He needs to return to his home where his mother waits for him," I said with little outward emotion as my heart filled with pity for the boy.

Looking down, I noticed that Jagger still held my hand tightly and his gaze returned to me as I spoke. He quickly dropped my hand and stomped away when he realized what he had been doing.

"Lily and I can return the boy to his home," Jonas had volunteered.

"We can go with them," Emilio offered while gesturing to Gus.

I nodded in acknowledgement as they began to lead the crying boy down the stairs. Taking one last look at Jagger before following them down, he met my gaze for a quick moment before turning back to the business at hand, which was collecting intelligence from the paperwork that had been discovered. Sensing his confusion and hesitance at allowing us to leave, I made my way down the stairs with a smile on face as the feeling of hope coursed through my body.

31

As we made our way down the dark muddy streets, my heart became heavy with the events that had just transpired. Jonas walked closely beside me holding my hand reassuringly as the boy tried his hardest not to sob as he walked beside us. I felt sadness for him. Sadness for him having witnessed his fathers' death. Sadness that he was growing up in a place so full of fear and hate. And I also felt sadness for being one of the sources of his pain. I knew full well what his father had been plotting with his co-conspirators but it still made me feel mournful for this very serious life experience at such a young age.

Jonas and I led our small group through the dark wet streets lined by the non-functioning streetlights, meeting no other living beings with the exception of a stray dog as it ran across our path. Jonas intentionally kept the skies covered by dark clouds that continued to threaten with possible storms, hoping that the residents would remain indoors until our business was complete. The Gonzalez brothers followed behind us, watching intently for enemies possibly lurking on the rooftops or in the shadowed corners. The boy walked quietly with his head hung until we reached his house. He stood outside of his door turning to Jonas and I silently asking for permission to enter. I gave him a quick nod before he ran inside shouting for his mother. She came running to him in her flowing maroon dress and matching Panjabi. Her headscarf came falling off of her black hair as she pulled her son into a tight embrace as the boy told her the story of his fathers demise. When she noticed our presence outside of her door she quietly reprimanded him for bringing soldiers to their home. Bringing my hands to my chest as if in prayer I bowed down deeply to her in an attempt to reassure her that they were safe from harm and to also silently apologize for the loss of her husband. She bowed her head slightly in return before shutting the door.

As we made our way back to the group, I could sense the brothers wanting to ask Jonas and I questions while we were away from the others.

"Spit it out Emilio. You want to know what we are and if you could be like us. Duals I mean," I said while turning to them.

"Yeah so, Gus and I have a very hard time when we are away from one another. Like, it's hard to think even. We noticed that the two of you are always touching or are really close to each other. How did you guys become like this?" he asked with a pause. "It's just that Gus and I have a really hard time when we are apart from each other." They both stood closely beside one another wide eyed with curiosity.

"This is a complicated story to tell right now. But I think that you deserve to know the truth. So I will tell you an abbreviated version and then expand on the details later on. Okay?" Jonas began as they nodded in understanding. "There is a top secret branch of the government called The Agency. They conducted experiments on orphaned children in the hopes of re-engineering their genes so that they would become 'enhanced'. Some of those children created deep bonds with other children. Those children became known as Duals. The other children, those who did not form the bonds became Solos. The Solos still went through the genetic mutations and testing, modifying them to be faster, stronger, essentially perfect soldiers. Some of the Solos, from what we believe at least, did form strong bonds, however those bonds did not yield in the creation of a Dual pair. Make sense?" Jonas explained.

Emilio and Gus stood with confused looks on their faces in silent shock over what they had just heard.

"We do believe you were perhaps failed Duals. You seem to have been successful at creating a strong bond, but not enough to create additional abilities or the Dual bond. We don't think. Your bond is true and real. We can help you explore what other abilities you may be unaware of that the modifications were able to achieve. We can help you," I assured them.

"Hold up. We had families growing up. We weren't orphans," Gus said disbelieving.

"We know this is a lot for you to take in. It took me weeks to come to grips with all of this myself. We were all made to forget our upbringing at The Homestead. That's where we all grew up. They erased our memories when were 17 or 18 years old before they sent us to live with our handlers. The handlers were charged with raising certain kids. Because you were groomed to be soldiers from a young age, your time on the outside was short. You both enlisted at 18 right?" I asked.

They both shook their heads in unison.

"The Agency scientists sent some of the soldiers into homes so that they could live civilian lives for a little while and to have a non-military connection to society. I actually don't know why some of you apparently were sent away and others remained at The Homestead. Jonas and I are just trying to learn some of these things ourselves. We don't have all of the answers," I explained.

"So what you're saying is that the people who raised us weren't really our family? But how do I remember them from when I was a little kid? This doesn't make any sense," Gus said with an annoyed tone.

"We know how this sounds. Trust us," Jonas said with an emphasis. "But here it is. You both grew up at The Homestead. All of your memories were erased before you were sent away and new memories were implanted. The new memories contained fake information about your childhood. The people who raised you were assigned to manage you for a short time. You both enlisted in the military because that was what you were supposed to do. That command was implanted as well. Your family, or the people you think are your family, they probably do care about you both. But ultimately they are not really your blood relative," Jonas continued.

"I'm sorry we are telling you this right now in the middle of a dark Afghani street. But you deserve to know the truth. We know you will have about a million questions. We are here to help you and answer as many questions as we can. I hate to cut this short but we really need to get going," I said as I held up my hands.

"Oh and you probably shouldn't mention this to your other team-mates. The truth will all come out eventually, I think. So for now mums the word okay?" Jonas explained as we slowly began walking again.

Emilio and Gus looked at each other in awe with small smiles that revealed their excitement slightly. I could feel their realization blossoming as they held each other's hand believing our words deep down in their soul.

Picking up speed I said, "We need to move quickly. There are many eyes on us."

We made it back to the rest of our team moments later and as we got closer we noticed that there were now two passenger HUMV's waiting for us. Marc and Jeff ran to us with open arms as we approached. They lifted me off the ground in a tight embrace and Jonas joined in on the group hug with a grunt.

When we broke away Jonas asked, "You guys Okay?"

"Yeah, we had been expecting some action but it seems Lily here did everyone's work for them," Marc said as he winked at me.

"Yeah, she was brilliant in there," Jonas said proudly while rubbing my shoulder.

I couldn't help but have mixed emotions about the events that had transpired. I just shook my head acknowledging their praise until suddenly my gold feather vibrated against my skin. Grabbing hold of it over my shirt, I turned to face the HUMVs where the rest of the men stood, immediately discovering that Jagger had been intently watching me. When our eyes connected, he began to make his way toward me with a serious look on his face. Holding my breath, he walked passed my boys to stand directly in front of me to then lean down to get a better look into my eyes. He got so close I could feel his breath on my face. My skin began to flush in a rush of heat while my heartbeat quickened. I tried to take a step back just as his hand had begun to move toward my arm. Noticing my hesitance, he quickly dropped his hand back down to his side.

"We need to leave immediately. Our presence is no longer secret," Jagger commanded.

Saddened by the emotionless tone of his voice, my eyes began to fill with tears again as I released the breath I had unintentionally been holding. It felt as though my spirit had begun deflating as he turned away from me and headed back to his men.

'I need to get my shit together. I'm acting like such a pussy! He doesn't remember me and it's probably for the best. Its cleaner this way, at least now I know he's alive. I have to stop crying damn it,' I said silently reprimanding myself.

My self deprecation was interrupted by the brothers, "You knew him...before he became Captain Jagger didn't you? We can feel your emotions for him. Your heart hurts every time he gets close to you," Emilio said as Gus stood closely beside him nodding.

Acknowledging their observation, I reached for Jonas for a quick hug and reassurance that through all of my emotional turmoil he would always be beside me.

I looked at my boys and said, "I'm flying back. I'll be okay," I said with a fake smile in an attempt to reassure them, but especially Jonas. "I need some space. I'll see you all back at the base."

Jonas was beginning to object when Marc put his hand on his shoulder to silence him. Jonas continued to look at me with concern until finally nodding in understanding.

I made my way, alone, to a small-darkened ally. Looking around to make sure nobody was watching me, I called upon the wind to lift me straight up into the dark sky in a zoom. It lifted me high above the buildings and away from the groups. My boys and the Gonzalez brothers watched me as I rose until the clouds concealed me from curious onlookers.

I could hear Jagger shout up at me as he ran to Jonas, "Where the fuck is she going?"

"She'll be OK Captain Jagger. She needs some space. She'll meet us at the base," Jonas explained confidently.

Hearing this encounter made me begin to sob as I lifted further and further into the sky. When I was well above the cloud cover I turned my body in the direction of the base and flung myself toward it. The sky at dusk was just as glorious as it was at dawn in the desert. I tried to relish in the beauty of it all, trying my hardest to pull my thoughts away from my doomed desires and focus on my current situation. I ultimately lost the battle as my sobbing continued despite myself. Responding to my emotional distress, my brother wind tightened its embrace on me forming a soft protective cocoon of air that held me afloat.

Not long after taking flight, I touched down in the courtyard of the barracks, immediately sinking down to the ground as my knees gave out beneath me. Sitting in the dusty dirt, I was able to stop my sobbing as the wind continued to softly spin around me drying my tear stained cheeks leaving behind only salt streaks on my skin. Not a moment later, the silence around me was broken by the sound of feet running towards me. Sensing his panic, I knew instantly that it was Marcus. He dropped down to his knees and pulled me onto his lap sending dust and sand up in a cloud around us. He held me tightly and breathed into my hair for a few moments.

'I have her Jonas. She's Okay,' he declared to my Dual.

Marcus held me for several minutes caressing my hair as he rocked me slightly until I pushed off of him to stand.

"I heard the mission was a success. You and Jonas did an excellent job. We heard it was quick and clean and that you got more targets than they had expected," Marcus said proudly.

I couldn't respond. I stood in a state of motionless silence until Marcus lifted me and carried me towards our bunker.

"You know what I think? I think you need a long hot shower," he said as he detoured to the bathroom building instead. Lifting my shirt over my head, he paused with a loud gasp.

"Lil, what happened here?" he said while gently rubbing the skin in between my breasts with his thumb. He leaned down to get a closer look, "It looks like a burn. Oh my God, you can see the markings of your pendant. It looks like your feather branded you. That's strange, you're impervious to fire," he looked at me quizzically.

I looked down and saw what he had been talking about. Nodding silently I continued to remove my own clothing with his help. I climbed into the scalding hot shower and stood still with my head beneath the stream. Reassured that I was going to be alright, he left me to shower alone but still checking on me every few minutes.

Jonas came storming into the bathroom about 30 minutes later, breathing heavily with a panicked look. The water had been running cold for a few minutes by the time he reached behind me and turned it off. After draping a towel around my body, he gently pulled me out of the stall and into his arms. Holding the towel tightly in place around my wet body, he sent me love and reassurance through my wet skin as he kissed the top of my head.

"We will figure all of this out darling. Not to worry. You were brilliant back in that building. Quick and clean," Jonas said as he rubbed my back.

"I killed that boys father," I spoke with a sullen voice.

The bathroom door swung open quickly and in stormed Captain Jagger. Startled by my state of undress as Jonas held me. He paused before saying, "Forgive my intrusion. Lily, I wanted to be sure you were Okay."

I lifted my head off of Jonas' chest to get a better look at him. "Yes, I am well thank you," I whispered.

Captain Jagger looked at Jonas giving him a slight nod. "The boys father has killed many innocent people including women and children in an effort to eliminate us and our efforts. He would beat his son and his wife every chance he had. They were frequent flyers in the emergency room because of broken bones. We saved many peoples lives tonight including theirs. You did a good job out there," Jagger explained before he turned around and leaving the building.

Unable to move, my eyes remained fixed on the spot Jagger had just been standing as my heart bled in my chest.

I DRESSED QUICKLY and left Jonas in the shower alone. The sun had gone completely down and all of the clouds had vanished, revealing a brilliantly starry night. I could hear the men laughing and joking in the distance as they recounted their versions of the day's events. I stood still for a moment, listening silently to the tales being told.

"...Those people had no idea what they were in for. Lily smashed the windows and then floated in like a ghost, just complete silence. She took them completely by surprise. She actually was very polite, she greeted them and then did something with her hands until suddenly poof they were all dead. We did not fire our weapons once!" I recognized Ken Martins' voice as he regaled the troops with our day's success.

"We knew they had abilities but I thought that just meant they could speak languages, read minds and shit. This goes beyond all of my expectations. I'm just glad she's on our side," Brody said.

"Yeah, they're really great people. I'm glad they're here," Emilio said. I smiled as I embraced his kind words.

Walking in the opposite direction from where the men were, I made my way outside of the bases light limits lusting for darkness and silence. I breathed in deeply, pulling the crisp night air into my lungs while I stood in the dark perimeter of the base. Counting each breath, calming my mind into a slight meditation, my thoughts were brought back to the present when my gold feather pendant began to vibrate on my chest again. I closed my eyes as I held the heated piece of gold until the sensation of my stomach dropping engulfed my mind as it sensed his approach.

"Lily?" Captain Jagger said in a whisper from behind me.

I opened my eyes but kept my back to him.

"Can I talk to you for a minute?" he asked me softly and politely.

I didn't turn to him. I knew that if I did that I would start crying in front of him again. I needed to maintain control and contain my emotions. Squeezing my hands into fists, I kept my right hand wrapped tightly around the pendant as my left hand reminded me to not give into the overwhelming need I had to touch him.

He continued to speak despite my silence, "I have this very funny feeling we have met before. It almost feels like really strong Déjà vu. Was it school or work perhaps? Where our paths have crossed before I mean. Do you know who I am?" he asked innocently. I didn't respond. "My wife and children live in Georgia. Perhaps we have met stateside before?"

"Holy shit," I mouthed silently. I could feel myself trembling as my eyes welled up. Fuck. Suddenly and silently, Marcus and Jonas appeared beside me. Jonas stood between Jagger and myself, blocking his view of me. Marcus stood in front of me.

"Hello Captain Jagger. Can we help you?" Jonas asked with a serious almost threatening tone.

Startled into silence, Jagger responded finally. "No, I was just talking to Lily. I have this feeling that I know her from somewhere and I was asking her if she had any memory of me," Jagger said as Marcus and I held each others gaze.

The blood in my body flowed like ice as Jonas sent me the cold in an effort to keep me in control. As I began to shiver, Marcus held his outstretched hand for me to take. Without a second thought, I grabbed hold of it tightly just before we began to walk away back toward the base and its brilliant lights. Jonas caught up to us quickly taking my other hand in his. Once we had reached the bases light limits, I turned back with tear stained cheeks to see Jagger standing motionless, watching me walk away.

Son of a bitch! Is this really happening right now? This is all so fucking painful it's making me exhausted. Is this feeling of Déjà vu that he is experiencing his brain trying to remember a little? How can I help him remember me?

When we got far enough away I stopped and said, "Of course he has a wife and children. What was I expecting? We had separate lives. I had a husband and children myself," I said laughing and crying at the same time. "This is silly and ridiculous. He is living his life and he's probably better without me and without remembering anything. I'm just so fucking selfish. Its stupid really...I'll be fine. I promise...I'll be fine. I need to get this job done so that I can move on and let it all go. He's alive and that's all that matters. Right? I'm happy that he's thriving and happy and that he has a life." I looked at Jonas and said, "Right?"

Jonas nodded at me with a concerned look.

"That's right Lil, let's just be happy he's alive," Marcus said. "What we do need to do is find out why we were lied to about him. And what else they're lying about. What if they know where Luna is?"

I took his hand and squeezed it, "We'll find her."

"Maybe we can find out what happened to the other Duals. How could they just disappear? Maybe we can disappear too once this is all done," Jonas whispered.

"Why were some of the soldiers memories erased and not others? I don't understand," I said.

As the questions continued to build without any true hope of finding answers we walked hand in hand toward the bright and starless military base.

32

The room we slept in was freezing cold again. All of the boys were wearing shorts and nothing else, sleeping over their blankets. I was in a sleeping bag that supposedly could handle minus 30-degree temperatures and still I shivered.

My sleep was restless as I relived the day in my mind over and over and over again. Reaching into Jonas' dream, I was not surprised to find him on the beach with Jack again. We need to figure out what happened to Jack. Poor Jonas...the same dream every night. This is a nightmare at this point, I thought leaving him to have his private Jack moments.

Turning my head slightly, I looked at the clock on the nightstand and saw that it was a little past four in the morning. Giving up the dream of getting any sleep, I slowly and quietly I climbed out of bed, put on my running clothes and went outside.

I began to run out in the same direction I had run the previous morning, hoping to see another spectacular sunrise. I ran past all of the bases buildings as the silence and solitude drew me away from it all, at least for a little while. Once I had found my comfortable pace, I began to sing songs to myself wishing I had an iPod and some headphones.

"It's a terrible love and I'm walking with spiders...and I can't fall asleep without a little help...it takes an ocean not to break..." I sang.

"That's one of my favorite songs, Terrible Love by The Nationals," Jagger said as he sneakily ran beside me.

Jumping with a scream, I instinctively threw my energy at him sending him flying into the air before ultimately landing in the sand thirty or so feet away from me. With escalating dread, I stood motionless waiting for him to move but he remained motionless.

"Oh my God, Did I kill you?" I asked in a panic as I ran to him. Landing on my knees beside him I began to shake him. "Peter! Can you hear me? Oh my God."

"Holy shit. Yeah, I'm okay. I just got the wind knocked out of me. I didn't mean to scare you. You've got quite the defense mechanism there," he said with a grunt as he rubbed his chest.

"What the hell are you doing sneaking up on me?" I shouted as I slapped his arm.

"Same as you, out for a morning run," he said with a smirk. "And I wasn't sneaking..."

"Well, I'm sorry if I hurt you. I would prefer to run alone please," I said pushing myself to stand and then breaking out into a sprint.

"Hey wait up," he said with a grunt as he stood and began to run after me. "Have I done something to offend you? I don't understand why you dislike me so much."

He caught up to me easily enough. I slowed my pace down to my comfortable speed, remaining silent as he ran beside me. Unhappy that he easily kept up my pace, I increased my speed again, which he had no problem keeping up with until finally remembering that speed had always been one of his abilities. I shook my head in defeat as I continued to run and ignore him. Well, attempting to ignore him.

After a few minutes, he firmly held my arm, forcing my legs to stop as he held me in place. "Stop. Look at me. Please," he demanded. After taking a deep breath he said, "Why do I feel this pull to you? I've been completely out of sorts for the past two days now. I'm having trouble concentrating on anything. I have no appetite. I tried to sleep and the moment I close my eyes, there you are. This is..." he paused,

"I feel entranced by you Lily. Every thought I have strays back to you. Please help me understand what is happening. Have you done something to make me feel this way? Who are you?" Jagger asked pleadingly while earnestly looking into my eyes. Tightening his grip on my arms as he came closer.

Telling myself that I needed to turn away and break free from his hold, I felt physically unable to move away from his grasp. I knew that I could make him let go of me, but I really didn't want him to. After a long pause with our eyes locked on each other, while my heart beating fiercely in my chest I gave myself permission to open up and accept the consequences, whatever they might be. After taking in a deep breath I began to explain it all.

"We grew up together Peter. In a place called the Homestead... It's a military funded home for orphaned children basically. A secret branch of the government called The Agency conducted experiments on us as infants while we lived at The Homestead. We were genetically modified as children. Experimented on in an attempt to be made into better fighters, weapons for the government essentially. That's how I can do what I do and how you can run so fast. You have been genetically enhanced." I paused allowing him to process a little bit at a time. "Jonas is my Dual...My other half essentially. We enhance each other's abilities; help with control and...where he goes I go. It's that simple. You were intended to be a Dual as well with a woman named Naomi. But due to genetic differences the bond was unsuccessful. So because of the abilities that you were able to develop, they sent you to another division of this top-secret initiative so that you could be trained as a soldier. Your military training began when you were a small child."

Pausing quickly to allow for him to process the information, he remained still and silent as he continued to hold my arms tightly. "When you turned 18, they sent you away to live with a scientist or a handler. I'm not sure who you were sent to live with actually. But anyway, before you were sent away, all of your childhood memories were erased. New memories, false memories were programmed into your mind. They were of you growing up surrounded by family and loved ones where you had happy childhood experiences and friends. Gap fillers basically so you wouldn't have any memory of what your life had really been like up to that point. Your life, the entire thing, was all planned out for you. The life experiences you have had outside of the military are all part of their design. Your wife and children bring you a sense of security. They bring balance and most importantly they make you feel like you're fighting for them. Keeping them safe from evil. But in reality we are all The Agencies pawns, puppets in their war."

He watched my lips as I spoke, transfixed by my words, uncertain of what to make of this tall tale I had just told him. The silence between us was so profound I began to hear his heart beat quicken and his mind processed all of the information. "I have parents and a family. I go home every few months to see them. You're insane," he said with a mocking laugh as he let go of my arms and began to walk away from me.

I grunted a laughing sound in response and then began to run again in the original direction I had been headed. Catching up to me quickly again and he said, "I'm sorry. Tell me more. This doesn't explain my pull to you. We grew up together in this Homestead place. Then what?"

After coming to a stop I turned to face him and with an irritated tone said, "We were in love Peter. You were my life and I was yours. The love I felt for you was... I loved you with every cell in my body. You will never know nor understand the pain that I feel right now, seeing you standing in front of me and yet you have no memory of who I am or what we meant to each other." I stopped talking for a few moments to try to collect myself while I began walking away from him. Keeping up with my pace, he followed me waiting for more information.

"I was told you were dead Peter. Killed in battle somewhere. I unravelled inside when I heard those words. It was as if the piece of you that lived inside of me had died as well and I would have died with it. Jonas kept me grounded while I mourned for you. He kept me going...Jonas and I, we were just brought back together not too long ago. Much like you I didn't know about all of this. I also had my memories cleared, new ones created. Sent to live with a handler for the sole purpose of gaining life experiences. I had a life too, on the outside. A life that I am beginning to believe was created for me so that I could grow and gain the knowledge they deemed necessary to consider me a conscientious adult," I explained mockingly. "I was married before they pulled me back in. I had a husband and two children. They're all dead now. And I wonder if they died because of me. Because of who or what I am. What I was made into." I looked at my hands and began to cry. "I loved you Peter. More than I can ever explain to you. Even when I had no memory of any of this, I unknowingly carried you with me." I reached into my shirt and pulled out the gold feather pendant. "You gave me this on the day we were separated. I have worn it almost everyday since. Keeping the memory of us with me always, even if just subconsciously."

"I know this," he said as he reached for the necklace. He held it in his hand and closed his eyes. "I have dreams about this. It's funny but I'm always flying in those dreams."

"You would fly with me all the time," I explained, cautiously reaching for his face. "Look at me. Please remember us." With a pleading look I stood on tiptoe and kissed him softly on the lips. I could feel the pull of the chain around my neck as he squeezed the pendant tighter and tighter in his hand sending a sensation of heat that moved down the chain like igniting gunpowder, burning all the way down to the pendant. It felt as if it were releasing a power I was unaware it contained. We both kept our eyes open as we kissed, seeing the glow from the chain reflecting in each other's eyes.

His body became tense as confusion flowed through his muscles. It felt as if the pendant itself had released something inside of him. Almost like opening a door that had been closed. He pulled away from me slightly and said breathlessly, "Lily. I remember this. I remember feeling this. Feeling you on my lips."

I opened my mouth to ask him what he remembered but he had already pulled me into his arms and began kissing me passionately with his eyes closed now. My stomach flipped and my face flushed while my lungs became incapable of breathing as I reciprocated his pull and kissed him back deeply and desperately. I wanted to dive into him so that I could stay with him, live in him and never leave him again. See what he saw and breathe his air. His hands traveled up the sides of body up to my neck and face, pulling and holding me to him.

"Lily," he breathed into my mouth. "I remember flying. I remember the feel of your lips and your body. I've been here, in your arms. This is all so familiar. I know this body. I know these lips. How they feel and how they taste," he said as he ran his hands over my breasts and abdomen, over my back and down to my ass. "Where have I been? Where have you been? What is happening to me? I didn't know that I had been missing you. Missing you from me. How is this all possible? These sensations...I can't explain it."

I cried as he kissed me, pulling his tongue into my mouth and tasting him again, feeling his tears fall onto my cheeks, mixing with mine.

"Oh my God Peter, I have missed you so much." I sobbed as I stroked his face. "Oh God," I breathed. "I'm so happy...Please keep remembering, even if it's just a little bit. It's all felt like it hadn't really happened. I thought maybe they had planted those memories too and that you weren't real. We weren't real."

"Lily," he said as he moved my hair away from my face. "What is happening to me Lily? What is happening?" he whispered as he kissed my eyes, my nose, and my lips. "When I close my eyes I see a lake...the two of us making love in the shade of an old weeping willow by a lake. There's a crow. I remember a crow flying overhead," he said with a quizzical look.

"His name is Raven. And yes he is a friend," I explained. "What you're seeing is our lake. Our secret spot where we would sneak away to be alone."

Leaning his forehead onto mine he started breathing deeply. With shaking breaths that matched my own, he continued to run his hands over my body. Desperately, he lifted my shirt over my head followed by my sports bra. He kissed my neck and made his way down to my nipples while cupping my breasts in his hands. I took off his shirt and ran my hands over his tight chest down to the top of his shorts, pushing them down to the sand.

The energy in my core began to rise, sending heat out of my skin as we lay in the sand kissing and touching, exploring with our hands and tongues, remembering each other's bodies until he climbed on top of me and pushed himself inside of me. I gasped as I felt his girth stretch and fill me. He kissed me intensely with a bottomless thirst, squeezing and holding my body tightly as he moved inside of me. Holding his face in my hands I pushed my hips up to meet his thrusts, pulling him deeper inside of me, kissing him hungrily between breaths.

"I remember this feeling. I remember how you feel, how you smell and how you taste. Oh Lily, what is happening to me? How could I love you so deeply? How can this be? I can't explain any of it... but I love you so much," he said as he cried into my mouth.

"I love you Peter. Remember all of me. Stay with me," I whispered.

The sun had begun to rise in the distance as we made love on the pink sand under the pink sky. We both climaxed with a shudder remaining linked long after, kissing and caressing each other's bodies. After a few minutes had gone by he fell to the side and leaned up on his elbow so that our faces could remain together. We watched the sunrise and the sky change colors.

"We need to get back," I said. "Jonas is worried about me."

He nodded while leaning in to kiss me again. "I feel like I've been asleep Lily. You've woken me up." He ran his hand down my neck and onto my breasts. "The gold feather marked you." Gently running his fingers between my breasts, he leaned down and kissed the mark before lifting his right hand to show me the mark on his palm. "Look. It marked me as well," he said showing me the burned brand of the feather on his hand. Lining up our marks so that they touched, he said. "I don't know what is happening to me but it feels...right. Like I am supposed to be here at this moment, with you. And I'm meant to remember. Remember my love for you," he said in a whisper leaning down to kiss me before making love to me again.

WE RAN BACK to the base at a normal human pace, trying to prolong our time together. Peter was positively jubilant. He would stop me every few feet to kiss me. Once we crossed into the bases border, Jonas came running to me pulling me away from Peter towards the showers.

"If you are going to run off like that, I don't care who you are with, you need to let down your shield every once in a while so I know you are safe. I have been out of my mind over here not knowing what is going on with you," he said frantically, bordering on shouting at me before pulling me into an embrace.

I looked over Jonas' shoulder and saw Peter standing there with a concerned look, readying himself to intervene. I smiled and shook my head, silently letting him know all was well. He smiled back and gave me a small wave as he turned toward his bunker.

"He remembers? And you had sex?" Jonas asked in a loud whisper completely flabbergasted.

"What?" Marcus asked as he approached with Jeff and Marc walking behind him.

"Look, all I'm going to tell you is that he remembers small bits. Glimpses really. But most importantly he remembers how he felt and how we loved each other. The rest doesn't matter if he ever remembers. I can fill in the pieces for him as much as I can," I said as I began to cry tears of joy. "Now I have sand in some very delicate parts and could really use a shower."

Before any of them could respond, I began walking towards the showers as Jeff asked Marc in a whisper, "Why does she have sand in her delicate parts? What did I miss?"

All of my boys started laughing as we made our way to the showers together.

33

I couldn't stop smiling as I relaxed under the hot shower while Jonas washed my hair. Marcus showered in his own stall while Jeff washed in another stall with Marc. Since the dividing walls were so short we could all continue to have face-to-face conversations under the water stream. The boys all talked while I remained silent in my bubble of bliss while having my scalp massaged.

The door to the bathroom building opened suddenly and in strode Peter wearing nothing but flip-flops and a towel. He took in the scene focusing especially on me, as I stood naked in the shower with Jonas. I could see the color leave his face.

"Hey there," I said to him with a wide smile.

He seemed deflated as he silently made his way to me, watching Jonas and I briefly before making his way to one of the other stalls and hesitantly turning on the shower. He began to wash with a sullen and confused look on his face. I walked out of my shower and went into his. I rubbed his back as the warm water beat down on his muscular body.

"Hey! I haven't rinsed the shampoo out of your hair yet," Jonas complained with a whine.

"It's Okay I can do it," I said quickly to dismiss him. "Peter look at me."

He turned and faced me. I rinsed the soap that was on his face and reached up to kiss him. "Jonas is my Dual. I know you don't understand what that is yet but trust me we are not lovers. We love one another deeply but our love does not go beyond that of siblings, friends. All of my team members are my brothers," I paused for a moment as I waited for him to relax his muscles a little. "Please tell me you understand. I am just finding you again and I don't want this fragile state we are in to be jeopardized. Please look at me. See me. I love you," I whispered into his closed lips.

He kissed me back deeply. When he finally pulled away he whispered in my ear, "I wash your hair from now on. Okay?"

I smiled and said with a nod, "Okay."

"She has really thick hair I just want you to know. It takes work to get that clean. And the conditioner has to sit in her hair for at least three minutes before you rinse it off. Otherwise it's a dry mess," Jonas said in a semi-joking tone.

We all broke out into laughter including Peter. He shook his head closing his eyes as he leaned down to kiss me. "I love you," he whispered.

Peter did rinse my hair with some coaching from Jonas over the wall and I conditioned my own hair.

WE SPENT the day reading and talking. It was an R&R day they said. They always have a day of rest between missions, when they can of course. When dinnertime rolled around everyone was ready for a little celebration. Roberts was so happy with how our mission had gone that he let everyone drink beer with dinner. We all ate together telling stories and rehashing our mission to Roberts once again, who seemed shocked to hear about how ultimately everything played out in the apartment.

"Well, Lily you certainly are a surprise. I must tell you I did not have very high hopes for you when I first saw you. Shy little thing, constantly clinging to Jonas, I thought you were going to be our weakest link. Well, you showed me. Welcome to the team," he raised his beer and everyone cheered. I turned to Jonas who was sitting beside me and gave him a bashful smile while blinking my lashes quickly. He leaned forward and kissed my forehead.

Peter held my hand under the table, not letting it go for a single moment. Roberts noticed this and at one point said as he cleared his throat, "Captain Jagger, your wife called this morning. She asked for you to call her back."

Well, that was a harsh wakeup call. I let go of Peter's hand and put both of my elbows on the table.

"Thank you sir," Jagger replied dryly, watching me take my hand away from his. He immediately reached for my leg and gently squeezed it.

Jonas began rubbing my back in an attempt to comfort me. I looked over at Peter and asked with a polite smile, "What are your kids names?"

Gazing out into the distance he seemed to be preparing himself to talk to me about his family, "Lily and Jonas."

Sitting across from me, Marcus spit out his beer, nearly covering me with it. "You're kidding!" Marcus shouted.

With wide eyes, goose bumps rose on my skin as I processed this shocking revelation. I couldn't respond. I sat frozen with a blank stare, as did Jonas.

"You've been with me this entire time too," Peter whispered turning to Jonas and me. I nodded in response. "I love you," he whispered to me with his eyes closed. "I don't understand how this is all possible and how I could feel this way so quickly, but I've never been more certain about anything in my life," he said. I took his right hand and kissed the feather mark on his palm.

"Ok boys and girls, we have an early day tomorrow. Don't stay up too late," Roberts said as he rose before striding off to bed.

"Goodnight sir," several men said.

We stayed up for several more hours. The Gonzalez brothers

were in deep discussions with Jeff and Marc. Marcus tried to explain to many of the men what his abilities were as they sat there in awe intently listening. Jonas and Brian O'Connell sat a few seats away from me, whispering closely to each other. I was a bit surprised when I secretly listened in to learn that Brian was very much attracted to Jonas. *'Well, I didn't see that coming'*, I thought as I smiled at him.

After several hours, I kissed Peter goodnight and said, "I'll see you tomorrow."

He kissed me back and said, "I love you. Dream of me."

With a fading smile I responded seriously, "Every night." Before standing and making my way to my teams bunker alone.

JONAS RAN after me and we walked arm in arm together to our bunker. We climbed into bed, Jonas half naked and me in the sleeping bag made for the Arctic Circle, facing each other smiling.

"I haven't seen you this happy in decades," Jonas said to me.

"I can't remember being this happy... and so scared," I responded sadly. After a few short moments I said, "So Brian O'Connell huh? He's cute," I said in a whisper teasingly.

Jonas rolled his eyes and smiled. "Yeah, he's cute and sweet," he shrugged.

"Well, he likes you back so don't worry about letting that guard of yours down," I said with a soft understanding smile.

His own smile slowly faded before responding, "What if Jack is out there, waiting for me? Like Peter was. All this time," he whispered with a sigh. I could see the wheels turning in his mind.

After a few moments I said, "I don't know if he is or if he isn't. What I do know is that he isn't here right now. And you deserve to be happy or at the very least have a fling with someone. I can't be as happy as I can be if you're not happy too," I said as I reached across to stroke his cheek.

"I love you darling. Sleep well," Jonas said.

"I love you too. Goodnight my loves," I said to the room as all of my boys responded sleepily.

I WOKE UP WITH STARTLED. Jonas was in his usual position, arm draped across me with his leg straddling my legs despite the divot between our beds. Turning away from him, I silently jumped and screeched when I noticed that there was someone sitting on the floor beside my bed. I could hear a slight snore coming from the slumped figure. With a bit of effort I was finally able to focus my eyes in the dark only to discover that it was Peter sleeping while seated on the floor beside my bed.

I reached over and began stroking his hair before whispering, "Peter! Peter, come on. Come up here," I said while pulling him up to my bed.

Without saying a word, he sleepily stood before climbing onto my cot, reaching his arm under my head to pull my body into his. It was as if we had been sleeping like this for years. Like all of the time that had passed didn't change how we were with each other. The cot creaked its complaint under both of our body weights making me nervous about how we would likely be waking up with a crash, but I didn't care. I have never felt safer than at this moment. My head on Peter's chest listening to his healthy heart beating as he held me tightly, while Jonas' arm and leg remained draped over my body. My two loves surrounding me. My life was momentarily perfect.

I WOKE UP HEARING JAMES' voice, "Captain Jagger. Wake up please. You are being summoned by Major Roberts."

Peter startled awake and said, "Thank you James. I'm on my way."

Rubbing his eyes he laid his head back down on the pillow. I leaned over momentarily to get a look over at the clock on the night-stand to discover that it was two in the morning. Reaching out with my senses, I felt an alarm sounding in the control bunker. There was a vehicle approaching the base and it wasn't friendly energy that I sensed.

Peter leaned down, "Stay here," he whispered while kissing me before walking out.

He and James left the building and made their way to the control bunker. I jumped out of bed followed by Jeff and Marc, who were surprisingly awake. Marcus and Jonas continued to snore undisturbed. The three of us ran outside, me in a t-shirt and underwear while Jeff and Marc sported boxer briefs. I instinctively encased the base in a shield sensing the negativity coming from the approaching vehicle as it made its way toward us in the dark. Once the three of us had arrived at the perimeter we sensed that there were two men, both heavily armed speeding through the sand with their malicious intentions, thinking of nothing but vengeance for their fallen friends.

Jeff and Marc reached their magnetic charges out pulling weapons from somewhere and were instantly ready to return oncoming fire. When the vehicle was finally within eyesight and the passengers could clearly see us beneath the bases brightly shining lights, they begin screaming at us in Pashto before suddenly opening fire. While Jeff and Marc began shooting, I instantly pulled the air around me, willing it to push me up high above the base.

As quickly rose up into the night sky, I heard Peter yelling, "Oh my God Lily. Stop!"

I continued my ascent until the altitude felt sufficient for me to do what I needed to do. Stretching my ability out to the vehicle, I wrapped the wind around the explosive laden car and lifted it easily off of the sand, keeping it far from shielded borders of the base. I lifted the hunk of metal with the infuriated locals until the air was thin and the men had clearly begun to struggle for breath. With single-minded intention and focus the men continued to fire their weapons at me despite their hypoxic brains. But I was not to be deterred as I continued to rise with the vehicle. Watching the men intently, I made my way to stand on the hood of the vehicle feeling its cold metal beneath my bare feet. With a sudden whoosh, Jonas descended beside me in his boxers. He took my hand tightly into his as we stood side by side, watching the men until they stopped struggling. Touching their minds with my own, I confirmed that they had indeed suffocated to death.

Jonas and I slowly began descending along with the vehicle and as my long brown hair flicked around my head, I turned back to Jeff and Marc sending them a quick signal to reengage the explosives from the buried mines we had unearthed. Hearing the mechanics reconnect, Jonas and I pushed the vehicle directly over the targeted pile and unceremoniously dropped it. We moved away quickly as the vehicle plummeted back to earth, directly above the mound of explosives. The moment that there was contact the mines began to violently detonate. Sending shrapnel and larger pieces of metal in a scattered pattern around the explosion site.

As the eruptions continued, we returned to the base to find Peter in a cold sweat panic standing at the border of my shield as Brian also watched our approach with concern.

The moment we landed, Jeff and Marc ran to us still holding their guns. But before they could say a word, Peter rushed behind them and reached his arms between them, to pull me into his arms while the rest of the military men made their way towards our small cluster.

"Lily you scared the shit out of me," he breathed into my hair.

"Ms. Lily what did you and Mr. Jonas do to those men?" Major Roberts asked us a little out of breath as he ran toward us.

I stepped a few inches away from Peter and looked at Jonas with a concerned look. "We um, killed them sir," I answered flatly.

"Well, why did you take them all the way up there?" Roberts said while pointing to the sky.

"I thought it would be nicer to suffocate them first sir. Then blow them up with their own explosives," I answered as I shook my head alarmed at how positively psychotic I sounded. "It was almost instinctual, I didn't really give it much thought."

Suddenly, the Gonzalez brothers broke out into laughter as everyone followed suit. Peter finally began laughing with relief that I was back in his arms safely. There was nervous laughter coming from the military men as they looked at each other in disbelief. Regardless of how ridiculous I sounded, I was happy that my words helped release the tension the sudden threat had caused.

After verifying the bases safety, everyone returned to bed except for Brian and Jonas who remained on watch for the night. Peter and I slept soundly the remainder of the night holding each other tightly on my creaky cot.

34

It turns out that there are many enemy targets plotting against us not far from our location. It became clear to me that the work that was being done on this base was incredibly important for the survival and success of all troops fighting the same enemy. I wasn't however, convinced that the elimination of terrorist activity in this part of the world would actually make a legitimate impact at reducing terrorism overall, and wondered if it could perhaps be making it worst. Were we just providing enemies with the psychological ammunition they needed to inspire others to rise against what they deemed enemies to their cause? It was like asking what came first the chicken or the egg.

Despite my inner dissection of this issue our lives on the base continued. The days that followed the attempted attack were filled with training exercises. Peter and I would begin our mornings with a run that was always interrupted by love making in the dunes. These were my favorite times of the day. Where I could relish in the feel of his skin against mine, his firm hold on my body and our long passionate kissing. Our bodies and minds seemed to melt into one, making me smile and cry all at once, overwhelmed by how beautiful we were together. The intensity of our love and passion for one another had just continued to grow surpassing anything I could have imagined.

We spent as much time together during the day as possible. His memories began to quickly resurface, remembering more and more everyday, frequently interrupting our activities when sudden flashes of a memory appeared to him. He would come running to me to share what he had just seen and confirm that his visions were accurate.

Brian and Jonas became quite enamored with each other as well during this time. I would catch them sneaking a kiss in the shadows sometimes. Jonas still had trepidations about Brian, but he was trying to open up and let down his guard. That's all I had ever hoped for him. Whether he and Brian would ultimately fall in love and spend the rest of their lives together didn't really matter to me. All I cared about was that for the moment he had found happiness and even maybe a little respite from the nightmare that Jack had become to him. And for that I was very thankful to Brian.

The Gonzalez brothers were under the watchful eyes of Jeff and Marc. With their help, the brothers were able to start shedding some light on their past as their memories began to slowly return to them as well. The brothers turned out to have quite the empathetic ability and at times seemed to be developing clairvoyance. Their Dual connection was quite strong as well making us often wonder if The Agency had deemed their abilities to not be very beneficial from a military perspective and so perhaps their abilities had not been encouraged when they were children. The Agency wanted efficient killers and the brothers ability would never evolve into something that would be beneficial in a time of war. What they were looking for was exactly what I had become.

We also learned that all of the Corvus soldiers had been at the Homestead, including Roberts who had known all of his men since infancy. All of the men, with the exception of Roberts, had had the same experiences as the Gonzalez brothers in terms of memory clearing and then living with handlers for a short while before enlisting. Roberts was a senior person at The Homestead. His role was that of a handler for all of the men once they had enlisted, monitoring and training them as adults, still seeing how far their genetic modifications had taken them. Despite Roberts' status within The Agency, his loyalty to their vision had been waning for several years because he cared for these men as if they had been his sons.

Curiously, all of the men began to experience memory recollections since our arrival. Their senses began to heighten and the abilities that they had been able to develop under the experimentations at The Homestead, strengthened with our presence. Despite all of the excitement surrounding these discoveries, there was also a great deal of anger about what they had endured and unknowingly sacrificed.

The Five of us worked closely with them in the hopes that they would continue to recall the reality of their lives and to also help them understand that each of them was special in their own way in terms of abilities. Roberts was completely on board with our training of his men and encouraged their memory recollections as much as he could, often helping them piece together the sudden flashes that would appear to them. His time with the men had been almost constant after their arrival at The Homestead as infants, with the exception of the short period of time when they were with their handlers. Other than that, he had been with them everyday since. The men did feel some anger at him for not helping them remember sooner but the love and respect they had for him led them to understand that like them, he had been following orders his entire life as well.

One afternoon while I was helping the team put away equipment in the training center we had used for hand-to-hand combat training, Steven Charvis approached me meekly. I smiled warmly at him and waited for him to build up his courage to say what he wanted say to me. His trepidation was thick in the air as he placed his hands in his pants pockets. He was a good-looking man. He was quite tall with black hair and honey colored eyes that watched me intently.

"I remember you Lily," Charvis said shyly. "So far many of my memories have been about you."

"What about me? My abilities you mean?" I asked.

He shook his head and just as he had opened his mouth to explain what it was he meant, Peter came into the room drawing my attention away from Charvis. Noticing my response to Peter, Charvis smiled sadly before turning to walk out of the room.

"Charvis wait. What did you have to tell me?" I asked him as he walked through the door and out of the room. He left me wondering for a few moments what it was he had to say until Peter approached and kissed me sweetly as he held my face, instantly making me forget what it was I had just been doing.

Marcus' determination to find Luna seemed to grow daily in the passing weeks. When he learned that Roberts had maintained his memories, his inquiry of him about Luna intensified. During this time, Marcus had also started working intensely with all of the men in a selfish attempt to facilitate the return of their memories in the hopes that maybe at least one of them could shed some light on the Luna mystery. Much to his deep disappointment, none of the men remembered her. Roberts wasn't much help either. He was only able to reinforce what we had already known. He explained that she had become uncontrollable after their separation. It became difficult to keep her abilities in control. Ultimately, she was transferred to another base for further management. Marcus was visibly upset and disheartened when he heard this information which corroborated what Naomi had told him. Roberts' sadness was clear to see when he shared this information with Marcus.

"It doesn't matter where she was sent Marcus. We are going to find her after this," I promised, holding him tightly as he wept on my shoulder.

Jonas and I tried to stay with him as much as we could. But he would often go for runs on his own, far enough away from the base where he could use his abilities. We would all feel the earth often quivering while he was away.

One day Martins came running to Marcus in a panic, explaining he had just had a memory about Luna. He explained that he remembered the day they were separated, when she was dragged away fitfully. Martins said that at night her screams were intolerable in their subterranean bunker beneath the Homestead. Many of the men had tried to comfort her but she was blind with fury. Martins also explained that he remembered her walking around like a zombie for a while in a drugged stupor. The doctors from the Agency had started to medicate her in an effort to calm her down until one day, after an episode in the mess hall where she was able to get her hands on a kitchen knife and had actually successfully killed one of the guards, she was sent away. That was the last time he had seen her.

This new information threw Marcus into a tailspin. He was more determined than ever to leave the base. He would have private meetings with Roberts asking for his help. Much to everyone's surprise, Roberts was more than willing to help with the little information he had. Sharing maps and locations of other Agency bases.

"I'm worried about Marcus," I said to Jonas one morning at breakfast. "He isn't sleeping or eating. He thinks of nothing else."

"Wouldn't you be the same way if something happened to me? I know I would be. I know I was, until I found you that night," Jonas replied. I reached for his hand across the table and squeezed it as I nodded in acknowledgement.

"We'll find her," Marc said determinedly beside me.

NIGHTS for the Five of us had changed astronomically as well. After Peter had begun to sleep in our barrack nightly, Brian soon moved in as well. Emilio and Gus followed not long after and then ultimately all of us were crowded into the small space. The energy in the room was filled with acceptance and love. We had all been reunited. All of us reverting to our childhood need of being surrounded by the energy that each of us uniquely exuded.

35

One afternoon we received information from another unit not far from us that there were militants in another city much further than the one we had already cleared. These new militants had essentially picked up where the others had been forced to leave off and were now involved in putting together additional foreign enemy cells.

"What other unit?" Marc asked.

"Units like ours?" I asked Roberts. "Did you know about this?" I asked turning to Peter.

"Yes, they are like us but much larger. With more soldiers and a bigger base. The Agency decided to introduce The Five to a smaller unit, our unit to begin your acclimation slowly. The other units are composed of other former Homestead kids," Roberts said with a slight sullenness to his tone. "The Agency is requesting that you assist them with cleaning this city up as well."

"Could Luna be with one of these groups?" Marcus asked firmly.

Roberts just shook his head and replied, "No son. She isn't." After a pause he continued, "Prepare to go in everyone."

"Okay ladies, you heard him. Prepare to leave in 10 minutes," Peter shouted.

Peter made his way to me once everyone disbanded, "I want you next to me always Okay?" he said as he held my face closely to his. I nodded before kissing him. I then ran to Jonas who had waited for me with his outstretched hand reaching for me. As Jonas and I made our way to our bunker, I looked back to find Peter and was surprised to discover that he had remained where he had been standing, intensely watching me with obvious concern. I smiled at him reassuringly but his demeanor remained unchanged as his gaze remained fixed on my departing form.

WE TRAVELLED into the city in Melissa of course, with O'Connell behind the wheel. He would often glance in the rearview mirror to sweetly make eye contact with Jonas.

Once we were in the city limits, I could feel intense eyes on us immediately.

"Let me out Brian," I said firmly.

"You will do no such thing. Remain in the vehicle!" Peter commanded O'Connell as he turned to me.

But it was too late. Jonas and I had already opened the door and had jumped out, locking it all up so that no one could follow us. Peter kicked at the door to get out but it was useless despite his strength.

"Jeff! Jam the towns signals," I said, as I looked Jeff in the vehicle.

Peter's face reddened with rage as he began to shout at us through the windshield. "Goddamn it Lily. Get back in this fucking vehicle."

Ignoring him, Jonas and I continued to walk as the HUMV followed closely behind. Reaching out into the homes, I could feel all of the individual hearts beating. I felt confident that I could stop those beats if I needed to.

We made our way through the winding streets often met by several curious pedestrians who would nervously turn and run away after getting a good look at us. The sun beat down on us as the dry sand and dirt filled the air around us. Sweat dripped down my back sticking my white tank top to my body while my beige camo pants became dust covered as my boots kicked up the parched earth. My hair remained under control in a bun at the top of my head while my eyes scoped out our surroundings through my dark sunglasses. Jonas wore essentially the same clothes minus the sunglasses. Even though I was relishing in how the heat felt on my skin, I knew that this would not be well tolerated by him for a prolonged period of time. We continued on our path as the local women watched me contemptuously through their windows. It was easy for me to detect their disgust at what they deemed my immodest attire and uncovered hair. They believed I should be ashamed for walking in their streets in this way.

Glancing back to the vehicle, I saw Peter white knuckle gripping the dashboard with fear in his eyes as he watched me intently. Motioning with my right hand, the locks in the vehicle clicked in release. Peter responded in a flash, jumping out of the shotgun seat and making his way to me. He continued to look at me with a mixture of fright and anger, all mixed with love and adoration.

I gave him a quick wink and smile before saying, "I can feel the other Agency troops on the far side of town."

"Let's make our way towards them," Peter said.

We continued walking as curious eyes followed our progression. I couldn't imagine how weird it must be for these town residents. It was time for their mid-day meals and the air was filled with the smells of food being cooked by the women in their homes. Children ran around in the streets playing in the debris of the destroyed buildings. Despite it all and despite our presence, there were still produce markets and people having coffee in the small corner shops.

"This is so surreal," I said. "Lives continue despite the threats, deaths and destruction."

While vigilantly scoping the rooftops for signs of danger, I happened to notice a young woman watching us as she stood in the hot sun with her long sleeves and head covering, while holding a small child in her arms. I smiled at her when we made eye contact, imagining what her life was like in the chaos. In a burst of spoke and sparks, a rocket was shot from the rooftop of a tall building a few blocks away from where we were.

Briefly caught off guard, my response was slightly delayed as I let out a scream before jumping up to intercept it, only to be immediately met with a bright flash as the bomb impacted the thick shield I had created around us. Peter and Jonas grunted when the bomb exploded as their bodies were propelled into the air and onto the hood of the HUMV. Catching site of the guilty shooter as he surveyed the damaged he had achieved, my body shook with rage as I pulled a concentrated ball of energy out of myself and flung it in his direction. Instantly exploding not only our attacker but also a large portion of the building he had been standing on. I remained airborne briefly watching the pieces of concrete come crashing down, still shocked at what I had just done.

With ringing ears I quickly descended back to the vehicle as Jonas stirred.

"Jonas, are you OK?" I screamed.

"Just got the wind knocked out of me. I'm Okay," Jonas replied as he pushed himself back onto his feet.

"Peter!" I shouted. I looked in the HUMV and everyone seemed Okay. Jeff and Marc had already jumped out with their weapons and returning fire from the other assailants who were now leaving their hiding spots to attack us.

"Peter! Oh my God. Peter!" I screamed as I searched the rubble around the HUMV.

"I'm all right. I'm here," I heard Peter respond.

Running to him, I was immediately panicked at the sight of his dust and debris covered body. After wiping dusting him off, I saw blood seeping through small tears in his uniform, but was relieved to discover that his injuries were not life threatening.

I kissed him fiercely, "Are you Okay? I'm so sorry, I must have let my guard down for a moment. I'm so sorry," I begged.

"I'm Okay. This is not your fault. Come on, we have to go," he said as he stood with a grunt.

Once I had made my way back to the front of the vehicle to where

Jonas stood, I turned to him and asked, "You ready?" To which he barely preceptively nodded in agreement.

The both of us rose into the air, hand in hand strengthening each other's abilities. Drawing the fire out from my body I created a large blazing sphere that hovered in front of us. Once the sphere had grown sufficiently and the heat intensified, I sent it hurtling through the air towards a group of combatants that had gathered in the street and had started to make their way toward us as they fired their guns. Several of the men and women who were engaged in the gunfire, dove out of the way but the flames found them regardless of where they hid, sending them running and screaming as their flesh painfully burned. With impressive marksmanship, Jeff and Marc quickly shot each victim in the head in the hopes of shortening their pain. Jonas extinguished flames that threatened innocent homes with freezing gusts of rain.

The remaining combatants continued to fire on the Corvus men until Marcus engaged. He jumped up into the air and with fisted hands he punched the dirt as he came forcibly down, shaking the earth aggressively, opening a crater beneath the feet of our attackers, swallowing them up as they fell into the newly formed deep crevices.

It was in that moment that The Agencies plan for us had truly come to fruition, we were lethal as a team, able to eliminate the enemy effortlessly and efficiently, with no casualties suffered on our side of the fight.

When all finally seemed quiet below, Jonas and I descended back to the ground. As soon as my feet were firmly planted on the parched earth I searched for the woman and her child, whom I had been watching so intently. I was sad to discover that they both had been victims of the initial explosion.

"Oh God I'm so sorry," I said to the woman as I bent over her and her child's lifeless bodies.

After a few moments of standing in the bloody debris, Peter took my hand and coaxed me away from the sad scene.

"You are the most amazing creature I have ever seen," Peter said into my ear as he held me in a tight embrace. "I love you so much."

I remained silent in his embrace processing the destruction we had all just brought upon this area of the city. Seeing Jonas stand behind Peter, I reached my hand out to him so that I could hold him as well. Brian walked over and rubbed Jonas' back. Jeff and Marc stood by Melissa still on high alert as they scanned the rooftops.

"Where is Marcus?" I asked as I looked around us.

In a panic, I quickly let go of Peter as we desperately searched our surroundings. But he was nowhere in site. *'Marcus! Where are you?'* Jeff shouted silently.

'I'm all right. I'm with the other troop,' Marcus quickly responded.

Looking at Jonas I said in a panic, "We have to go. Now!"

"What's going on?" Peter asked the group of us.

"It's Marcus. He's made his way across the city to the other troops. We have to go to him. You all go back to the base, we will meet you there as soon as we can. Jeff and Marc, go with them please. We can reach out to you if we need help," I said to everyone.

"No way," Peter said flummoxed.

"Peter. Lily and I can do this. We need to retrieve Marcus and then we will return. The three of us can fly back. We can take care of one another. Please go back to the base," Jonas said firmly.

Almost as if on cue, Ken Martins' voice boomed through the communications device calling for Captain Jagger. Ken had stayed back with Roberts to serve as navigations coordinator for the team.

"This is Jagger," Peter said with an annoyed tone as he spoke into the speaker still tightly holding onto my hand, fearing that I would leave him.

"Your wife called into the base using the emergency number. Seems there was an accident at home. She seemed hysterical sir. You should call her back pronto."

I could feel my heart drop. All of the time we had spent together, she had never come up in discussion. All I knew about his life outside of the military was that his children were named Jonas and Lily. I suddenly felt ashamed to admit that I didn't even know what his wife's name was.

"You need to go and call her back Peter. We will be fine," I said in a sad tone. I tried to not feel jealous.Our circumstances were quite bizarre. We had no clear definitions about what we were to each other, the boundaries were skewed because of our past and we had no guidance. "Go," I said while nodding with false reassurance. "We'll be fine, I promise."

He took in a deep breath and pulled me into a kiss. "Be careful. Please," he pleaded.

"Okay, let's go," Captain Jagger commanded.

Jonas and Brian embraced and quickly kissed goodbye, promising to see each other shortly.

Jonas and I stood, hand-in-hand as we watched Melissa back out of the rubble and drive away from us. Brian and Peter were visibly panicked at leaving us behind. While Jeff and Marc gave us a reassuring nod through the back passenger window. Once they were all out of site, I allowed just one tear to escape, creating a muddy streak through my dust-covered skin.

"I'm scared I'm going to lose him again," I whispered in a panicked tone.

"I know darling. I know," Jonas said while squeezing my hand.

"Let's go get our boy back," I said determinedly.

In the sudden silence, the city people had started to make their way out of their homes to survey what had happened. Some of them became frozen at discovering Jonas and I standing at the center of a round clearing that was seemingly undamaged. A piece of road that had clearly been protected while the surrounding area had been severely damaged and destroyed. I was bombarded with the people's sense of fear and disbelief at seeing that the stories about Jonas and I had been real and not just a tall tale created by imaginative children.

Silently, Jonas began a torrential downpour of cold rain in an effort to camouflage us from prying eyes while encouraging other potential onlookers from coming out of their homes. In my protective shield we lifted into the sky and quickly made our way across the city, to Marcus' location.

The troops were easily discovered standing in the rain with Marcus yelling at them over the sounds of the heavy downpour. Once

I saw what was happening, I covered them with a shield so that not only were they protected from the rain, but Marcus could also ask them what he had been yearning to know.

Jonas and I dropped down beside him quite suddenly, making several of the men jump back startled while the rest of the troops stood open mouthed watching us in awe. Their stares moved between Jonas and myself, and the invisible bubble that blocked the rain from reaching them.

"You Okay?" I asked Marcus who had been trying to show the men a picture of Luna.

"It seems that their memories are not as advanced as the Corvus men," Marcus responded in a huff.

Turning my attention to the gawking men, I couldn't help but smile as a familiar face approached us from behind the teams' vehicle. Making my way toward him, I reached up on my tip toes for an embrace and was quickly lifted into his thick warm arms, "Hello Gunther," I greeted him warmly.

Jonas and Marcus made their way to him shaking his hand in greeting after he had put me back down.

"Glad to see you're all right Miss," Gunther said warmly to me.

I smiled at him and said, "I'm glad to see you as well Gunther."

"We heard a lot of commotion on the other side of the city. Your Sergeant notified us that you would be there and that things might get a bit rowdy," Gunther said with a chuckle as he lifted an eyebrow.

"Everything go alright out there?" a short stocky man asked from behind us.

"Yes, everyone from our team is fine. Someone shot a rocket missile at us from a rooftop... They've been taken care of," Jonas responded without emotion.

"You all with the Corvus team?" the short stocky guy asked Jonas.

"We are. I am Jonas. This is Lily and Marcus. And you are?" Jonas asked.

"I'm Captain Perry and we're the Blue Bird Squad. We heard that Corvus might have the Duals with them," Captain Perry said.

Well, that came as a surprise.

"Really? You heard about the Duals?" I asked Captain Perry, having to look down to make eye contact. I seemed to tower over him in my 5 feet 8 inch stature.

"We were told about the experiments, yes. We were also told about the Homestead. They said they were releasing the memories in stages," Perry explained bitterly.

I turned to Jonas and Marcus raised my eyebrows in surprise. The Agency is making a move. Why would they be releasing everyone now? Was this part of the experiment? Part of the overall plan?

"We are looking for someone you may remember then. She was a dear friend of ours. Her name is Luna. Marcus here has a picture of her. Have any of you seen her perhaps? At any point at all?" I asked gesturing to Marcus to show them the picture he tightly held.

Captain Perry took the picture in his small hand and looked at it closely. I could tell he recognized her. "I think I remember her from the Homestead. I don't believe I have seen her since then though. I'm sorry," Perry said as he passed the picture around.

The three of us stood there with anticipation, waiting for the picture to make its way around to all of the men. They were 25 men strong with multiple vehicles to shuttle them around, most were much larger than Melissa.

A man in the back of the group stepped forward and said, "Yes. I remember her. She was a feisty one...Very strong. I believe I saw her about 2 years ago, we were stationed in Stockholm," he said.

Marcus walked to him and asked, "Stockholm. Was it a base? Where was she planning on going after that? Do you know where she went?"

"Yes, it was a small base in the far North of Sweden. In a town called Lycksele. I was with her just before we were sent here. I'm not sure where she was sent after that." the man said.

"Thank you," Marcus said while shaking his hand. "Tell me your name please."

"Cooper," the man responded.

Marcus radiated with joy as he smiled at Jonas and me. I couldn't help but feel suspicious of this information.

"Neat trick with the rain here. Does it stop bullets too?" Captain Perry asked motioning to the shield.

"Yes, it does," I said dryly.

"You three want to come spend some time with us? Show us what you can do?" Captain Perry asked. "God knows we could really use the help."

"No," I said quickly and firmly. "We need to get back to Corvus. But thank you for the offer."

"I'll leave the rain so you can leave under its cover," Jonas said.

"Thank you. It's nice to feel rain actually," Perry said with a wink. "I hope to see you all again soon."

"How long have you all been here?" I asked as I looked around at the group.

"Two years," Perry said flatly.

That time span seemed to be very common these days. Two years seems to have been the date The Agency had chosen to re-engage their creations.

I walked over to Gunther and said, "It was nice to see you again my friend. Take care of yourself," I said as I squeezed his arm. "Hey, did you know who we were back in Tunisia?" I whispered to him.

He smiled and nodded his response. "I did. But the other fellas had no idea."

"Well, its good to see you again," I said warmly.

"You take care now Miss Lily," he said sweetly before quickly glancing at my gold feather necklace.

Before turning away from him, I pulled him further away from the group of men and asked, "How is it that The Agency is having you all remember? What are they doing? Is there someone from The Agency at your base?"

"Yes Miss, they make us all drink this bitter green medicine every morning. It makes about half of us sick to our stomach. But that's when the flashes come...with the pain in our stomachs," he responded seriously. "I don't know if there is anyone from The Agency there. But there sure are a lot of secrets being kept though, that's for sure."

Nodding in understanding I whisper, "Be careful Gunther."

With a last goodbye, I took Jonas' and Marcus' hand just before removing the shield, allowing the downpour to reach the men. After shielding us during our assent into the sky, Jonas increased the intensity of the downpour further so that Captain Perry and his men could experience a nice rainstorm that could also provide them with a thick cover so that they could safely make their way out of the city and back to their base.

Wanting a little space, Marcus let go of my hand and dropped to the ground with a loud rumble. He made his way back to the base alone as his mind filled with plans, further strengthening his determination to find his missing Luna.

36

J onas and I had landed safely back at the base and moments later Marcus came barreling down after us. Marcus couldn't contain his smile and his joy felt contagious. Jeff and Marc along with Emilio and Gus ran to welcome us back and to inquire about the other squad and if they had any information about where Luna was. Realizing that there was nothing else that bring such a bright smile to Marcus' face.

Scanning the group for Peter my attention was drawn to Gus as he said sullenly, "He's in his bunker." Knowing exactly who I had been looking for.

I ran to his barracks in a panic, discovering that he had been packing his bag. "What's going on?" I asked.

He took in a deep breath before answering as he paused from packing. "There's been an accident. It's my son Jonas. They were in a car accident. Jonas didn't make it," he said as he sobbed silently. I placed my hand on his shoulder and tried to pull him into an embrace, but he resisted and pushed away before saying, "I have to go home. My wife needs me. My daughter needs me."

He began packing again, more frantically this time with an obvious need to run away from me and my touch.

"I love you Lily, so much. But I can't do this to them. I made a vow when I married Cara. I have a daughter I love...Who will painfully remind me of you everyday," he said softly while intentionally keeping his gaze from me. After a few breaths he turned around and kissed me hungrily with his tear stained face. Once he pulled away from me he put his nose into my hair and neck as he held me tightly. "I'm sorry. I'm so sorry. I love you. I love you so much. You are my deepest and most important love."

Trying to remain as strong as I could, I held onto the tears and pain with all of my might. "I understand Peter. I love you. I love you so much," I said as my voice shook with despair. I slowly let go of him and sat on his cot feeling myself becoming lightheaded. I closed my eyes trying to control my panting breaths while the pain from what had been happening began to course through my body. "I feel like you're dying all over again," I said as my body shook and uncontrollably released a flood of tears I could no longer contain.

"I know. I am so sorry. I just can't do this to them," he pulled me into a desperate kiss and said, "I love you," into my open mouth as we breathed in each other one last time. "Forgive me. Please," he pleaded.

In one swift move, he pulled away from me and picked up his full duffel bag throwing it over his shoulder as he took long and quick steps out of his bunker. His stride forced me into a jog as I followed him to the hangar where a small plane waited for him. Picking up his pace he ran up the steps without turning or saying another word to me.

I stood at the bottom of the steps, hoping that he would change his mind and come down to me. I reached out to him with my mind and felt the overwhelming pain and despair that flowed through his body. I soaked up his pain, drawing it into myself so that I could then push it to all of my cells, infecting them with his aching.

The steps were quickly moved away from the plane, as I stood immobile and in shock, watching one of the pilots close the planes door. Forcing my feet to move, I walked down the length of the airplane until I found him sitting by a window. He sat stiffly facing forward, stoically and intentionally not turning to face me.

"Peter...please look at me," I begged through my tears while shouting in despair.

I could feel him shattering and knew that he didn't have the strength to look at me. I began to shake uncontrollably as the plane began to move away. Running after the plane, I screamed his name over and over again. But he remained unmoving self-contained despite my pleading. Just before I disappeared from his site, he turned to look at me one last time before placing his open hand on the glass showing me his feather brand.

I fell hard on the tarmac as the plane lifted off. My despair turned into an animalistic scream before it morphed into silence, as my mouth remained open but unable to make a sound. Jonas fell to the ground beside me and lifted me up onto his lap pulling me into a tight embrace. Marcus fell in on the other side, followed by Jeff and Marc. They all held me tightly as I continued to silently scream and shake. Emilio and Gus sat beside us holding each other as they cried along with us. Brian kneeled behind Jonas and stroked my hair as my hysterical crying persisted.

JONAS CARRIED me to my cot, where I lay in silence with my knees drawn to my chest, silently oozing tears. I held Peter's pillow tightly beneath my head soaking in his scent. Night had fallen without much notice. The boys had tried to feed me as I lay in an almost catatonic state, tears long since dried up. They carried me to the showers and bathed me in scalding hot water as Jonas hummed while washing my hair. But my shocked state persisted with only the occasional tear making its way down my cheek. I closed myself off, plunging deep into the blackness that was always there waiting and hoping that I would someday find my way back to it. I found solace in that deep and dark crevice as it blanketed my mind as if shielding me from any additional pain.

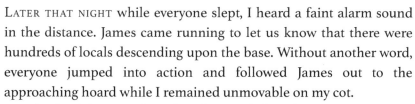

LATER THAT NIGHT while everyone slept, I heard a faint alarm sound in the distance. James came running to let us know that there were hundreds of locals descending upon the base. Without another word, everyone jumped into action and followed James out to the approaching hoard while I remained unmovable on my cot.

The loud bursts of gunfire shattered the silence around me. I could hear that anger in the words locals shouted through the bases gates. I could feel their burning rage as they fired their weapons at the Corvus men.

With a deep breath I drew their malice into my body, drawing power from their pain, feeding my own fury as it bubbled to the surface, begging me to release it. My legs shook as I pushed myself up from the cot and began to slowly make my way outside to where the chaos had been ensuing. Jonas' back clearly stiffened as I approached the group. Once the locals caught sight of me with my long disheveled brown hair blowing wildly in the wind. In nothing but a tank top and underwear, I could hear what they called me in their minds. *Witch.* They believed that I was a witch here to bring them bad omens. The shooting stopped as they silently watched me approach. The site of me filled them with fear and shock, all now believing the stories that had been circulating in the town about us.

Making my way slowly to the front of the line while the military men remained behind their covers. Jonas continued to hit the crowd with freezing rain and gusts of wind as Marcus shook the earth beneath their feet until everything stopped and there was nothing but silence. Slowly, I lifted my outstretched arms in front of my body while turning my palms to the crowd. Their fear paralyzed the locals, freezing them in place as they watched me with wide eyes performing auspicious movements with my hands.

Feeling the churning power within me itching to break loose, I molded its strength, pushing and pulling at it within myself, stretching it beneath my skin, turning my eyes into glowing flames that watched them remorselessly. With rising anxiety and fear, the crowd began to fire their weapons frantically at us, only to discover that their efforts were wasted as each of their bullets deflected or melted as it came in contact with my shield.

Releasing a primordial scream, I closed my eyes as the burning pain enveloped my body, forcing me to push and project all of my power out until it hovered in front of my now floating frame, in a big ball of fire. Drawing on all of my strength and control I could muster, I pushed the sphere of terror further out so that it hovered in front of me. Slowly, I extended my arms out to the sides of my body and then forcibly brought my hands together with a loud clap causing the fiery orb to burst out toward the hoard.

The licking flames rushed over their heads bringing with it all of the misery I had collected from the locals, harnessing power from them to only then send it all back to their owners and into their chests. Until I could feel each beating heart as I were holding it in my bare hands until, with nothing but a small squeeze, their hearts burst in their chests. The force with which I did this was too much for their chests to contain, creating an eruption of blood that covered my entire body in the sticky hot liquid. Once my feet were again rooted on the sandy earth, I stood in silent shock, petrified, feeling the blood drip down every inch of my skin, as I stared at the dead bodies that lay before me.

Jonas and the others stood behind me in silent shock, unmoving just processing the events that had led to demise of half a city at the bases gate. Jonas was the first to regain his composure and as he ran to me, my body collapsed into his arms just before it violently hit the ground.

I REGAINED consciousness in the shower. The hot water pouring over my head as Jonas and Marcus held me upright in the stream while Jeff scrubbed my head. I could see the blood mixed with soap bubbles running down my naked body as my head limply hung from my flaccid neck. When I was able to focus my eyes, the first thing that came clearly into view was my gold feather pendant hanging from its gold chain and the brand it had left on the delicate skin between my breasts.

"Lily?" Marc shouted at me. "She's coming to," he said to the others.

I picked my head up and looked at Jonas. His eyes were swollen and red, "Well hello darling,"he said half laughing and half sobbing.

"Your heart stopped beating for a few moments honey," Marcus said as his voice shook. "You gave us quite a scare."

"I'm sorry." Was all I could say as the anguish returned to me and I began crying.

"I know darling. I love you. We all love you. And we need you with us. Okay?" Jonas sobbing as he held me under the water, drenching his own clothes.

I closed my eyes and sobbed silently into his wet shirt as they continued to wash the blood off of my body. Once I was clean, they carefully dressed while they took turns bathing themselves. When we were all clean, they led me to the meal tables where Gus placed a hot cup of tea in front of me. Not far from where we were sitting, I could see the commotion at the entrance to the compound. Ken, Lawrence, Steven and Isaac were piling the bodies of the deceased onto a truck so that they could be driven to a site a few miles from the base where they could be buried in a mass grave. It was a horrific site and I knew that my lack of remorse over what I had done to those people did not bode well for my psyche.

"What have I done?" I whispered to myself in shock as I watched them working to clear the area. Jonas stroked my back as he continued to hold me close to him. Marcus gently moved my long unruly hair away from my face.

Roberts then approached and sat across from me. After clearing his throat he said, "Look there's no way that I can say this without it sounding alarming so...The Agency is quite pleased with what they are hearing about you all and the work that you have been doing out here. They got wind of what happened here tonight and they want to start sharing you with all of the other Squads. It turns out the Blue

Birds really like you Lily and they want you to go and spend some time with them. They will split the rest of you up so that all of the Squads get at least one of you. They don't seem to comprehend the strength that comes from the Dual bond no matter how many ways I try to explain it to them." He looked at Jonas sitting beside me as he explained with an annoyed tone.

"Now, I'm going to deny ever having said this, but the five of you need to run before they come for you," Roberts instructed.

His words brought me out of my stupor slightly and as we all looked at one another, we nodded in silent agreement knowing exactly what it was we needed to do.

"We would like to go too please," Emilio and Gus asked Marcus in unison.

Marc and Jeff immediately walked to the brothers. Marc placed his hand on Emilio's shoulder and said, "Yes. You both need to come with us."

Jonas turned to Brian who was sitting on the other side of him and said, "We'll be on the run for a bit I imagine. I'll understand if you..."

Before Jonas could finish his sentence, Brian leaned forward and kissed him deeply. When he pulled away he said, "You're not going anywhere without me."

AFTER PACKING OUR FEW BELONGINGS, we began boarding the cargo plane that had been waiting for us. Roberts and his remaining men came to see us off. Before I began making my way up the ramp, I turned to him and said, "Thank you for everything Sir. You're a good and kind man Major Roberts. It is clear you truly care for these men... and that you always have. Keep each other safe out here."

"You are very special Lily. All of you are. You are not together by accident remember that. I put a suitcase on the plane for you all. It should help you get started out there," he said before pulling me in for a hug.

I kissed his cheek before pulling away. "Can you tell me one last thing before I leave sir... it's about Peter. Where did he go? Where does his family live?" I asked as my eyes began to fill with tears.

He shook his head and motioned for Jonas to come and take me onto the plane. Nodding in understanding, I said my final goodbye to him as Jonas took my hand and pulled me onboard.

We buckled ourselves in and within minutes we were airborne. Quickly making our way to Lycksele, Stockholm to search for Luna. Search for our lives away from the Homestead and The Agency. Search for meaning to all we had endured and a peaceful future that seemed impossibly out of our reach.

ACKNOWLEDGMENTS

This book was written with much care and love. I could not have done it without the support and understanding from my husband and two incredible kids. I know that I was sometimes intolerable while my mind remained focused on Lily and Jonas. Thank you for letting me spend every spare moment I could writing. I love you guys ferociously.

I want to thank my sister and her family for all of their love.

I would also like to thank my GLEM girls for always believing and supporting me through all of our years together. May our adventures together continue.

A very special thank you to Ashley K for always being kind and supportive. But most importantly for being my very first fan. Thank you darling!

Last but certainly not least I would especially like to thank the people reading this book. You will never know how much I appreciate you spending time with these characters that have lived inside of me for so long. Thank you thank you thank you.

Stay tuned. Lily's story continues in Book 2, Incandescence.

Made in the USA
San Bernardino, CA
11 January 2019